HEAVEN IN OUR HEARTS

'Always love life' was the message Briony Stone's first sweetheart left with her before he was killed in an air crash. It seems strange that the same thought should be voiced by Robert Baker, the young vet whom she has known such a short time, but to whom she is so unaccountably drawn. Briony, now married to the snobbish, unimaginative Charles, realises too late that she has disregarded her lover's advice, running away from life into marriage with a man she likes and respects but doesn't love.

HEAVEN IN OUR HEARTS

Heaven In Our Hearts

by

Patricia Robins

Dales Large Print Books
Long Preston, North Yorkshire,
BD23 4ND, England.

British Library Cataloguing in Publication Data.

Robins, Patricia
    Heaven in our hearts.

    A catalogue record of this book is
    available from the British Library

    ISBN   1-84262-401-6 pbk

First published in Great Britain in 1954 by Hutchinson

Cover illustration © Helen Smith by arrangement with
Artist Partners

The moral right of the author has been asserted

Published in Large Print 2005 by arrangement with
Claire Lorrimer

Dales Large Print is an imprint of Library Magna Books Ltd.

Printed and bound in Great Britain by
T.J. (International) Ltd., Cornwall, PL28 8RW

I

The girl sat by the glowing red fire, the coppery tints in her cropped, curly head gleaming in the flame's light. The thin, heart-shaped face, generally pale, was flushed to an unusual colour; the large beautiful eyes were quiet and pensive.

Only her hands were restless as they lay in her lap, the short, square, boyish fingers playing with one another in thoughtless agitation.

Her mind was concentrated on her husband's homecoming. Any moment now she would hear the car turn into the drive. But for the first time in the three years of her marriage, she was not looking forward to his homecoming. As a rule, the long lonely hours of the day dragged all too slowly and, by half past six, Briony was relieved and immensely cheered by the thought that Charles would be home within a few minutes and her solitude dispelled. It was all very well for Charles, busy all day at the office, to treasure the peace and quiet of their country home. But for his young wife, the isolation and friendlessness of their house spelt loneliness. Charles could not understand why she should find time hanging heavy on her hands.

'There's the housekeeping to be done, the dogs to exercise, flowers to cut and arrange – all that kind of thing. Mother always used to say she had so much to do there were never enough hours in the day.'

But Briony was not Charles's mother, dead now, but still so very much alive in her husband's memory ... so much a part of their marriage. Although she had never known Mrs. Montague Campbell Stone, Briony knew instinctively that she would have had very little in common with her. Charles's mother was, or rather had been, a snob. There were people you did or did not know. There were things you did or did not do ... rigid lines that never deviated cutting between the right and the wrong of life ... as she had seen it. Perhaps more important, as she had brought Charles up to see it.

But for Briony there could be no definite rules without she first knew the conditions or personalities to whom those rules might be applied. Essentially guided by her heart rather than her head, she had always believed that there was good in everyone ... in everything, until it was proved otherwise. She would never condemn without hearing indisputable proof of someone's guilt; must always defend the underdog, the weakling, the attacked. How often had this essential backbone of her character led her into heated discussion with Charles ... and so often earned his disapproval.

Tonight, because it was the first time she had ever *consciously* acted against his wishes, she was not looking forward to seeing him. Unlike his mother, who apparently did no wrong, she had deliberately done something today of which she knew he would disapprove ... and she was aware that there would be a heated discussion ... if not actually an argument, because of it. As a rule, she never argued with Charles, chiefly because there were no two sides to any argument with him; no two points of view. Since he was consequently completely sure of himself, and because as a rule the outcome was of little importance to her, she acquiesced without bothering to state her views. Where Charles's principles were involved, there wasn't any use in trying to make him see her angle! So it had been easier to give way and see him happy and as much in love with her as the average woman expects her husband to be.

Perhaps, she thought dreamily as she stared into the glowing fire, she had always felt a little guilty about Charles ... marrying him. He had known, of course, that he was not the first man in her life, the first love. She had told him openly – even proudly – about the glorious six months which had constituted her life with Robert. She had not been married to him; somehow marriage had not seemed necessary in those crazy, dangerous, live-by-the-minute days of the war. Bob had been a fighter pilot ... twenty-two years old; she had been a WAAF driver, twenty-one years old. Two days after they had met at a camp dance they had openly avowed their love for one another; within a week, Briony had given with her whole heart the body that had, after all, been so willing to lose its innocence and which brought him such comfort in the long hours of the night when he had not been flying and when, without her, he had re-lived in nightmares the terror and horror and fear which never by word, deed or expression had he shown in the day.

Of course, he had been killed. Both of them had known it was practically inevitable. That was one of the reasons she had discarded convention and upbringing and had lived only for love ... for Bob. Afterwards, she had flung herself into a whirl of gaiety, activity, work, dances, parties – anything to help her forget. She burnt the candle at both ends until she was utterly exhausted. Then she had met Charles ... ten years older than herself ... a Major in the Army. And Charles had fallen in love with her.

There had been immense comfort in the calm ordinariness of Charles. He was like a character in a book, never variating from his basic self, never out of character.

Briony could remember her mother – who so seldom spoke seriously to her these days, for they had lost touch in the war, and never really regained the intimacy of their earlier relationship – saying one night after she had become engaged to Charles:

'Darling, don't you think this might be a mistake? Charles is very nice – very eligible – and will no doubt make someone a good husband, but not *you*, Briony. You're impulsive, impetuous, emotional. It's the French blood from your father's side, I expect. Charles is very, very English. Don't you think, dear, that you haven't a great deal in common? Not the way you and–'

'Bob?' Briony had spoken his name to her mother for the first time since Bob had died, over a year ago. 'That's just it, Mummy! There never would or could be another Bob. Charles is Bob's opposite – as he is mine. We shall complement one another. Charles will calm me down – keep me safe. That's what I want more than anything, Mummy, *to be safe*. I'm tired of chasing life. I want to relax and be quiet – and domesticated and – and normal.'

'Of course, darling – *now*. But later on, when you've had time to rest, you'll want to be yourself again. Do you really love Charles?'

For a brief moment Briony hesitated.

'Yes, I do. Not the way I loved Bob – that could never happen twice in a lifetime. But in a different way. I think one never loves anyone or anything the same way, do you, Mother? This is different. I respect Charles enormously. And I know he loves me. I can make him happy.'

'I believe that. But can *he* make *you* happy? And, Briony, can you be happy if you are not yourself? Can anyone? After a little while, when you become yourself again, it won't be so easy to make Charles happy either.'

'Mummy, I don't know what you are talking about. What is myself? Aren't I myself now? If I've changed, it's because life – unhappiness, experience, if you like – has changed me. This is how I am now. I've grown up – grown out of the impulsive, laughing, impetuous tomboy I used to be. I'm older and naturally I'm quieter!'

'Older? You're twenty-two, Briony. That's very young. Life has dealt you a blow and you're suffering from reaction. It'll pass, and you'll be young again. I've known your father, when he was alive, pass through just such phases as you are going through, Briony. You're very like him.'

'Don't you *like* Charles, Mummy?'

'But of course I do. I just don't think you'll be giving him, or yourself, a square deal if you marry him. Think it over, very, very carefully, Briony. I won't speak of it again.'

Strange how she could remember that conversation almost to the word today, three and a half years later! Perhaps it was because her mother, escaping from the loneliness of early widowhood, had moved into a gay, smart, insincere set of women who lived three-quarters of their lives at the card table, in clubs, drinking quite heavily, interested only in four suits; talking only in card language, revoking, trumps, tricks ... good luck ... bad luck ... big wins, large losses. It was far from Briony's own world, for she had never in her life cared for cards, and there was so little that she and her mother had in common to discuss with any intimacy, that conversation had remained imprinted on her mind. After she had married Charles, her mother had never mentioned her antipathy to the marriage again; she was always very charming to him when they met; interested, so she said, in Briony's letters telling her of the few exciting events of her life in the country. She never, of course, visited Briony. A week-end in the country – unless there was some first-class bridge – would have been the same to her as a week-end without drink to an alcoholic.

"Silly of Mother to worry about me!" Briony thought. "I've been very happy here with Charles. I'm very fond of him, and I know he loves me. There would be nothing at all wrong with my marriage if only there were more to do down here." When had she first started to feel time hanging heavy on her hands? Last winter ... when Charles spent most of his week-ends shooting and she had had the 'flu and not been able to go round with him? How quiet everything had seemed all of a sudden! Cook and James were downstairs in the basement. The old family butler was still in service though he had only Nancy, a young girl who came daily from the village, and Cook to help him. The days of a large staff had long since gone with the war and rather pathetically James tried to keep up appearances. Nancy, in spite of her unwillingness, was required to wear a frilly cap and apron and serve tea in the drawing-room from the enormous silver tea-pot, even if it were only for Briony!

Nancy had been nursing Briony through the post-'flu stages. Alone that Saturday afternoon in front of the fire, the girl had brought in tea as usual and Briony had found herself opening a conversation in order to detain her. Although Charles disapproved of her gossiping with the servants – meaning, of course, Nancy – she had felt she must talk to someone! How cross Charles had been when a heavy thunderstorm had brought him and his two friends back from their shoot early to find his wife excitedly engrossed in war-time reminiscences with his parlourmaid, who had amazingly enough turned out to be an ex-WAAF as well!

Somehow or other, that conversation with Nancy about the old days of the war had brought back memories of the companionship ... the many friends she had had ... the *fun* of it all. Since then she had hardly known what to do with herself all day. The two labradors were kept outside in kennels ... though Charles sometimes allowed them indoors after a day's shoot, which, while being in one sense a reward for their hard work, was also a very impractical arrangement, since they were inevitably plastered with mud on such occasions. So Briony did not even have the dogs for company except when she took them out for walks. She had always loved dogs, but these two retrievers were Charles's and had little interest for her. As for women friends ... well, the nearest house was five miles away and the few friends of Charles who lived within driving distance had wives who were either many years older than Briony or else with young babies who kept them tied to their homes. Briony had called once or twice on the younger ones, hoping to strike up a friendship with them, but after a little while she had ceased going; partly because they were always so busy they could not spare the time for a return visit, and she could never therefore repay their hospitality – partly because the sight of the children only increased her own desire to have a baby.

Unfortunately, Charles had made up his mind not to start a family just yet. The world was upside down, he had said, whenever she broached the subject. It was no fit place as yet for his sons and daughters. Why, there might even be a war with Russia, and who could be so callous as to bring a child into the world only to have the danger of an atom bomb hanging over its head!

'I'd risk it!' Briony had argued passionately. 'If everyone thought like that, Charles – I mean waited until everything was perfect before they had babies – there wouldn't be any "coming generation".'

'But the masses will always have kids – whatever the circumstances. Look how many children were born in bomb shelters – and just as many, no doubt, conceived during air raids. No, darling, you might take the risk, but I couldn't agree to it, I'm afraid. You're very dear to me, Briony, and I'm well aware that as a Territorialist I could be called up in an emergency and pushed off to Korea or Malaya or somewhere where you couldn't be with me. We'll have a family as soon as the world has settled down a bit. You're only twenty-three, darling. What's the hurry?'

'Only that I rather *want* a baby!' Briony said.

'But that's a purely selfish outlook. Look,

darling, why not have one of Jessie's pups? I intend to breed from her, you know.'

'As a substitute for a baby? Charles!'

He gave her a friendly, fond hug.

'Well, not as a substitute, but to give you something of your own to pet and spoil. Briony, perhaps I'm being selfish, but let me have you all to myself for a little longer.'

She had given way readily enough then ... as much to the impassioned love-making which followed his kiss as to his wishes ... after all, they had only been married a very short while. Men felt differently from women about children. She could understand that Charles did not want her tied to the nursery and pram-pushing as were the wives of his neighbours.

Instead, she threw herself feverishly into further efforts to be the kind of wife he wanted. She started spring-cleaning the house, paying more attention to some of the lovely heirlooms that were for the most part stored away now. She cleaned pictures, polished silver, washed and re-packed the precious china. She resorted all the linen, renewing moth balls. At weekends she entertained Charles's friends from London – mostly businessmen and occasionally their wives – whom she found dull company but who did at least make more noise round the house than there was during the week!

But her zest for housekeeping wore off in

due course and once again she had found time hanging heavy on her hands.

Maybe, just because there was so little event in her life, today's happening had assumed a far greater importance than it might otherwise have done. She had taken in and kept a stray mongrel puppy!

After all, why should Charles mind so much? she reassured herself. He had two dogs of his own. The trouble lay in the fact that it was a mongrel! For Charles there were, as in other things, two kind of dogs, the pedigreed ones he kept and the mongrels who were not really dogs at all! She had refused Jessie's pup because she didn't really care for labradors, and perhaps also because Charles had spoken of the training he would have to give it, since he automatically assumed it would join the shooting expedition with his pair. When Briony had a dog, it was to be hers ... heart and soul her own dog. She would train it to her voice, her command, feed it with her own hand.

Now, here was the kind of dog she had always secretly longed for. Once, when she had been about ten years old, she had saved up her pocket money for ten weeks; unknown to her parents, she had caught a bus into Brighton and by herself gone to the Lost Dogs' Home and brought home a black-and-tan mongrel. Her father had been so impressed by her saving so much and by her thoroughness in presenting him with a *fait accompli*, that he had allowed her to keep it. Two months later it had been run over and killed. This little stray had reminded her poignantly of that same black-and-tan mongrel she had had as a child. She had found it wandering, wet and forlorn, in the laurel bushes by the drive gates, and carried it back to the house and fed it. Afterwards, it lay on the carpet in front of the fire staring up at her from enormous brown eyes, its ragged tail thumping appreciation once in a while as it woke from a doze. Briony loved it! Only by a great effort had she brought herself to telephone the police and inform them she had found the dog wandering in her garden.

'Nobody reported a dog missing as yet, madam! Would you like us to collect him and bring him back to the station?'

'Oh no – I'll look after him!' Briony had cried. 'It's such a pathetic little thing. If no one does claim him, I'd like to keep him.'

'Well, as like as not he'll be yours!' said the police sergeant. 'Licences fall due in a couple of months and some folk have a way of turning out their unwanted dogs rather than pay seven and six for them. If it's a puppy, I daresay it couldn't be got rid of any other way.'

'Well, I'll keep him until he's claimed or the time is up for anyone to claim him. There's no collar or any way of identifying

19

him. He's all colours – about the size of a small terrier pup. He has pointed ears that are sometimes up and sometimes down ... really, there's nothing to distinguish him from thousands of other mongrels.'

'No idea as to his age?'

'I'm sure he's only a puppy. His teeth are like needles and his coat is still almost fluffy, though it's wiry on top.'

'Thank you for letting us know. We'll ring you if we have any queries about a lost mongrel. Good night, madam!'

So he might remain hers – that is, if Charles did not promptly turn him out of the house.

Towards evening, Briony had made up a bed for the puppy by the radiator in the downstairs cloakroom. She had felt that it might be better to break the news to Charles before he saw the dog, who was certainly not a very handsome little fellow looked at from a pedigree point of view ... Charles's view! At the same time, she could not bring herself to put the dog in the now disused stable. It still shivered occasionally and she believed it had been out all the previous night, though it did not seem terribly hungry.

Briony started as she heard Charles's car turn into the drive. Colour suffused her cheeks and receded again, leaving her pale with some strange inner excitement. She knew there would be trouble, but she would not be over-persuaded. Unless someone claimed him, she was going to keep that puppy, whatever Charles might say.

She left the matter until Charles had changed into more comfortable clothes and had joined her for a pre-dinner drink as was his custom. Then she told him.

At first Charles seemed merely amused.

'A mongrel! Probably covered in fleas. I hope you didn't put it in with Jessie and Jane.'

Briony lit a cigarette and said slowly:

'No. As a matter of fact, I thought it ought not to go outside. It doesn't seem very well, Charles, and was wet through. I – I put him in the cloakroom.'

Charles swung round to look at her, his expression clearly indicating that he thought she was mad.

'In the house? But for heaven's sake, Briony, there's no knowing what kind of livestock it will be scattering around. And it's probably not house-trained anyway. It'll have to go out to the stables.'

Briony's lips set in a firm line.

'If you don't mind awfully, Charles, I'd rather keep him indoors. I don't think he has fleas. He was just wet and muddy ... not really dirty. And he whined to go out, so I'm sure he's house-trained. I've told the police, of course, and if he's claimed, then I shall

21

naturally have to let him go. But if not, Charles, I'd like to keep him.'

'I say, are you serious?' Charles asked.

'Quite serious!' Briony said with a firmness she was far from feeling. 'You said I might have a puppy, Charles, and I've taken a fancy to this one.'

'One of Jessie's pups, yes, but a mongrel! Look here, my dear, I really think you're letting sentiment get the better of you. You're always on the side of the underdog and I can quite see that you feel sorry for a stray and all that kind of thing. But we can quite well find a decent home for it if it isn't claimed. I daresay the gardener's boy would have it if I paid the licence each year. I'm quite willing to do that, you know.'

'That's very generous of you, Charles,' Briony said, softening a little at his words. 'But I really would like to keep him myself. He's just the kind of dog I've always wanted. Wait till you see him! He has the most beautiful and intelligent eyes and he's attached to me already. Come and have a look at him, darling. I know you'll fall in love with him, too.'

'Now look here, old girl–' Charles began, but Briony's look halted him for a moment. How often had she told him that she could not bear to hear him address her as 'old girl' – the same term, meant undoubtedly as an endearment, as he used to his labrador bitch! 'Look here, Briony, I'm going to put my foot down about this. You must see that we can't have a mongrel running round the house. It's just absurd.'

'I don't see why!' Briony argued, growing heated in spite of her determination to argue this out coolly. 'He's smaller than the labradors and won't make anything like as much mess.'

Charles tapped out his pipe on the edge of the fireplace and his mouth set in a stubborn line.

'That's not the point, my dear. To begin with, it's a dog. What do you suppose will happen if Jessie or Jane get out when they're on heat? A fine litter of pups we'd get from them then! And both bitches ruined into the bargain.'

'Then you'll just have to keep your dogs under control, Charles,' Briony said. 'After all, it's only for three weeks twice a year.'

'And have the mongrel howling its head off outside the kennels all night?'

'He wouldn't be outside at night. I intend to let him sleep indoors, Charles. He's to be a pet.'

'Why not get a peke or a pom!' Charles said scathingly. 'They make better lapdogs.'

'Oh, for goodness' sake, Charles, try not to be childish about this. I've every right to choose the kind of dog I want – just as I respect your wish to have Jessie and Jane although they aren't the kind of dog I happen to care for. There's no point in discussing this further if you just wish to be rude.'

Charles flushed an angry red.

'On the contrary, there's every reason for discussing the matter. I have no intention of letting a flea-ridden mongrel stay in *my* house–'

'Your house, Charles?' Briony broke in furiously. 'It's also supposed to be my home. I think you sometimes forget that fact. You brought me here as your wife, and I think you sometimes imagine I'm just part of the furniture. Well, I'm not an antique you purchased for *your* house. I'm your wife, Charles, and have as much say in the organizing of our home as you have.'

Charles looked at his wife, surprise mingling with annoyance. Briony had never spoken so openly of her 'rights' before, far less accused him of denying her her wifely due.

'You've had everything in the world you wanted!' he said. 'I let you re-decorate most of the rooms, although I was dead against modernizing the place, as you well know. But I gave way because I thought that was your affair rather than mine. I let you keep Nancy although I think she's cheeky and far too forward for a servant.'

'You're out of date,' Briony broke in. 'Girls like Nancy are very hard to get and she works like a Trojan keeping this great house clean.'

'So she should, seeing the wages we pay her. It's a disgrace!'

'Well, let's not argue about Nancy!' Briony said sharply. 'As you said, the servants are my affair. I would have thought the choice of my dog was also my affair. It's not even as if it were to be your dog, too. You have Jess and Jane and as far as I'm concerned you can have fifty more like them. I don't complain when they bring dirt into the house and leave hairs all over the carpet which even the Hoover won't budge at times! Why should you complain because I want a puppy of my own choosing?'

'All right, keep the beastly dog!' Charles said furiously. 'But let me tell you this much, Briony. The first time it does any serious damage inside or outside the house, it'll have to go. Is that understood?'

Briony faced him across the room, her eyes bright.

'I understand that you have graciously condescended to let me keep the puppy,' she said clearly. 'For which generous gesture I thank you very much. Now, if you'll excuse me, I'm going to have a look at him.'

She closed the door behind her and stood for a few moments with her hands against it, hesitating. This was the first serious argument she had ever had with Charles and she was very unhappy about it. She would have liked to go back into the room and say to him: "Oh, darling, don't let's quarrel about this. I've been so happy all day. Say you really don't mind. I'm sure you'd fall in love with him if only you'd come and see him..."

But deep in her heart she knew that Charles would not 'fall in love' with a mongrel. He was too prejudiced. And if she weakened now, it would give him the opportunity to exert his will over hers. And she had no intention of letting the puppy go – not unless she had to.

She sighed, then, shrugging her shoulders, went quickly down the passage to the cloakroom.

As she opened the door, the dog's head turned towards her and the deep golden-brown eyes stared up at her. Very slowly the stumpy tail started to wag. Then his head dropped to the rug on which he lay and the pricked ears drooped.

Briony dropped to her knees beside the pathetic little creature, her face white with concern. The dog feebly licked her hand as she stroked his head. Then a fit of trembling was followed by a sudden attack of sickness.

There was no doubt that the dog was ill – very ill, Briony thought as she rushed off to the kitchen to get a floorcloth and a hot-water bottle. It would give Charles plenty of opportunity for sarcastic remarks but she was going to telephone his vet to come and see the puppy tonight. What was the man's name? Edwards? ... no, Elliot. She had never much cared for him, but their social relationship hardly mattered. It was the dog she was worried about.

Her heart melted as the dog tried once more to turn his head at her approach. He seemed pathetically pleased to see her and once in a while his tongue came out to lick her hand as she tried to make him more comfortable with another rug and the hot-water bottle against his back.

Mr. Elliot, Briony was told by his wife, was out helping a cow deliver twin calves. She could not say when he would be back. If it was urgent, perhaps she might care to ring the new vet, Mr. Baker.

'Thanks very much,' Briony said, taking down his phone number. 'I'll ring Mr. Baker right away. I'm really concerned about the puppy.'

A quarter of an hour later, Briony was watching the young man as he ran gentle hands over her dog, probing, testing, feeling with his long, sensitive fingers. Fascinated by his hands, Briony found she could not take her eyes off them. She herself caressed the dog's head and ears soothingly although he seemed unaware of the vet's touch.

The young man looked up and met Briony's questioning gaze.

'I don't think there's any internal injury,' he said. 'I believe you told me over the phone he could have been hit by a car – something of that sort?'

'I – I don't really know what's wrong,' Briony said. 'You see, I only found him this afternoon. I mean, he's not my dog ... at least, he is now ... I mean, he will be if nobody claims him!'

She broke off, smiling apologetically.

'What I'm trying to say is that I found him straying. I want to keep him for my own. He *is* going to be all right, isn't he?'

The young man bent down to examine the dog again. Then he turned back to the girl who crouched on the floor beside him.

'I think so. It's rather hard to say just exactly what is wrong. It may be the onset of distemper, but he looks pretty strong, even if he is thin. He seems fond of you already, Mrs. Stone.'

Briony stood up.

'I'm sorry to have dragged you out so late, Mr. Baker,' she said. 'We usually have Mr. Elliot. He attends my husband's dogs.'

The young man smiled.

'I'll ask Mr. Elliot to call in and look at the pup first thing in the morning. He'll be all right tonight. I'll give him a bromide to help him sleep ... and if you've got any glucose in the house, give him sips of that in milk.'

'Glucose? Yes, I think there is some,'

Briony said.

She broke off, watching the vet as he washed his hands at the basin. Automatically she handed him a clean towel from behind the door, and for a moment their eyes met and he smiled.

'Can't – I mean – couldn't you go on attending to my dog?' Briony heard herself saying impulsively. 'I know Mr. Elliot comes to see Jessie and Jane, but – well, I'd like *you* to look after this puppy, if you will.'

'Well, of course, if you'd prefer it. But wouldn't your husband prefer to have his own vet?'

'My husband isn't very fond of mongrels, so won't mind one way or the other!' Briony said bitterly. Then, seeing the dark eyes looking at her askance, she said again:

'It's awfully late to have dragged you out. Please come and have a drink before you go home.'

Robert Baker hesitated for a moment, then nodded his head.

'Thank you very much. I'd like it!' he said simply.

Briony, too, had wondered, as soon as she suggested it, what had made her ask him. For a brief instant she regretted her invitation, then as the young man paused before replying she knew that she wanted him to stay.

So, as simply as that, it all began.

II

'This is Mr. Baker, Charles. He's been having a look at the puppy. It isn't very well.'

Charles greeted the newcomer civilly enough. He did not look at his wife.

'You're a vet, Mr. Baker?'

'Yes. Mr. Elliot, whom you usually call in, I understand, was busy. When that happens, he passes urgent calls on to me and I do the same. The arrangement works out quite well for both of us, since we neither of us have partners.'

Charles nodded, and recalling his manners, said:

'You'll have a drink, Mr...?'

'Baker – Robert Baker,' the young man said politely, wondering if Mr. Charles Stone had forgotten his name on purpose.

'Whiskey?' Charles asked.

'I'd rather have beer, if that's all right.'

'Don't seem to have seen you round this district,' Charles continued.

'No, I've only been here six months. Mr. Elliot has been very kind giving me so many introductions. Naturally I don't like to poach on his preserves, so if you'd prefer to have him call to see the puppy tomorrow—'

'Elliot wouldn't be interested in that dog, I can assure you!' Charles said with a hearty laugh. 'He can appreciate a good blood strain if ever a man could. Wouldn't waste his time on mongrels!'

Briony dropped her gaze from Charles's face and looked back to the younger man. Inconsequently, she noted that he was taller than Charles, less stocky; that he was as dark as Charles was fair; that his hands were as long and sensitive as Charles's were square and blunt; and his name, by some odd mischance, was Robert. Was he, too, called Bob by his friends?

Robert Baker turned towards her and again their eyes met. He looked back quickly at Charles.

'Well, I can appreciate a good pedigree too, Mr. Stone. But a dog is a dog whatever its breed and we're as deeply pledged to do what we can to save the life of a mongrel as of a valuable champion.'

'Waste of time!' said Charles flatly. 'Only live to breed a lot more mongrels. Have the country swarming with them if they weren't allowed to die off.'

'Charles, that's inhuman. You know you're fond of dogs...'

'A mongrel isn't a dog, my dear,' he broke in on his wife's words. 'It's a four-legged animal.'

Briony gritted her teeth, determined not

to argue in front of their guest. But those flat assertions of Charles's always raised her temper. If only he could be made to understand that other people had different points of view, that some people loved mongrels just as he loved Jessie and Jane!

Robert Baker voiced her thoughts:

'You may not care for cross-breeds, Mr. Stone, but some people would rather have a mongrel than any other type of dog. They are very often exceptionally intelligent and nearly always intensely loyal and devoted to their masters.'

Briony listened intently, her eyes on the young man's face.

'Shoot the lot of 'em, I say! Small wonder someone turfed this dog out of their house. Would have done the same myself!'

'But, Charles, that's cruelty to animals. This puppy was soaking wet. And Mr. Baker thinks it may have distemper. You surely don't advocate turning out a sick dog just because it's a mongrel? On a night like this?'

'Wouldn't turn it out till tomorrow. Sleep in the stable,' Charles said calmly.

Robert Baker put down his empty glass and stood up, timing the interruption very well.

'I really ought to be pushing along,' he said quietly. 'I'll call again first thing in the morning. I'll give you that bromide for the pup, Mrs. Stone, before I go. I think I left my bag in the hall.'

Briony followed him to the door, where he stood aside to let her pass through before him.

'Good night, Mr. Stone,' he said.

''Night, Parker. My wife will see you out.'

Briony wanted to make some apology for Charles's behaviour but she could not. Her voice seemed strangled in her throat. Only the young vet seemed completely at ease. He smiled down at her when he gave her the bromide tablets.

'Don't worry!' he said. 'We'll pull the little chap through. I'm rather prejudiced too, you know, in favour of the world's oddities! You know, I'm surprised at what your husband said about Elliot. I didn't know he was like that.'

'A snob?' Briony checked the words too late.

'Yes. I suppose that is the word. One can be just as much a snob about animals as about people! Come to think of it, I believe his practice does tend to exclude the poorer homes where the dogs are less genteel.'

'I'm glad *you've* come to treat my puppy,' Briony said sincerely. 'I have a feeling Mr. Elliot and my husband might have cooked up some good reason for having him put to sleep … and I'd never have known. I know it seems silly, when I've only had the dog a few hours, but I'm really terribly fond of it already.'

33

'It isn't silly. One can take to a dog in just the same way as one can take to a person.'

'Love at first sight!' Briony said, smiling.

But there was no answering smile, and as she looked upwards and met the dark intent gaze of the young man she felt the hot colour rush into her cheeks. It was absurd, of course, to imagine that he had intended to convey anything to her by that look, following so closely upon her own words ... and yet ... and yet...

'I'll be along to see you tomorrow, Mrs. Stone. Don't worry about the puppy. He'll be all right.'

Briony opened the great oak doors and her eyes followed the man to his car. Then she turned hurriedly and went back into the brightly lit hall. It was not the cold night air that had left her shivering but some nameless apprehension tinged with a breath of excitement. She did not try to fathom out the cause but went slowly back to the sitting-room where Charles awaited her.

'...ask him in here for a drink!' Charles voice broke in on her inner thoughts. 'It's different with Elliot – he's a personal friend. Besides, he's an Oxford man.'

Briony gave Charles her full attention. Her face was bright with indignation.

'Am I to understand you are objecting to Mr. Baker having a drink with us, Charles?'

He looked at her coolly.

'Certainly. Don't even know the fellow. You know nothing about him, do you?'

Briony gave a sigh of exasperation. That Charles could be so incredibly Victorian at times!

'He seems a very nice young man,' she said, vehemently stressing the 'nice'. 'His manners were beyond reproach and I'm willing to vouch for the fact that he hasn't walked off with any of the family heirlooms!'

She turned her back on Charles, who gave his usual 'humph' which Briony understood would precede a lecture on 'People One Knows' and 'People One Doesn't Know'. She did not feel up to arguing with him.

'Please, Charles!' she said, turning to face him. 'I know you're displeased about the puppy, but since you have been forced to give way, please try to behave a little graciously. Mr. Baker is hardly important enough for us to have an argument about, is he? He's here to attend to my puppy, not as a friend. I merely thought it would be good manners to ask him to have a drink since it is so late to call anyone out.'

Charles poured himself another glass of sherry and joined Briony by the fire.

'I've no wish to quarrel, my dear. I merely wanted to point out that it's surely past our dinner hour?'

Briony glanced at the clock and saw that it was barely eight. She knew that Charles had

35

put himself in the right without being strictly truthful but was glad enough to let the matter drop.

'I'll go and see what Nancy is up to,' she said.

But even as she spoke the door opened and the girl announced that dinner was ready.

'Where's James?' Charles asked, always a stickler for the etiquette he tried to preserve in spite of the times.

'It's his night off!' Briony said, for a brief instant relishing the opportunity to snap at Charles. Then her kinder nature reasserted itself and she regretted making Charles look silly, in front of Nancy too. Nancy's grin had not escaped her even though, fortunately, Charles had had his back to the girl.

Dinner over, Briony led the way back to the sitting-room, determined to re-establish the friendliness that usually existed at this time of evening between her husband and herself. But she was not to be given a chance. After coffee, Charles departed to the cloak-room, only to return a few minutes later in an irate temper.

'That bloody dog has been sick all over the lavatory floor!' he said furiously. 'It's not good enough, Briony. It'll have to go. Damn it all, I'm not going to have my house made a stinking mess just because–'

'Please don't swear at me, Charles,' Briony

said, curbing the desire to lose her temper, too. 'I'll go and see to it. I'm sorry!'

Nancy was helping Cook with the washing-up when Briony called in for a floor cloth and a bowl of disinfectant.

'I'm sorry the dog's so poorly, ma'am,' the girl said sympathetically. 'Do you think it'll be all right?'

'I don't know, Nancy,' Briony replied, suddenly near to tears. At least someone else other than herself cared whether her puppy lived or died. 'I'm afraid it's been very sick again.'

'Maybe it would be better upstairs out of the way?' Cook said, causing Briony to wonder, not for the first time, how servants always seemed to have overheard her private conversations with Charles. Maybe they had raised their voices … certainly Charles had been all but shouting at her!

'It could go in your bathroom, ma'am,' Nancy suggested helpfully. 'No one goes there excepting you. It'd be easy to keep that oilcloth clean, too, and there's the radiator by the window to keep the poor scrap warm.'

'That's a good idea, Nancy!' Briony said. 'I won't have far to go if I have to be up in the night.'

'You fix him up a bed there, ma'am, and I'll clear the mess in the cloak-room. Won't bother me!'

'Thank you,' said Briony.

Upstairs in her bedroom she paused for a moment beside the great triple mirror that stood on her glass-topped dressing-table and surveyed her reflection in the mirror.

"Why couldn't Charles have helped me?" she asked herself.

The grey eyes stared back at her in bewilderment.

"I'd have been grateful to him," she thought. "Now I'm resentful and hurt and ... Bob would have helped me ... been just as keen as I am to keep the puppy and get him well ... Bob..."

She turned away from her reflected self in sudden dislike of what she had heard herself say. She had vowed never, never to compare Bob and Charles. She had never yet done so, at least never openly made comparisons to herself. What had led her to do so tonight? It must be the fact that Bob was in her mind, brought back from being a distant memory by the young vet. How kind and sympathetic and understanding *he* had been! How strange the way they had seemed instantly to understand one another! With some people one felt at ease immediately – with others, never, in spite of years of knowing them. Time did not matter – it was something else. Some people you knew instinctively would be your friends...

Friend? The word hung for a moment on the silence of the room. What chance was there that she should make a real friend, here in the isolation of her home with Charles? Certainly she and the young vet could not be friends! Charles apparently considered Robert Baker outside their social circle, though heaven knew on what basis he had judged the stranger! And even if Charles accepted him, how could a young man come to her house for tea, or friendly walks or talks, even a game of tennis? It was all very well to talk of sex equality – Charles did not believe in it anyway! – but it didn't – couldn't – exist in everyday life. People would soon start gossiping if a young married woman was seen frequently in the company of an attractive young bachelor.

Briony caught up on her last words. Was Robert Baker attractive? Certainly he had the most amazing large dark brown eyes – and such beautiful hands! They were Bob's hands, Bob the artist who had turned flier and used his hands to kill because his country wished it. But how he hated destroying the life he had so loved to immortalize on paper! What a brilliant life had been wasted by that utter futility, war!

What was it Bob had once said to her? Something which until now she had completely forgotten. Now – yes, now she was remembering. It was to do with life... 'Always love life, Briony. It's so easy to turn a blind eye to the beauty of life. Only artists really see. Ordinary people are blind, either because they are too selfish, too prejudiced or too afraid to look. Not you, Briony. You're alive. Never be afraid of life, darling!'

Briony sat down, suddenly weakened by the remembered words of one so dearly loved. How could she have forgotten, in her unhappiness, the strange intensity of Bob's message? Was she blind now, too? Was she one of the millions of others who were afraid to see what life meant? Had Bob meant to protect her from the possible consequences of his death? He had known and understood her so well. Perhaps he had realized that in the deep aching loneliness after death, she would close herself into a shell where life could not hurt her again.

"Is that what I have done?"

Briony was suddenly afraid – afraid of her thoughts as much as of her isolation. Her impulse was to leave that beautiful grey and white bedroom of hers and run down to the friendly warmth of the sitting-room, to the comfortable security of Charles's presence. He would be sitting in his armchair, puffing contentedly at his pipe, listening no doubt to 'Take It From Here'. 'Only really funny programme on the wireless,' he would say when it was over. Dear Charles – so much a creature of habit – and prejudice.

She caught herself sharply on the word. Too prejudiced to see life. Yes! It was true that Charles was one of the blind. But it didn't matter. It must not matter. After all, it was the utter reliability of Charles that made him so dear to her. She could stake her life at any time on what he would say or do; on what were his opinions, his wishes.

'Here's the puppy, ma'am. He seems fair sorry for hisself!'

Briony jumped to her feet and took the limp bundle from Nancy's arms.

'There's a travelling rug in the bottom of the wardrobe, Nancy,' she said, almost guilty that Nancy should have caught her day-dreaming. 'And he can have that garden cushion in the basket chair.'

Together, the two young women made the dog comfortable. Then Nancy went down to the kitchen to warm the milk so that Briony could give the puppy his bromide. Presently, the little animal seemed to be sleeping comfortably and Briony, glancing at her bedside clock, saw that it was almost ten o'clock.

Charles would undoubtedly be wondering if she had deserted him for the evening. Poor Charles!

She ran downstairs and went hurriedly into the sitting-room. As she came in, Charles switched off the wireless and said:

'"Take It From Here", my dear. Only really funny programme on the wireless!'

Briony felt laughter creeping up from her

41

throat and then, unaccountably, turn to tears. Impulsively she flung herself into Charles's arms and sobbed on his shoulder.

Charles looked down at the coppery head in perplexity.

'Look here, old thing, you mustn't do that, you know. I'm sorry for swearing at you and all that. Didn't mean to be rude, old girl. Now cheer up, there's a dear. There's nothing to cry about. I've said you can keep the animal if you want to. Now buck up, darling, and dry your eyes. Nancy will be in to take the coffee-tray and you don't want her to see you've been crying.'

"You mean you don't want her to see!" Briony thought, but she didn't speak the words aloud and when Charles gave her his handkerchief she did her best to remove all traces of the sudden storm of weeping.

'Better?' Charles asked tenderly. And when she nodded: 'Give us a kiss and we'll call it quits, eh?'

Briony nodded and obediently raised her lips to his.

But the tears still lingered on in her heart.

III

'I'm afraid it's pneumonia, Mrs. Stone. I'll give him penicillin, of course, and we may pull him through.'

Briony looked at the vet from anxious eyes.

'May? There's real danger, then?'

'I'm afraid so. If you'd like to have Mr. Elliot give a second opinion–'

'Oh, damn Mr. Elliot!' Briony said, and seeing the expression in her companion's eyes, she flushed and then smiled and said: 'I'm sorry. I just don't care about Mr. Elliot. I know you'll do your best and that's all I ask. What are his chances?'

'About fifty-fifty. He's only a pup and he isn't any too fat. But mongrels' – the brown eyes turned to meet hers with a twinkle she could not miss – 'are constitutionally pretty strong. We'll hope for the best.'

'Have you got a dog?' Briony asked as Robert Baker prepared the penicillin injection.

'Unfortunately not. I don't feel it's very fair to keep an animal unless you can look after it properly, and I haven't the time to give a dog the exercise it needs. I did have

43

one, of course, when I was a kid. It died when I was up at Cambridge, fourteen years old. I still miss him.'

'Dare I ask what he was?' Briony asked sympathetically.

'Poodle cross spaniel, I think! But he was a grand dog.'

'Is that why you have a soft spot for mongrels?'

Robert Baker looked into the serious green eyes only a foot from his and his reply died suddenly on his lips. It was a moment of unaccustomed embarrassment for him. He had been acutely aware of this girl on his previous visit last night, aware of her physical attractiveness, of her charm and strange quietness. After meeting her husband, he had felt intensely sorry for her that she should be married to such a pompous boor. Then, as he had bade her good night in the doorway, he had seen her eyes, large, lonely, oddly pathetic, and he had felt the most ridiculous and intense desire to put his arms round her and kiss that sad, drooping little mouth into laughter.

Most of the night he had lain awake thinking of her, wondering just what it was about her that had made such an impression on him. And now, suddenly, he knew. He was in love with her – in love for the first time in his twenty-eight years, and at the same time painfully aware that she was a

44

married woman.

A smile suddenly twisted his lips. Trust him to find himself in such a predicament. It was typical, too, that he should discover romance kneeling side by side with a woman whose Christian name he did not know, on the cold linoleum of her bathroom floor! What a confounded idiot he was! Quite suddenly he laughed.

It broke the tension of the moment, for Briony had not been unaware of his failure to reply to her question or of the strange way in which he had been staring at her for the past minute – or was it only a second? The colour had rushed to her cheeks and she knew that her hands were trembling as she held the puppy's head on her lap.

Her companion's sudden smile ... then his young, spontaneous laughter, was like a bright ray of sunlight streaming into the darkness of her spirit.

'Joke?' she asked.

His eyes were suddenly serious again.

'Not really a joke,' he said quietly. 'It's just that – well, it struck me suddenly that life is so peculiar. If you don't laugh at it, you'd have to cry. Laughing seems easier, doesn't it?'

'Yes. I know what you mean. But it isn't always easy to see the funny side.'

'You have to be apart from life to be able to do that,' he said thoughtfully. 'Once you're living in a situation, then it's not so easy to see it objectively. But I don't think it matters terribly whether you laugh or cry so long as you are alive.'

Bob's words ... Bob's thoughts ... how could he possibly know that they were in her mind last night? What was happening to her so suddenly? Why did everything this man said seem either a repetition of her own thoughts or Bob's words? It was as if her life was in an instant uncannily controlled by some supernatural power. Or was it just that she had been asleep, asleep in an apathy from which, like the Princess, she had been suddenly touched into wakefulness, awareness?

'I'll inject him now. Hold him steady. I'll try not to hurt him.'

Obediently, Briony held the puppy's head, but there was no need. He did not seem to notice the quick efficient prick of the needle in the scruff of the neck.

'He ought to have these twice a day, Mrs. Stone. I'm afraid it'll be rather an expensive business—'

'Expense needn't be considered!' Briony broke in quickly. Then regretted her words in case they sounded boastful, but he merely nodded and continued with the business of packing up his instrument bag.

'There! That should help him. Has he got a name yet?'

Briony gave a shy smile.

'I haven't liked to name him. You see, I was afraid it would be bad luck. Not that I'm really superstitious but I don't think I could bear it if the police told me someone was claiming him!'

Robert Baker nodded his head again.

'Surprising how fond you can get of a dog in twenty-four hours. Don't worry about him. We'll pull him through. It's nice and warm in here too.'

Briony felt oddly comforted by the coupling of their names. It was to be a joint effort to save the puppy's life, and that showed that this strange companion of hers was on her side.

'You'll have a drink before you go?' she asked, as they turned and walked back through her bedroom on to the upstairs landing.

Robert Baker gave her a quick smile.

'I'm rather busy at the moment. Thank you for asking me though.'

'You'll be back later today?' Briony asked.

'On my way home. I can't say exactly what the time will be. Does it matter if I'm a little late?'

'Not at all! I'm seldom out at night, and I certainly wouldn't go out while the puppy is ill. I'm the only person he'll take food from. He won't look at a saucer of milk when Nancy – that's our maid – tries to give it to him.'

They were downstairs in the hall now and Robert was slipping into his overcoat.

'Your husband taken to the dog a bit more now?'

Briony bit her lip.

'He still hasn't seen him. Knowing how Charles feels about mongrels, I felt it was best not to force the issue – just let them meet naturally.' She felt a sudden desire to explain Charles's attitude, to defend him. 'He's really very fond of animals and always kind to them. It's just that – well, he'd hardly had time to get used to the idea of my puppy.'

Robert Baker gave her a sudden searching look.

'You're quite sure he wouldn't rather have Elliot? Your husband's attitude may have something to do with the fact that I was called in. I telephoned Elliot, of course, and gave him a brief outline of what had happened. If he had insisted on treating the case himself, I could hardly have insisted that I should continue to come. Fortunately – for me, I mean – he seemed quite willing for me to carry on. He said, of course, that he was very friendly with your husband.'

'I'm glad that's all settled!' Briony said earnestly. 'I quite appreciate that there's a certain amount of etiquette involved.'

'Well, there is, in our case. We have never been rivals because we came to an understanding before I set up practice here. Elliot knew an aunt of mine very well and when he heard I'd qualified he suggested I came and helped him out as he was the only vet in the neighbourhood and very overworked. But he didn't want a partner – says he prefers to work single-handed. In a way, I agree with him. It was very decent of him to give me the chance to set up in the same district.'

'Then you like him – as a person?' Briony asked curiously, also a little awkwardly, since she could recall that she had voiced her own dislike of Charles's vet in no uncertain terms.

Robert Baker gave his quick, boyish smile.

'Just between you and me and the gate-post, no! But he's been pretty good to me and so we keep up a sort of friendship.'

'I don't see that he's actually lost such a lot!' said Briony. 'After all, I presume no one has exclusive rights to any one district, and if you hadn't come then someone who might have been a rival might have set up in competition. Then he may have lost some of his best clients instead of handing you his worst ones!'

'I realize that,' the young man said, smiling. 'But once again, between ourselves, I have every hope that I can build up a good enough reputation for myself so that some of the "good" clients insist on having me. And there are a lot of new people moving out this way. There's plenty of work for two men.' He glanced at his watch and said regretfully: 'Well, I'll really have to push off. I'll see you later, then.'

'I'm sorry I've kept you gossiping,' Briony apologized. 'It was thoughtless of me when you're so busy. I am always glad of an opportunity to pass a few minutes away!'

Driving away from the great ugly mansion, Robert Baker thought about those parting words of his client, and they explained a great deal. Clearly the girl was lonely. And she was only a girl – sweet, shy, uncertain of herself. How could she have married that old stuffed shirt, Charles Montague Campbell Stone! Not that he knew him except by sight and their brief introduction yesterday evening. But he knew him well enough by reputation. He was very well off, even in these days, and completely Victorian in his attitude to life; a snob of the first order. Rather like Elliot, in fact. He must be years older than his wife.

Robert rejected the thought that she might have married Stone for his money. The girl was not like that; and what's more she was clearly not enjoying the fruits of her marriage. If anyone looked mortally unhappy and lonely, she did. Surely she couldn't be in love with her husband? Or did he have some quality or other that he, Robert, knew nothing of?

'Hell!' he said to himself, suddenly angry with life. 'Why did she have to marry him? If he'd been older, and she was his daughter...' His mind played contentedly with the thought of the friendship that might have developed under such circumstances, a slow awakening in the girl's heart of the same intense feeling he already felt for her. They would fall desperately in love. Stone, the Victorian father, would probably insist that Robert had no right to court his daughter, since he was all but penniless! But somehow he'd make money – and it would all come right!

'I'm crazy!' Robert pulled himself up sharply. 'I ought not even to see her again, feeling as I'm beginning to feel about her. She's married and we can't even get to Christian names. What is her name? I don't even know that much about her.'

His next call put Briony out of his thoughts until he was once more in his car, looking for a decent pub for lunch. Then his mind wandered again to the picture of her, with her short reddish hair and curious, exciting eyes, standing in the hall looking up at him like a shy child.

Briony, at that precise moment, was sitting alone in the large chilly dining-room, toying with the steamed fish that Nancy had put on a tray before her.

'I'm really not very hungry, Nancy,' she

51

said at last to the girl. 'I think I'll skip the pudding, whatever it is, and just have coffee in the sitting-room.'

'Oh, ma'am, you should eat a bit more than that!' Nancy said maternally. 'Why, you're losing so much weight, you're naught but skin and bone.'

Briony smiled.

'Well, I know I'm not exactly fat, Nancy, but I'm not wasting away. I weigh at least eight stone, as far as I know.'

'That's not enough by a long chalk!' Nancy said stoutly. 'Leastways my Jim reckons a girl needs a bit of fat on her if she's to attract the opposite sex. My trouble is keeping me weight down! All that starchy food in the forces did for me.'

'We used to eat very well,' Briony said, smiling. 'In fact, you might have tempted me today with a bit of Spam, Nancy. Wonder why we don't get any nowadays? Dollar shortage, I suppose!'

Nancy sighed.

'Them good old days is gone for good, ma'am. Still, I do hear that the Yanks is back in force in the North. Don't see many down here though, do we? We could do with a few handsome fellows around these parts. Only really glamour boy we've got in the village is Mr. Baker.'

'You mean the vet?' asked Briony unnecessarily.

'Who else?' Nancy retorted. She gave Briony a wink. 'Now don't pretend you haven't noticed those gorgeous dark eyes of his! Why, you'd have to be blind to miss 'em. I'd go for him in a big way if he was in my class. Bet he was RAF, don't you, ma'am? Just picture him in one of those dandy blue officers' uniforms with wings across his chest. Coo, I'd as soon sit looking at him for a couple of hours as go to the pictures to see Burt Lancaster, and that's saying something, because he's my second best favourite after Alan Ladd.'

Briony laughed.

'You do me good, Nancy! I do hope you don't rush off one of these days and marry your Jim. What would I do without you?'

'Me, ma'am? I ain't nothing special.'

'I think if you were, I shouldn't be so fond of you!' Briony said honestly. 'It's just that you're so normal, Nancy, and so good-tempered and cheerful about life.'

'I've got plenty to be cheerful about, ma'am. Not the same for you shut up in this great barn of a house–' She broke off quickly, as if afraid of what she might have said if she had continued. 'Sakes alive, Cook'll have the hide off me if I don't fetch your pudding. Try and eat a bit, ma'am. It's caramel custard and you like that.'

Left alone once more, Briony's thoughts turned, not unnaturally, to the young man she had been discussing with Nancy. Was he really so good looking? Yes, when you thought about it, he was unusually handsome. He had one of those nice, strong, masculine faces. And his eyes were his most striking feature. She bit her lip, remembering the moment when she had found him staring at her.

"I wonder if he's married?" she asked herself, and rejected the idea as unlikely. He was too young, or at least too newly qualified, to be able to afford to marry yet. But he probably had a girl – several girls, in fact. He must be attractive to women.

"If I'd been free, I'd have been only too pleased to be asked out by him," Briony thought – and then blushed furiously at the idea.

"I'm behaving like a silly schoolgirl!" she reproved herself sharply. "I'll stop thinking such absurd thoughts and try to make up my mind what to do with myself this afternoon."

But deep in her heart she knew that she would be wondering what to do with herself until the young man called again.

'Thought we might have a house party this week-end,' Charles announced after dinner. The vet had still not come to see the puppy, who Briony thought seemed a lot worse, and her mind had not taken in what Charles had been saying.

'I beg your pardon?'

'I said,' Charles repeated pompously, 'that I thought we might have a house party this week-end.'

'Yes, yes of course, if you'd like it, Charles,' Briony replied.

'Does that mean you wouldn't be pleased with the notion?' Charles asked.

'No, darling, of course not. You know I enjoy entertaining. It helps to pass the time.'

'Fact of the matter is,' Charles continued with his planned announcement, 'there's a chap I used to be friendly with years ago. He's just over from America with his wife and sister-in-law. Settled out there before the war and hasn't been back until now. Took out U.S.A. citizenship when he married an American girl. Done very well for himself, too. Pots of money. I saw him at the Club today and he suggested we had a get-together to discuss old times. So I asked him and his family down for a long weekend.'

'How many will there be?' said Briony, without much interest.

'Four. That's to say Gerald Martell, his wife, and the sister-in-law, and they've a kid of seven or eight, I think – a girl. They said they could probably find some nursery to park the child in for the week-end, but I told them I didn't think you'd mind looking after her, being fond of kids. After all, you don't

55

care to come shooting and I expect we'll play a bit of Canasta after dinner, and you don't like that. So it would give you something to do.'

'I'd be very glad to look after the child,' Briony said truthfully. Deep down inside her she was hurt by Charles's obvious inference that they would be a foursome without her. At the same time, she was the first to admit that she didn't as a rule 'mix' with Charles's friends. She had tried, and failed, to get on with them. Charles accepted it, presumably, for they had never discussed it, and made his arrangements accordingly. She thought of the little American girl who was coming and wondered if she would be a precocious, spoilt child of the Shirley Temple variety.

'I'd like to put on a show, my dear,' Charles was saying. 'Fact is, Gerald has made the grade in America, from what I can gather, and I don't want him to think we're incapable of having a good time in the jolly old Mother Country. That's why I thought I'd suggest a dance, or something, for the Saturday night; evening dress, of course – the ladies always like to get themselves up. I believe Gerald's wife plays the piano, so we could dance to that, or the radiogram. What do you think of the scheme, old girl?'

Briony felt a sudden stirring of interest. This would be the first really big party they had ever given. As a rule there were select house parties that numbered four or six at the most. Besides, if others were invited, perhaps she would meet someone congenial to herself. Why, she could presumably even invite... She broke off the thought, unwilling to admit that she was hoping this would give her an opportunity to meet Robert Baker socially, have him included as one of their joint friends. After all, he was nice! And they could be good friends, of that Briony was certain. Perhaps, being new to the district, he was lonely too. He would be glad of the chance to meet other people.

'It's a fine idea, Charles. How many people shall we ask?'

Charles puffed contentedly at his pipe.

'As many as you think we can cater for. We'll have to get extra help for Cook, of course, unless we get one of the London caterers to do the buffet properly. Maybe that would be best.'

'I think it would,' Briony agreed quickly, thinking of the remarks Cook would make at the suggestion of so much extra work. And Nancy would be unwilling to give up her local Saturday night dance with Jim.

'Well, I'll get that organized, leave you to fix up the flowers for the ballroom and get it opened and aired and that kind of thing. Great Scott, it's years since we used that room – not since Mother died! I can remember the wonderful parties we used to have – an orchestra down from town and potted palms all over the place. Mother used to organize them beautifully ... as I'm sure you will, old girl!' he added with such obvious tactfulness that Briony smiled in spite of herself.

'Perhaps we'd better make a list of the people you'd like me to invite,' she said. 'You know them so much better than I do, Charles.'

Charles laboriously considered and enumerated some of their neighbours. Briony listed them under two headings – men, women.

'That should be enough, eh?' Charles asked at last.

Briony counted the columns.

'Twenty women and nineteen men, including ourselves and our week-end guests,' she said at last.

'Dash it, that won't do. Must have even numbers for a dance!' Charles complained. 'Whom have I left out?'

It was on the tip of Briony's tongue to suggest Baker, but something prevented her. She was silent while Charles considered the problem.

'Can't think of anyone else we *can* ask!' he said at last. 'There aren't any unattached men in our circle. Of course, we could ask Elliot. He may be a vet but he is an Oxford chap. Yes, we'll ask him!'

'Why not ask Mr. Baker, too?' Briony heard her voice, coolly calm and casual in spite of her inner excitement. 'He's a Cambridge man. What's more, he's fairly young and probably a good dancer. Your American friends will probably appreciate that.'

'Yes, I suppose they might,' Charles agreed after a second's hesitation. 'Very well, my dear, ask him too. Should be quite a gay week-end, what?'

'I'll wear my red velvet,' Briony said, her eyes shining. 'Why, I've only worn it once, Charles, since I bought it for my trousseau. It'll be quite in fashion, too, because it's full-skirted and off the shoulder. I'll take the bus into town tomorrow and get some nice invitation cards. Those old ones in your desk are brown with age.'

She felt excited, exhilarated, young again. This was something at last to look forward to. She felt grateful to Charles, as if he had just given her a longed-for present. Impulsively she dropped a kiss on his cheek and said:

'I'll make myself really beautiful for the occasion, Charles. You'll be proud of me!'

'My dear, I always am!' said Charles simply. Briony was touched and a deep affection for him caused her to kneel beside him as she had not done for years, and rest her chin on his knees.

'Dear Charles!' she whispered. 'You are very kind to me.'

The older man looked down at the heart-shaped face raised to his own and, unaware of the shadows beneath her eyes and the transparent thinness of the face, saw only the flush of excitement.

'You're very beautiful, Briony,' he said at last. 'How could I help being kind to you! You know, my dear, I've sometimes wondered if I did the right thing forcing you to marry me ... wondered if I've made you happy, I mean. You're such a quiet little soul. A chap never really knows what you're thinking.'

Briony felt the tears starting to her eyes. Tears for herself? For Charles? She could not say.

'Charles, you didn't force me to marry you. You mustn't say that. I *wanted* to marry you.'

'Well, yes, I know,' Charles said with unusual perception. 'But that may have been because you wanted security. You were on the rebound, my dear, as we both knew, and I took a chance. I haven't regretted it – but I wondered if you might have done.'

'But Charles, why should I? What reason could I have for being unhappy?'

'That's something only you can answer,' he replied rather pompously. 'But you don't always *look* happy, Briony. Maybe you're just remembering that fellow who was killed?'

'No!' Briony said sharply, the moment of intimacy with Charles foreshortened by his bluntness. 'No, I don't think of him. That's past. Quite past.' She jumped to her feet and went across the room for a cigarette. At that moment James knocked on the door and announced that Mr. Baker had come to see the 'animal'.

'I'll come immediately, James!' Briony said, welcoming the interruption, and not a little amused by James's snobbery that was such an exact replica of Charles's.

Robert Baker stood at the foot of the stairway, waiting for her. Their eyes met and each looked quickly away.

'Sorry to be so late, Mrs. Stone,' Robert said. 'It's been a pretty hectic day, I'm afraid. How's the puppy?'

'He doesn't seem too good,' Briony said, as she led the way upstairs. 'I'm rather concerned about him.'

'I thought he must be better,' the man replied. 'You looked so happy when you came into the hall just now.'

"So he was aware of my mood!" Briony thought in wonder.

'We're going to have a party!' she said by way of explanation. 'A really big one ... in fact, a dance. It'll be evening dress and it's always fun dressing up, at least for a woman.'

She looked at him, suddenly shy. 'You're to be invited,' she said. 'I hope you'll be able to come!'

Robert had resolved to make his visit purely professional and as brief as possible. But he knew himself weakening – knew, even as he wondered whether part of this girl's excitement was due to the fact that *he* was to be invited, that come what may he would not refuse the invitation.

'My d.j. is at home,' he said. 'But I'll ask them to send it off to me immediately. I'd love to come!'

Relief flooded through Briony and for a moment her knees felt weak and she was desperately afraid her expression might betray her feelings. It had mattered a great deal that he should come, only because it was someone she knew she'd find an interesting and likable companion, she told herself hastily. Nearly everyone else was really Charles's friend, and however hard she tried she could not find anything in common with them. There was a French word one used about people, saying they were *sympathique* – but it was more than just 'in sympathy with', which would be the nearest translation. It really meant a kind of communion of spirits. It was there between herself and Robert Baker, although they had only known each other such a brief time.

They did not speak again until Robert had injected the puppy and announced him not too seriously ill. Then he said:

'You didn't mention when the party was to be.'

'Next Saturday,' Briony told him. 'I know it's rather short notice but Charles – my husband – has some American friends coming for the week-end and we thought we'd like to give the dance in their honour.'

Robert Baker pushed his arms into his overcoat and said:

'I'd better phone my mother tonight or my d.j. won't be here in time. That really would be a tragedy!'

She looked quickly up at him and her face relaxed as she saw his smile.

'I don't suppose you know many people round here, do you?' she asked. 'It'll be an opportunity to meet some possible clients, too. Most of Charles's friends either shoot or hunt and so they all have animals of one kind or another.'

'It's really very kind of you to ask me,' Robert said, watching her changing expressions and thinking how odd it was, but true, that the two of them seemed to be entering some kind of conspiracy together. 'Not because of the possible clients, but because I'll so much enjoy a dance. Are you fond of dancing?'

'Oh yes, terribly!' Briony cried eagerly. 'I used to do masses of it during the war. But – well, my husband isn't too keen and anyway there isn't much opportunity down here.'

'I hope you won't be so busy as hostess that I won't have the chance to dance with you!'

Briony felt again that unaccountable shyness and was conscious of her heightened colour.

'No! I mean, I'm sure there'll be plenty of time for us to dance together.'

They stood for a moment in silence, not looking at one another but each very aware of the other's presence.

Presently Robert said:

'Well, thanks again for asking me. I'll see you tomorrow, of course. I was just about to say "Good-bye till Saturday".'

'And my puppy ... he's going to be all right?'

'I think so – he's no worse than I expected – just feeling a bit sorry for himself. Don't worry about him.'

'I won't,' Briony said quietly. 'Good night! And thank you for coming.'

As if he wanted thanking, Robert told himself caustically as he drove away from the house. If he continued to feel the way he felt right now about young Mrs. Stone, she would soon be thanking him for staying away.

'Hell!' he said, as he pressed his foot on the accelerator: 'It's no good pretending. I'm head over heels in love with her. Whatever happens, I must not give myself away on Saturday. It's a pretty ghastly thought, but if she ever found out, I could never see her again.'

Miserable, lonely and frustrated by the blow Fate had struck him, he took himself back to his digs to a cold supper and an even colder bed.

IV

Briony had not been looking forward to having the American child to stay. Her whole being was wrapped up in preparing for the dance and the thought of a bumptious, precocious child underfoot irritated and worried her. She was, however, to be greatly surprised.

Tea time on Friday Charles arrived home in his car with his guests. Briony went to greet them in the hail. They were talking noisily in high nasal voices and she looked from one to the other as Charles introduced them.

'Gerald – my wife Briony ... and Marion, Gerald's wife, my dear. This is Vanessa Gough, Marion's sister.'

Gerald was surprisingly like Charles, Briony thought, as she murmured a conventional welcome to her guests. At least an

American counterpart of Charles. They were both tall, slightly rotund, bluff, hearty, with high complexions. The only difference lay in their glasses – Charles's horn-rimmed, his friend's rimless, and in their voices.

The two American women were also very alike. Marion, the taller of the two, and probably the older, had what most English-women believe to be the usual superb American figure – long-legged, broad-shoul-dered, narrow-hipped. She was beautifully dressed in a smart grey tweed dress beneath a perfectly beautiful mink coat. Her heels were inches high and her nails, when she drew the violet suède gloves off, were long and scarlet tipped. Briony felt unhappily conscious of her own short, square, unvarn-ished fingers – of her tweed skirt and conventional 'twin-set'. She wished she had dressed more smartly.

Vanessa looked like a younger counterpart of her sister. Her hair and eyes were light brown, as were Marion's, and her figure and clothes just as admirable, except that she wore a sable instead of mink.

These were her first brief impressions made in the few moments before Charles said:

'And this is Belinda, Briony. I think the car ride upset her a bit. You might like to take her up to her room. I'll show the others where to go.'

The two tall American women stood slightly apart and from the narrow gap between them Briony saw a tiny, pale, much-freckled little girl staring at her from huge dark eyes that were a mixture of apprehension and acute fatigue. The child's mother said sharply:

'Where are you hiding your manners, Binny?'

'How are you, Mrs. Stone? It's very good of you to have me here.'

The child's eyes were suddenly full of tears and Briony stepped quickly forward and took one of the small, damp hands. In the other was held a rather grubby rag doll.

'Come upstairs with me, Belinda! I expect you'd like a nice wash and some tea. You must be tired after that long car journey. You can tell me all about it.'

The little girl went with her, not once, Briony realized, glancing back to where her mother stood, talking now to Charles and her husband.

Upstairs in the small dressing-room next to her own bedroom, Briony sat the child down on the pretty chintz bedcover and, kneeling beside her, began to take off the smart little coat.

'I hope you're going to like being here, darling,' she said, feeling the child's bewilderment and fear in her own heart even had she not been able to read it in the great dark eyes. 'As a matter of fact, I've got something very special to show you. Can you guess what it is?'

The little American girl bit her lip and shook her head. Briony realized she was making every effort to keep back the tears that she did not trust herself to speak. Her own voice was carefully casual.

'It's a puppy!' she went on. 'The sweetest little dog! I found him straying at the bottom of the garden. If nobody claims him, I'm going to keep him for my own. I thought you could help me choose a name for him.'

But it was no good. The child burst into floods of tears and it was several minutes before Briony could make out what she was saying between the great, body-shaking sobs.

'I want to go home. I want to go home. Please, please let me go home.'

Briony lifted Belinda on to her lap and for a moment or two the sobs continued. When she was a little calmer, Briony asked gently:

'Home to London, you mean?'

The great dark eyes, filled with tears, stared into hers.

'No! Home to Daddy. I want my Daddy. I want to go home to my Daddy.'

'But, darling, your Daddy's downstairs. He's here with you.'

For a brief instant the eyes lit with incredulous hope. Then the spark died and in a quiet little voice Belinda said:

'He's not my Daddy. He's my stepfather. My Daddy lives in California.'

Briony could have cut out her tongue for raising those pathetic hopes, even for so short an instant.

'But you can't go all that way back to California!' she said gently. 'It would take ages and ages. Why not stay here with me for a few days and we'll have a good time together? Then perhaps later on Mummy will take you back to America.'

'No, she won't. Not for six months. I'll be eight then. You see, my Mom and my Daddy are divorced. I can go and live with my Daddy for six months every year and the other six months I have to stay with Mommy. Daddy says it's only fair to Mommy that she sees me sometimes, but I'd rather live with my Daddy. I don't like my Mommy. She made my Daddy unhappy.'

Briony felt momentarily nonplussed by the quiet, grave voice explaining the adult complications of life to her. She also felt desperately sorry for the unhappy little girl. She could not think what to say to comfort her.

'I think you're nice!' Belinda said suddenly. 'You've got a swell voice – soft and funny! I expect that's 'cos you're English. What's your name?'

'Briony. And you're Belinda, aren't you?'

'Well, my Mommy calls me Binny, but

Daddy calls me Lynn. I like Lynn best. You can call me that if you'd like to.'

'All right, Lynn. And who's this?'

There was a little more colour in the cheeks now and the tears were in check.

'Oh, that's my baby, Susie. She comes everywhere with me. I'm her Mommy, but she hasn't got a Daddy at all. It must be terrible not to have a Daddy, but Susie says she loves me so much it doesn't matter. I love her, too.'

Briony suddenly recalled her other guests. She stood up and said.

'We'd better get you washed and then we must go down to tea! We'll be keeping the others waiting.'

A hot little hand clutched hers.

'Downstairs? But can't we have tea together up here – you and me? I don't want to go down there. Mommy...'

'Yes?' prompted Briony as the child hesitated.

The reply was almost a whisper.

'I felt kinda sick in the car and she was angry 'cos we had to stop. Please don't make me go down!'

Briony knew that she would always hate Marion Martell. However nice she might appear on better acquaintance, nothing would ever undo the fact that her own child was afraid of her. No wonder Lynn was such a tiny, undersized, pathetic creature! And

70

she had expected such a noisy, precocious, spoilt brat!

'Well, I'll tell you what. I'll say you aren't feeling very well. Then, after Nancy has brought in our tea, I'll tell her to bring up a tray to you. You'll like Nancy. She's great fun and very kind, too.'

'Then I guess she'll be like you, Mrs. Briony!'

Impulsively, Briony gave Lynn a hug.

'You'll see! I'll come up again and see how you are as soon as I can get away. And, Lynn, shall I tell you a secret?'

The freckled face looked at her expectantly.

'I'd much rather be having my tea up here with you and Nancy! Will you be all right till I come back? You'll see I've put some picture books on that table by your bed. They used to be mine when I was a little girl. You can look at them until Nancy comes.'

Briony did not feel, when she went into the drawing-room, that she had been greatly missed. Gerald Martell and Charles were standing by the huge log fire, talking to the two American women, who had made themselves comfortable on the sofa. Conversation ended as she came in.

'Hope the child hasn't been a bother, Mrs. Stone?'

Briony turned to Lynn's mother and could not keep the coldness from her voice.

'No! She's tired and a little upset by the car ride. I thought she'd be happier upstairs by herself.'

'Sure can be a drag on you, kids!' Marion drawled. 'I guess I ought not to have brought her to Europe but it seemed such a swell opportunity for her to get educated, and learn how the other half of the world lives!'

'Isn't she a little young for so much travelling?' Briony asked quietly, as she rang the bell for Nancy to bring tea.

'Young? I should say not. By the time I was Binny's age I'd been to half a dozen foreign countries and loved every moment of it. She's just odd – I can't seem to knock this timidity out of her. Got a lot of her father in her. But she'll grow out of it.'

'Perhaps she's naturally rather sensitive?' Briony suggested quietly.

'I declare, I don't know! She's been to two psychiatrists and they say the divorce upset her, but how could it? It's not as if she could understand the rows Lance and I used to have! And, anyway, she's had two years to get used to the idea.'

'She doesn't dislike Gerald!' Vanessa entered the conversation brightly. 'And Gerald is perfectly swell to her!'

'I guess I just try to be a good father to her,' Gerald said heartily, smugly. 'Say, did she show you that doll I gave her for

Christmas, Mrs. Stone? Sure is the cutest thing! It can walk and talk, and you actually have to change its diapers after feeding it!'

They laughed uproariously while Briony remembered the torn rag doll that was Lynn's 'baby'.

Nancy came in with the tea ... the silver tea-pot, milk jug and sugar basin glittering on the highly polished silver tray. Briony saw Charles's little nod of approval and felt suddenly sickened by the whole idea that was behind this week-end – impressing three Americans, none of whom she felt she could ever like.

She drew Nancy aside and explained briefly about the child while Charles told his guests about the silver heirlooms that had been in his family for four hundred years. Lynn was forgotten by her mother, aunt and stepfather.

During tea Briony had a better opportunity to consider her week-end visitors. Marion she knew she hated. She was hard, self-opinionated, 'bossy'! Gerald was the weaker of the two – agreeing with every comment his wife made, clearly infatuated with her; and by the sound of it, rich enough and more than willing to indulge every whim. Vanessa was not quite so easy to assess. She was quieter than her sister and brother-in-law. In her way, prettier than Marion, but she also seemed more artificial. At least Marion and

Gerald took no pains to pretend they were other than they appeared! But Vanessa seemed almost to be playing a part. Her movements were graceful, but studied. The tilt of her beautifully coiffeured head was surely not quite natural as she listened to something Charles was telling her about the shooting rights he held in the neighbourhood. Now and again she turned to include Briony in the conversation, but the way in which she did so made it seem, to Briony at least, that she was the 'odd man out'.

Briony looked at her husband, obviously very pleased with life as he helped himself to another cucumber sandwich. His face was flushed and his voice was raised, slightly bragging, Briony thought, with sudden dislike. It was strange how she could sit back like this, feeling herself to be an unobserved onlooker! She could even see herself, mouse-like, rather dowdy between her two American women guests, rather nastily criticizing them in her mind as if she were superior. For a moment or two she disliked herself as much as everyone else in the room. Then tea was over and Nancy had come to take the tray.

'What say a hand or two of Canasta before dinner?' Gerald was suggesting. His wife and sister-in-law agreed instantly. Charles looked at Briony.

'I have to go upstairs and see to one or two

74

things,' she excused herself thankfully. And was grateful to Charles for not forgetting her!

Lynn lay curled up on the bed, Susie's ragged head close to hers as she bent over a book. She looked up as Briony came into the room and her cheeks were no longer pale, the eyes sparkling now with excitement rather than with tears.

'Oh, Mrs. Briony! This is the *Water Babies*. Daddy read it me last holidays. It's our favourite. Daddy can't let me have a copy when I go away because his is a very, very old and special one that's very valuable. I did ask Mommy to give me an ordinary copy for Christmas, but I guess she forgot.'

'I'm so glad, Lynn,' Briony said, as she sat down beside the child. 'Did Nancy give you a nice tea?'

'Oh, swell. There were things she says you call "crumpets". I ate two. I like Nancy. She's nice, just like you said, but not a bit like you after all!'

'Nice people aren't always alike!' Briony said, smiling. 'And, Lynn, just call me Briony – never mind the Mrs. part of it. Would you like to come and see my puppy now? He's not very well and the vet has to come and see him and give him injections.'

Lynn jumped off the bed and stood beside Briony, one hand slipping naturally into hers.

'We've got a dog at home,' she said. 'He's a spaniel. Daddy takes him for walks when he gets back from the office. Daddy's a business man. We had to have a vet to our dog when he got distemper. But he soon got better.'

The child was still shy – her voice was still quiet even while the words ran off her tongue as if she hadn't had a chance to talk to anyone for weeks. Maybe she hadn't! Maybe the beautiful Marion did not like to be reminded all the time of 'Daddy'.

'You'll be able to write and tell your Daddy about my puppy,' said Briony gently.

The little girl looked at her unbelievingly.

'You mean – you'll help me write a real letter to my Daddy? Oh, Mrs. Briony – I mean, just Briony, you're swell! He'll be so pleased. I can't write to him very often. I'm not very good yet at spelling, and that kind of thing. It sure takes me a long while to write even a post-card. Of course, Daddy writes to me, but he has to do block letters because I can't read his ordinary writing, so he can't say a lot either.'

"Can't your mother read his letters to you?" thought Briony angrily. "Can't she find time from her amusements to help you write to him?"

She felt suddenly immensely sorry for the man who must love his little girl dearly for her to love him so much, and yet who had to live for six months of the year on a few childish words.

'We'll write a long, long letter together – on Sunday afternoon,' she said. 'Not tomorrow because I've got to do the flowers for the ballroom. We're going to have a dance and the room must look beautiful. You can help me.'

'I'm not very good with my hands,' Lynn said, obviously repeating an adult comment she had overheard. 'Except when I'm at home. Daddy says I'm really a great help around the house. Sometimes I make him a cup of coffee. He says it sure is the best coffee he ever tasted. You drink tea in England, don't you?'

'Well, we have tea at tea time, but we drink coffee too,' said Briony. 'Shall we go and see the puppy now, Lynn?'

They spent a happy half-hour together with the dog, who seemed better. Lynn, when pressed, decided he should be called Tom, after the little boy in the *Water Babies*. Briony approved – after all, it was a nice plain, everyday kind of name for a mongrel pup!

As they were about to go, Robert Baker was shown into the room by Nancy.

Briony introduced Lynn, who looked at the vet shyly.

'We've just christened the puppy "Tom",' Briony said, inwardly conscious of her own dishevelled appearance and the peculiarly searching look in the young man's eyes.

'Is Lynn tomorrow night's belle of the ball?' Robert asked.

The child looked puzzled and Briony explained.

'Oh no!' Lynn said, when she understood. 'I'll be in bed and, anyway, the most beautiful lady there is sure to be Mrs. – I mean Briony!'

It was Robert's turn to look puzzled. He still did not know that this was her name. Lynn, answering his question, said:

'Didn't you know? I think it's such a pretty name and it just suits her.'

'So do I!' said Robert. 'And I think you're right about her being the "belle of the ball", too.'

'Just wait till you see Lynn's mother and aunt!' Briony replied, laughing. 'Real glamour!'

'Being glam'rous doesn't mean being pretty, my Daddy says!'

Her companions laughed.

'How old is she?' Robert asked.

'Very, very old and so very young,' Briony replied, wondering if Robert would understand her remark. She watched him as he bent down and explained what he was doing to the curious child. He was very gentle, very sweet with her, but Briony felt she had known instinctively that anyone who was so fond of animals must be fond of children too. She liked him for it.

'Won't it hurt him?' Lynn asked.

'Not if we're very careful! It's all over so quickly, he hardly knows it has happened. He has to have it to make him better. Will you hold him now, Mrs. Stone?'

'No, she doesn't like to be called Mrs.,' Lynn said, gently explaining. 'You have to call her "Briony".'

Robert looked embarrassed, but Briony laughed.

'Why not? After all, it's the party tomorrow night and no one will be very formal then.'

'Then you must call me Robert! It's only fair.'

Robert ... Bob ... but Bob was dead. This was another Robert with dark brown eyes instead of blue.

She looked up and met his eyes. For a brief instant time stood still and her heart raced in utter confusion.

'I think Tom's thirsty. He's trying to get to the saucer of milk!'

The child's high treble broke the moment. They both turned towards the dog. Robert knew his hands were trembling, but he didn't care. Nothing in the world mattered but the look he had seen for a moment in Briony's eyes ... a look of appeal, of loneliness, of understanding ... of love?

'My – my d.j. has come,' he said at last. 'I was afraid it wasn't going to turn up. Will you have the last dance with me, whatever happens in between?'

She didn't seem to be surprised by his request, but nodded her head.

'I'll come before lunch tomorrow to give the pup his treatment. I expect you'll be pretty busy in the afternoon.'

'We're going to do the flowers!' Lynn said. 'Briony has promised I shall help.'

'Then I'm sure the room will look beautiful. I suppose I can't very well hope for the first dance with you, Lynn?'

The freckled face broke into an amused grin. She looked suddenly like any other child – the scared, forlorn look vanished in amusement.

'I'll have to go to bed ... but you could come and say good night to me – couldn't he, Briony?'

'Well, I expect we can smuggle him up the back stairs!' Briony said, rightly assuming that Lynn's mother might object but not caring anyway.

'It's a promise,' Robert said. 'I suppose I ought to go now.'

Lynn spoke for Briony when she said:

'Oh, what a pity! I like you. I like Briony and Nancy too. I thought I wouldn't like anyone in England. The people in our hotel are just horrible and I guess I thought it was because they were English. But I suppose it isn't what you are but how you are that matters.'

'Out of the mouths of babes and sucklings!' Briony said thoughtfully. 'So much wisdom in one so young is quite frightening.'

'Are you really coming to the dance tomorrow night, Robert?' the child continued. 'I wish I was grown up and you were my date. You sure are handsome!'

Briony laughed until the tears were coming to her eyes. Robert, embarrassed but equally amused, said:

'I wish I could date you, Lynn, if that's the correct way of saying I'd like to have you for my girl.'

'Haven't you got a girl?' Lynn asked, fulfilling Briony's expectations of a precocious American child now, but in a sweet way to which neither she, nor apparently Robert, objected.

'No, I haven't got a girl,' Robert said, his eyes once more turning to Briony although he addressed the child. 'I did once nearly get engaged to a girl, but she decided to marry someone else before I got up courage enough to tell her how I felt about her. Since then ... well, I just haven't met anyone I liked enough.'

Lynn considered him gravely.

'It's an awful waste of you, isn't it?'

Robert grimaced.

81

'I don't know. I'm a dull kind of chap really.'

'I don't think so – do you, Briony? I think he's real fun, don't you?'

Robert watched while Briony tried to answer both questions at once and with reserve. At last she said simply:

'Yes, I think he's very nice too.'

'Well, I'd better push off,' Robert said abruptly. The conversation was getting a little out of hand, and he was unsure whether they were talking for each other or merely for the child. If only his emotions were less confused, perhaps he could think more clearly. It was more than time that he started to tighten the reins. His heart was fast beginning to take control of his head and he was scared to death of where it might lead him. "Briony – Mrs. Stone – yes, remember that 'Mrs.' that Lynn wishes to forget!" he told himself sharply. "It isn't your line to fool around with another fellow's wife, however much you think you dislike the 'other fellow'." And he would stake his life on the fact that *she* wasn't the type to have idle flirtations. It wouldn't be good for either of them to – to what? To fall in love?

Robert bade them an abrupt good-bye which puzzled them both, not having telepathized his train of thought! After he had left them, Lynn said thoughtfully:

'Isn't it a pity, Briony, that you're married?

I mean, if you hadn't got a husband you could marry Robert, couldn't you? Then it would be just like a story book with you as the Princess and Robert as Prince Charming.'

'You're only a little girl!' Briony said sharply. 'You don't understand what you're talking about.'

Lynn looked at her from a face suddenly drawn and white.

'I'm sure sorry I offended you, Briony. I know I'm only little. But I do know about married people. You see, Mommy couldn't marry Uncle Gerald because she'd already got a husband. So that's the same as you, isn't it? Of course, there's always a divorce thing, isn't there? But then it's not very nice for the one who's left behind. My Daddy was left all alone and he's very unhappy. I'm glad I'm not old enough to fall in love.'

Briony stooped to one knee and for a moment hid her face against that flat little chest. Tears were in her eyes and her voice was barely audible as she whispered:

'I wish I weren't either, Lynn. Oh, how I wish I weren't!'

V

Briony was putting the finishing touches to her hair when Charles, who had dressed an hour ago and had been to see about the drinks, came into their room. He looked at his wife's reflection in the mirror and nodded approvingly.

'You look very lovely, my dear!' he said. 'Thought you might like to wear these. They were Mother's.'

He dropped on to the glass-topped dressing-table a beautiful diamond and ruby necklace with matching drop earrings.

Briony cried out in admiration.

'Charles, they're beautiful! I've never seen them before. They'll look just perfect with my red dress. How clever of you to pick them out for me!'

She held them against her white throat, where the rubies twinkled and caught the even more red gleam of her velvet dress. They made her appearance perfect.

'Of course, they're worth a great deal of money,' Charles warned her, 'so be careful what you do with them. They look very nice, my dear. I must go down again now. Time to mix the cocktails. I think it should all go off very well tonight. As a matter of fact, Gerald is pretty staggered already by the set-up, as he calls it. Incidentally, I had a look at the ballroom, Briony. The flowers look perfect. Mother would approve, I know. Tell me, what d'you think of Marion and Vanessa?'

Briony fastened the beautiful necklace, and because she was feeling so excited and happy and confident of the radiance of her own reflection in the mirror, she tried to be charitable.

'They're both very attractive women,' she said truthfully as far as looks were concerned. 'But I think Vanessa is the prettier ... and nicer.'

Charles looked pleased.

'Just what I think. Dashed attractive girl, Vanessa. Wonder she hasn't married again. Lost her husband in the war, y'know. You'd think a pretty girl like that would be snapped up.'

This was an uncommonly long speech for Charles and Briony looked at her husband curiously. Could Charles be attracted to the beautiful Vanessa? Well, more than vaguely attracted as any man must be? Charles, mistaking her glance, said quickly:

'Of course, she isn't a patch on you, old girl! Prettiest woman there tonight. Very proud of you. Well, must be getting down. Don't be too long.'

Briony winced as she heard him shut the

door behind him. How she abominated that favourite 'endearment' of his – 'old girl'! After all, she wasn't old and the term itself was contradictory, since you couldn't be old and a girl. Still, you could hardly say 'old woman' as a term of affection! Where had he picked up the phrase in the first place? Surely the long-dead Montague Stone couldn't have called Charles's mother 'old girl'! That hardly fitted in with her picture of a tall, gracious, highly dignified Victorian Mamma.

Briony looked at herself again in the mirror and for a moment she allowed herself to dream a little. This was her first party – her very first party dress. Soon she would go downstairs and her mother and father would be greeting their guests and presently Robert would appear ... Bob ... the war-time Bob? In her day-dream, it was both of them ... it was her own dear love coming into the room towards her. She looked beautiful and her beauty was all for him. In a moment the orchestra would start to play a tune – slow, dreamy music, and his arms would be round her–

'Briony?'

She nearly cried out in surprise at the sudden unexpectedness of the voice in her room. She swung round and saw a forlorn little figure in a pale pink night-dress that made Lynn even more shrimp-like in appearance than she had been in her day-clothes.

'Darling, you'll catch your death of cold. What are you doing out of bed?'

But the last words were smothered as the child rushed into her arms and, heedless of Briony's immaculate appearance, clasped her in a positive agony of unhappiness.

When the tears had ceased for a moment, Briony smoothed the damp hair from the hot little forehead and said:

'Lynn, dearest! What's the matter? We were so happy this afternoon – why tears now? You must be overtired.'

'It's just – just that I thought suddenly – I only just thought – when I was waiting for you to come and say good night to me – I thought – oh, Briony, there's only tomorrow and then I'll never ever see you again!'

Briony rocked the thin little body to and fro. All the happiness of a moment ago had drained away from her and her heart was filled with this child's need for her and her fear of the future. She did not know what to say to comfort her.

'Darling Lynn, you mustn't let yourself be so upset. We'll always be friends. I'll write to you often ... that's a promise. And maybe you can come and stay with me again.'

But the sobs continued and through them came broken words that Briony slowly pieced together. It was awful to love people. If you loved anyone, it hurt you to leave them. It was better to hate everyone, then nothing mattered. There was only Susie, the rag doll.

'But Daddy–'

Daddy was three thousand miles away, and five long months. Five months could mean five years to a child.

Why, why did Marion Martell, when she obviously had no use and very little affection for Lynn, insist on taking her away from her father? How could any woman deny her child those few little acts of love that meant all the difference between happiness and misery? There was so little she, Briony, had been able to do in the past twenty-four hours and yet already the child loved her. Couldn't Marion Martell have done as much? Just a little time, a little understanding, a few endearments? Lynn, like a puppy, was the kind of child who only needed a pathetic amount of encouragement in order to give her whole heart to that person.

'Lynn, try to stop crying! I tell you what I'll do – I'll ask Mummy if you can stay on for a little while ... perhaps until she goes on to France. Do you know when that will be?'

'In February!' Lynn said. 'We go to Paris then. Oh, Briony, do you really mean it? Do you think she'd let me stay? It would be swell!'

'I'll certainly ask,' Briony said carefully, 'but don't count on it too much, darling, in case Mummy has other plans for you. And in case you do think too much about it in bed tonight, think instead of the letter we're going to write to Daddy tomorrow. Lynn, have you got a calendar?'

'A – a what?'

'A calendar. All the days of the weeks and months are written on it. I'm going to give you one. It's to be a secret between you and me. You can tick off the days then until you are going to see Daddy again. You'll soon see how quickly they go when you do that.'

When she promised to get the calendar immediately, Lynn went back to her bed without any further tears. For a moment, her attention was distracted. The calendar delighted her. She was quick to understand what it meant and eager to start striking off the days.

'Do you know when you go back?' Briony asked, feeling a little guilty but not really caring what Marion would say to this new 'game'.

'No, I don't, Briony. It'll be six months from when I came to Mommy, and that was the day before Christmas Eve.'

Briony helped Lynn work out six months from that date and they underlined the day in the middle of June with Briony's lipstick. That's what they mean by a 'red-letter day', she explained.

The thin arms went round her neck and

the freckled face was pressed against her cheek as she said good night.

'I do love you so much, Briony. And I forgot to tell you that you look just like the Princess tonight. Do you think Robert will remember he's coming to say good night?'

'I'm sure he will, Poppet. Now, cuddle down and I'll leave this little light on until Robert comes. Good night, Precious, sleep well.'

'Briony, thank you for the calendar. I can tell Daddy, can't I? It isn't a secret from him?'

'No, Lynn, you can tell Daddy.'

'I always tell him everything,' said the voice softly. 'At least, as much as I can.'

Briony had a quick mental picture of those carefully scrawled words: *'Darling Daddy, I do want you...'* or *'Dear Daddy, I'm so longing to come home'*. Poor wretched man – he must long so much for the sight of those letters and yet know so much misery for what they contained. Was there nothing he could do? Or did he not realize just how much his child needed him?

"Maybe I could write to him, too!" Briony thought on an impulse. "I could let him know how it looks to me ... say I might be wrong, but hint. I'm sure if he knew how miserable Lynn is away from him, he would find some way to keep her all the year round."

90

'Darling, I must go downstairs now. I shall be late. I'll peep in again later on just to see if you're safely tucked in and asleep.'

"That is what her mother should be saying, doing!" Had Marion been to see the child before bedtime? Not as far as Briony knew and she would not question the child.

Lynn, however, answered her unspoken question by saying:

'Please tell Mommy and Uncle Gerald and Aunt Vanessa good night for me, Briony.'

It was with some satisfaction that Briony joined the Americans in the library and sought out Lynn's mother.

'Your little girl asked me to tell you good night,' she said coldly.

'Oh, for crying out loud! I'd forgotten all about her,' Marion said, laughing. 'She's so mouse-like I declare I sometimes don't know I've got a child. Why, at her age I'd have been clamouring for Momma and Poppa to come and tell me good night!'

'Maybe she doesn't want to bother you?' Briony asked icily.

'Now there you are!' Marion replied, waving a slender white hand vaguely in the air. 'That's Binny all over. She just isn't natural. Why she can't be like other kids beats me.'

Briony suddenly hit on an idea.

'Maybe she isn't too well,' she suggested. 'I think ... that is, if you don't mind my

91

voicing an opinion—'

'Go ahead, dear! I'll take any advice on that one I can get.'

'I was just going to suggest that she doesn't strike me as being very strong. I think the travelling upsets her. She needs a bit of a rest.'

'Say, you think she's sickening for something? Measles?'

'No, just run down. I don't know what your plans are, Mrs. Martell, but if it would be convenient, I thought if she could stay on here for a little while we might get her really fit before you go to Paris.'

'Say, that's a swell idea!' Gerald said with a little too much eagerness. 'Kind of freshen her up for the rest of the vacation.'

'It's very kind of you to offer, dear,' Marion said, 'but I couldn't possibly take advantage of your hospitality.'

'Why not?' Charles suddenly interrupted the conversation. 'Give Briony something to do. She's fond of kids. Do 'em both good.'

'When Charles puts it so nicely, I don't see how you can refuse, Marion.'

Briony looked round at Vanessa, who was regarding her with an amused expression.

'It's okay by me!' said Marion. 'And I'm grateful. Fact is, I sometimes just don't know what to do with my own child. She's like a stranger to me. I'll admit I don't understand her. Fact is, I'd let Lance have her all year round, only it doesn't seem kinda right to shove a seven-year-old kid – a girl at that – on to her father. Lance wanted her, of course, but he'd have to have some woman in to take care of her while he was in the office and I'm not having my friends say I've abandoned my kid to a strange help. It'd be different if Lance married again.'

"So that explains it all," Briony thought. "She admits she isn't really fond of Lynn – doesn't even want her. But is worried what her friends will say if they know her ex-husband has hired a housekeeper to take care of the child." In other words, for the sake of appearances, Lynn was having to suffer as much as her father. Surely the man did not realize this? If so, it should be easy enough to refuse to let Lynn go back at the end of her next six months' visit and that would take care of everything. Marion would be vindicated by her friends, since Lance was acting by force. And she would certainly not take the matter to Court, since it resulted in just what she wanted. Then everyone would be happy.

'Charles is embarrassed by all this, Marion,' Vanessa said suddenly. 'You forget he's an Englishman. In England, they don't discuss their intimate domestic affairs in front of strangers!'

Charles coughed, then gave a sheepish laugh.

'Dash it all – hardly strangers, what?'

The conversation ended abruptly when James announced the first of their guests. Briony slipped into the rôle of hostess and was so busy that she only caught a glimpse of Robert when he arrived and then lost sight of him again. She assumed he must have gone upstairs to Lynn.

When she next had time to glance round the now crowded ballroom, she saw him dancing with Vanessa. Briony stood perfectly still, watching him, knowing that the colour had drained from her face and that she was desperately, bitingly jealous. Robert was laughing at something that Vanessa had said. Her hand, holding a transparent square of chiffon, was resting behind his head, her cheek was very close to his. Then the fierce, almost primeval emotion drained away, leaving her utterly miserable. They had every right to dance close to one another ... to do whatever they wished. Vanessa was not, like herself, married. If she was attracted by Robert and he by her – and how could he help but find her attractive, for she looked like a Varga girl in that gold lamé dress split up one nylon-clad slender leg, the neckline of the dress cut almost to the waist! – then they could let their feelings develop without a qualm. Briony had no right to wish herself in Vanessa's place, far less to be jealous.

With a sick feeling in her stomach she turned away from them and went back to the servants' quarters to find James and see how long it would be before the buffet supper was ready.

Half an hour later Briony saw them together again, Robert handing Vanessa a plate. This time Gerald was with them. He looked flushed – almost as if he might have been drinking rather a lot. Unable to prevent herself, Briony excused herself to her companion and moved over to join them.

'Good evening, Mrs. Stone!' How polite Robert sounded! She glanced briefly at him and looked quickly away again.

'Swell party,' Vanessa remarked. 'Guess I wasn't aware you could have this kind of fun in England. Robert's a grand dancer, too. I always thought Englishmen were pretty hopeless dancers.'

Gerald looked annoyed, whether with Robert or Vanessa, Briony wasn't sure.

'It would be very difficult not to dance well with you, Miss Gough.'

'Now come off it, Robert. We agreed on Christian names!'

"Did you?" Briony thought. "So did we. But I'm Mrs. Stone again! Oh, Robert, I was mad, quite mad ever to imagine there was something between us! How could there have been? You knew I was married. Why should you have cared anyway? But I thought... I thought... How can I have been so stupid!"

She heard her own voice, cool, controlled:

'I'm glad you're enjoying the party, Vanessa – and you, Mr. Baker.'

'The flowers are really beautiful!'

Her heart leapt and pounded. Robert knew she ... she and Lynn had done the flowers.

'It's time you danced with your host!' Charles broke into the conversation, addressing Vanessa. 'Can't say I'm up to young Baker's standard but I'll not tread on your toes.'

Vanessa laughed, a low husky laugh.

'Your wife will vouch for you, Charles. I'll go by what she says.'

'Charles dances very well,' Briony said. 'He may not know the latest steps or the newest dances, perhaps, but he's always in time.'

'Sedate, that's me!' Charles said, pleased with Briony's praise.

'Perhaps I might have the pleasure, Mrs. Stone?'

'Yes, thank you – I'd like to dance!'

A moment later she was leaving the dining-room, Robert's arm guiding her back towards the ballroom ... no, beyond the ballroom on to the staircase that led to the east wing of the house. He mounted a few steps and then sat down, pulling her down beside him.

'You don't mind ... Briony?'

She raised her head and met his eyes and knew that nothing he ever did could be wrong with her.

'It was so hot and crowded,' Robert said hesitantly. 'And I've barely caught a glimpse of you all evening – you've been so busy. It's time you devoted a few minutes to this guest!'

'You seemed quite busy yourself, Robert!'

The words slipped out in spite of her determination not to say them.

'You mean Miss Gough? She's a good dancer, but oh, oh! what tiresome females these Americans are! So much superficial gossip! It's good to relax.'

Briony felt the tension leaving her body and she relaxed in so far as the awakened nerves of her body permitted.

'Did you see Lynn?'

He smiled.

'Yes – she's really crazy about you, Briony. Thinks you're the most wonderful person in the whole world – except her father, of course.'

'You remember what I told you today about the general set-up with father and mother? Tonight she had another break-down and it seems she is desperate because she has to leave here on Monday. That poor child needs love and security, Robert. Do you think I'd be wrong if I wrote to her father and told him so? Marion admitted tonight that she couldn't be bothered with Lynn but she felt she ought to have her half the year in case her friends thought she was neglecting the child! Surely if he knew – and he must love her to have inspired such devotion in return – he would find some way to keep her.'

Robert shook his head.

'One doesn't always get thanked for interfering in other people's affairs. You don't know how he'll take it.'

'I'd risk his disapproval of me if it helped Lynn in the end,' Briony cried. 'At least Marion has agreed to let Lynn stay here until they go to Paris next month.'

'That's fine – for both you and Lynn!' Robert said. 'That might give you more time to cope with Lynn's father. I mean, you could drop the odd hint that all isn't well in your first letter and see how he replies. If he presses for further information you can let your back hair down. If he ignores the reference or doesn't pay any attention, then I think you'd better steer clear.'

Briony gave a little sigh.

'I felt sure you'd see a way out, Robert. That's just what I'll do. You know, I'm getting so fond of Lynn and so maternal about her, I shall feel as if I've lost my own child when she has gone.'

Robert took his pipe from his pocket and with a glance at Briony to see if she objected, carefully packed it and lit it. Then he said:

'Lynn doesn't look like you, but I have the feeling with her that she might be your child. I mean, there's so much in her make-up that is also in yours. Oh, lord, what am I saying? How can I possibly know what you are really like!'

Briony clasped her hands on her lap and said:

'Everyone forms instinctive first opinions of other people. I understand how you think you know – about me, I mean. You see, I know a little about you, too. Shall I tell you?'

Robert nodded.

'You're shy – but self-confident. I mean by that you always rely on your own judgment rather than on other people's. You're gentle but firm. Once you've made up your mind, little or nothing can change it. You're kind but exacting. You'd hate anything but a square deal for everyone, yourself included, but you'd put yourself second.'

Robert laughed.

'Well, you're right about some things. I'm a stubborn devil. I've got a temper, too, when roused. Now you've broken the ice I'll tell you what I think about you, shall I?'

It had been a semi-humorous conversation until that moment, but suddenly Robert became serious and, in spite of his inner self telling him to be quiet, he heard himself saying:

'You're like Lynn because you are sensitive; because you are afraid of life. At least, you seem to me to be frightened. It's as if you didn't trust yourself to be happy. Does that make sense?'

Briony bit her lip. Robert had told her something about herself which she had not acknowledged even while in her heart she knew it now to be true. She was afraid of life – afraid to let herself embrace life as she had once done because, like Lynn, life had hurt her. Her marriage to Charles had been an escape from reality, from emotion. Robert, without realizing the cause, had guessed at the truth and forced her to admit it.

'You aren't denying it, Briony? I hope I haven't offended you?'

She shook her head numbly.

'No. You're right, of course. You see, I lost someone very dear to me in the war. After-wards I was very unhappy. I – I've been afraid since then to let myself come alive again. Do you know that Lynn, in spite of her very tender years, actually told me in her childish way that it might be better never to love anyone because it hurts so much to lose them.'

Robert looked at the grave, delicately moulded face, and felt his own heart aching with a combination of tenderness and fear. It was true that to love invariably brought pain in its wake. For himself there could be nothing but unhappiness in loving this girl who was, first and last, a married woman. *He could not and must never forget that fact.* There could be no happy ending to his love story. Any more than there had been for her. Her words had at least explained the probable reason for her marriage to Charles Stone – rebound from the war-time affair.

'I suppose it's wrong, or at least cowardly, to retire into a shell, shutting yourself away from life,' Briony was saying softly. 'But life itself had become unbearable. If you can turn yourself into a being without emotions, then it is possible to go on living. Unfortunately something or other is always finding a way in beneath that armour – Lynn, for instance, and my puppy. One loves in spite of wishing not to.'

It was on the tip of Robert's tongue to tell her then that he loved her; that in spite of the insupportable barriers that would always lie between them, he had fallen in love with her nonetheless. But he refrained ... as much for her sake as for his own. At least while she was ignorant of his feelings, he could be her friend ... perhaps help her a little to be less lonely, less unhappy. Once she knew how he felt, she would of course send him out of her life, possibly even despise him. And yet ... there was something in her eyes, in the way she looked at him, that made him wonder whether, perhaps, had she been unmarried, he might not have made her care for him.

'I – I suppose we should go back to the ballroom,' Briony was saying. He could not know that she had been afraid of the intimacy of their conversation betraying her into saying more than was possible. For she knew now that she loved the man beside her; knew that if she allowed herself to be controlled by her heart rather than her mind, she would fall in love again ... she, who had believed that with Bob, all love had died. How wrong she had been! How simply and easily this second love had come into her life! She had known Robert less than a week, but already she felt she had known him always, and that if it were possible for them to speak their minds without reservation, he would understand.

A wry smile touched the corners of her lips as she asked herself whether he would also understand if she told him now that she loved him! He would probably think she was a mental case and be extremely embarrassed into the bargain. After all, she had no indication of how he felt towards her. He liked her ... that much she knew ... and there was that special bond between them that made them sensitive to each other's thoughts, moods. But if there was anything more, she must not know, or even think about it. 'I've been wanting to dance with you very much,' she heard Robert's voice as he helped her to her feet and they started back down the stairs.

Someone had put 'Blue Tango' on the radiogram. The haunting romantic strain of the violins filled Briony's ears as they joined the other dancers. Then Robert's arm was round her and she was conscious of his hand holding hers tightly, his body leading hers into the beautiful rhythm of the dance.

There were ten or twelve other couples on the dance floor but Briony did not know or care who they were. She was too carried away by the desperate force of her emotions. They had not, after all, died with Bob; they had slept through the long winter years and now, as if the spring had touched her nerves to life, they had reawakened with dreadful, frightening intensity. Every nerve in her body was aware of the contact with the man in whose arms she danced. Each nerve throbbed and her knees felt weak. Somewhere her brain told her that Robert's cheek was touching hers, that his arm had tightened round her waist, that his voice was whispering against her hair:

'Oh, God, Briony – you're so very lovely, so lovely!'

Had he spoken? Was she dreaming? If she

opened her eyes would she find that this was not reality?

'Briony!'

She felt the wildness of the music in her veins and in sudden abandonment she clung to Robert, pressing her cheek closer against his. The dance had become nothing now but an excuse to be in his arms. She felt him trembling and knew that he felt as she did. She was suddenly desperately afraid.

Then abruptly the dance ended. A voice said:

'Wish I knew how to tango properly, John!'

Someone else said:

'Let's go and get a drink and sit the next one out.'

Then Robert released her and she knew that he was leading her off the floor, away to a quiet corner of the room, his hand supporting her beneath an elbow. She felt herself guided into a chair. She knew she must look at him but was trying fiercely to get her emotions under control before she did so. Someone far less perceptive than Robert would read in her eyes what was in her heart.

'Did you mind?' he asked, so quietly that she was not quite certain if she had heard him correctly.

She looked up at him then and awareness of her own feelings was swamped by recognition of his. He was in love with her! He felt the same.

'Oh, Robert!' she whispered, and turned her head quickly away.

It was an admission, a silent admission of the truth for both of them. Each knew now how the other felt. Robert, unable to trust himself not to ignore the room full of people who might, for all he knew, have been observing their strange wild dance, felt that he must leave this girl before he threw the last vestige of reason to the winds and made violent love to her. He must get away before he said too much; before further damage was done.

'I'm going to get a drink,' he said quietly. 'Then I'll try to dance with someone else. Briony ... we'll still have the last dance, won't we? You promised!'

'Yes,' she replied, still not looking at him. 'Robert, give me a cigarette before you go.'

But even the act of holding a cigarette for her, of lighting it, for him was a further betrayal of their overstrung nerves. Their hands trembled as they touched briefly and darted apart. Then their eyes met and suddenly there was quiet after the storm and they looked into each other's eyes and smiled.

'Crazy, isn't it?' Robert said gruffly. And before she could reply, he was walking away from her towards the door that led out of the room.

'All by yourself, old girl? Feeling all right, I hope?'

Briony looked up at her husband and felt as if she had been knocked into another world. Charles seemed a complete stranger. Slowly his face came into perspective and she said with an effort:

'It's a little warm in here, Charles. I was resting for a few moments.'

He sat down on the empty chair beside her and mopped his forehead with a handkerchief.

'Jolly good party, though. Must say I'm enjoying myself. That Vanessa's a pretty fine dancer. She's been teaching me to samba! Never thought I'd see the day when I'd do that. We must have a dance, old thing. Must dance with my wife, what? Next one, shall we?'

'Charles – not just now. Later. I must rest for a moment. I'd like a cup of coffee if there's one to be had.'

'Try and get you one ... back in a jiffy. Jolly good party – do say so myself...'

And he was gone.

Briony looked round the room a little wildly. Robert had gone and with him all the warmth and security and life and enjoyment. He had gone to the bar, of course. He would come back later. They were promised for the last dance.

For a moment her heart jolted at the thought that Robert might have gone home. But he couldn't ... he couldn't do that! she thought desperately. However sensible it might be, however much it was the right thing for him to do, he couldn't! They must have that dance, she must be in his arms just once more. Tomorrow would be like yesterday. She might see him but that would be all. They would never, never speak of this evening ... of what lay in their hearts. But tonight was theirs. Robert must feel that, too. She couldn't have misjudged him on that point. He had felt as she had done. For a few brief moments in eternity they had been one person and she had known that their beings existed with the same thoughts, desires, fears, bewilderments, and the same hopeless, all-powerful love.

'I'm having such a wonderful time, Mrs. Stone! It was so good of you to ask us.'

'Briony dear, this is the greatest fun. I sure am glad we haven't missed the opportunity to see how you English enjoy yourselves!'

'Had a little more champagne than is good for me, I think, Briony. Lovely party, though. Jane wants you to come to dinner and bridge. Oh, I forgot – you don't play. Well, come to dinner all the same!'

Voices beat on her mind and Briony heard her own voice, quiet, oddly commonplace, making formal replies to her guests as she moved like an automaton among them. Only her eyes searched the room incessantly for Robert's tall figure, the brown head, the dark eyes.

An hour passed. Briony danced with several of her guests including Gerald Martell, who held her far too close for her liking. Gerald, it seemed, had had 'a little too much champagne'. Still she did not see Robert. Then Charles was beside her, saying:

'You look rather pale and tired, old girl. It's nearly one a.m., you know. Think it's time we packed it up. Shall I announce the last dance?'

Briony looked round the room for the thousandth time and still could not see Robert. So he had gone home! She nodded wearily to Charles.

'Think we'll give 'em that good old hinter!' Charles said. 'That'll give 'em the idea of going home. We've still got that old record, haven't we, my dear? You remember, "Good Night, Sweetheart"?'

He hummed the words a little out of tune while he searched amongst the pile of records, broke off as he found it and put it on the gramophone.

'We still haven't had our dance yet!' Charles turned towards her.

'I – I did promise the next one to somebody,' Briony said frantically. 'As a matter of fact – I–'

'That's all right, old girl. I'm sort of committed myself. Oh, there you are, Vanessa. This is to be the last one. Let's see if I've improved a little under your jolly good tuition, what?'

As they moved away, Briony saw Robert. He was coming straight across the room towards her. Almost rudely, he pushed between the couples who inadvertently barred his way. His eyes never left Briony's face.

'I assume this is the last one?'

She nodded.

Robert turned to the radiogram and carefully nudged the pick-up so that it slid back to the start. No one seemed to have noticed except Briony, who met Robert's smile with a grateful look. Then she was in his arms again.

'I thought you'd gone home!' she whispered. Her relief was so enormous that she had to say it.

'But I wouldn't have broken a promise, Briony.'

"I can always trust you. I should have known," thought Briony. Then the music claimed them. She heard Robert's voice half-singing, half-humming the words of the old song: 'Good Night, Sweetheart'. She knew, as he intended she should, that he was speaking the words for her. Then Vanessa's strident voice broke in with:

'Don't be so British, Charles! Cheek to cheek is how I like it!'

'That goes for me, too!' Robert said, almost laughing in the brief ecstasy of the moment. Roughly he pulled her yielding body to him, and Briony knew that never, never could she be in his arms again. If it were not for the restraint imposed on them by the other people in the room ... if they were dancing alone, then she could not answer for her own behaviour. As it was, she knew that she did not care who saw them, who could read on her face, guess by her closed eyes, Robert's tight embrace, that they were wildly in love. Hysterically she thought that they were playing the wrong tune. It should have been 'People Will Say We're in Love'. Then Robert said:

'I shall always remember this night, Briony, as the most wonderful in my whole life!'

For him it was the first time he had known the full power and the pain of being hopelessly in love.

VI

'Briony, shall we write the letter to Daddy now? You're quite sure you don't want to rest, too? You look tired!'

Briony smiled at the little girl and shook her head. Sunday lunch had ended at last and Marion and Vanessa had pleaded head-aches and the need for a sleep. Charles, with

Gerald, had departed to the library with the Sunday papers, which Briony guessed would soon be placed over their heads as they, too, slept.

But she could not rest. What hope was there of sleep when, tired as she had been in the early hours of the morning when the last guest had gone, she had lain wide-eyed, dreaming, knowing that it could only be a dream, and crying then as if her heart would break? No wonder Lynn said she 'sure looked tired'. But in Lynn's company she might forget for a little while the hopeless mess she had made of her life. Her mother had warned her ... and she had believed that she, Briony, knew best. 'One day you'll wake up, Briony! It won't be so easy then to make Charles happy!'

How true that was! Already she felt she could not bear Charles to touch her. She had lain far away from him in the big double bed and been thankful that sleep had claimed him almost the instant his head touched the pillow. Guilt – for she was guilty in thought if not actually in deed – had forced her to a tenderness she had been far from feeling when Charles woke up next morning with a mild 'hangover'. But as his spirits revived later in the morning, she had caught herself criticizing things in him which she had never really noticed much before ... his heartiness, his playfulness with

111

Marion and Vanessa ... or was it just with Vanessa? His habit of ending most of his sentences with 'what?' or 'eh?' and his superior way of saying 'the servants'. She had pulled herself up sharply when she had been aware of herself watching him with a cold, dispassionate, critical air. Charles was her husband ... the man who had given her so much; not the man she had ever loved, but her husband nonetheless. He had always been kind to her, more than generous, and he loved her, depended on her in many ways. She had always been fond of him. Had? No, would always be fond of him. "Oh, Robert, Robert! Where are you? What are you doing? Was last night true? Did it really happen? Will you come to the house again? What will happen to my puppy?"

'Briony?'

'Darling, I'm sorry, I was day-dreaming. Come, let's get some writing paper and we'll go into the sun porch. No one will disturb us there.'

"If I could stop thinking... If I could go back to the calm acceptance of life that was my peace of mind last week!"

My Dear Daddy...

"Darling, darling, Robert..."

I have a new friend. Her name is Briony and I

love her very much. She is a sweet English lady and you would love her, too. We are staying with her for a long week-end. That is from Friday, when we came, until Monday, when we have to go back to London. I wish...

'Briony, did you say anything to Mommy?'

'Lynn, I did. And I clean forgot to tell you. How awful of me! Mummy says you can stay, darling, until she goes to Paris. Isn't it wonderful?'

'Oh, Briony!' The child's eyes were like saucers. 'That's the most heavenly surprise. It's really true? You're not joking?'

"Why do we always find it so difficult to credit good news... so easy to believe bad news? Poor, pathetic little Lynn! I'm going to write to your Daddy, too. At least I can try to see *you* are happy!"

...I'm to be allowed to stay here with her until we have to go to Paris. I'm very happy here. Briony has a puppy which I call Tom. I miss you very much, Daddy. June seems a very long way off but Briony has given me a calendar to make the days go quicker...

'Briony, why does time always hurry up when you're happy and go slow when you're miserable? The six months I'm with Daddy are gone in a week ... at least, that's what it seems. And the six months with Mommy

113

just never end.'

'I know what you mean, Lynn. It's because we don't notice time when we are happy, and because of that, it seems to us to go fast. If we are unhappy, we are always looking at the clock and the hands never move. The number of hours in the day is really just the same although it doesn't seem so.'

Lynn sighed and chewed the end of her pen.

'You always understand, Briony. I do wish you could have been my Mommy. Didn't you ever want a little girl like me?'

'Yes, Lynn. I've often wanted a little girl or boy. But Uncle Charles thought it would be better not to have a family until we know if we are going to have another war!'

"I'm glad now we have no children. And yet, if I had borne Charles a child, would I have felt more deeply towards him? Would I have felt less lonely? Been less susceptible to the impact of Robert's coming?"

'Daddy and I wanted a baby brother for me, but Mommy said I was quite enough. I didn't really mind very much when – when we lived with Daddy, but when we went away, I wished we had had a little boy to leave with Daddy. I think he must be very lonely without me. He mightn't have been so lonely with a baby to look after.'

"Nor I! Lynn, when you grow up, marry for love... only for love. I hope someone will

114

guide you."

'Let's go on with the letter, Poppet. The post goes at half past four on Sundays and it's nearly half past three now.'

...Briony is helping me to write this letter ... that's why the spelling is right and it was her what drew the lines on the paper so I'd write it straight for you to read. I'm getting quicker at writing but the teacher at my New York school says I'm behind with most things 'cos of being at a different school when I'm in California. Daddy, if I came to live with you always, I wouldn't have to get quicker at writing as I only want that to write to you.

Briony says it's tea-time. English tea-time is at four and they have lots of buns and sandwiches and things to eat. I like being here but I'd rather be with you. There's a hundred and fifty-one days to go on the calendar before I see you. It's a lot but Briony says they'll go quickly if I don't think about it too much. But I always do think of it because I want to come and be with you.

With love from your Baby Honey,
Lynn.
P.S. – Briony calls me Lynn, too.

'Baby Honey is Daddy's very special name for me. Briony, do you have a nice Daddy?'

Briony shook her head. No – her father had died when she was very young. Her mother lived in London.

'Then you've really nobody either – except Uncle Charles, I mean?'

"And the memory of a dead love and the hopelessness of a new one that can never be born."

'Crumpets, Lynn! Nancy must have toasted them specially for you.'

Half an hour later, they were walking hand in hand down the lane to the post-box when Robert's car passed them. He drew up as he recognized them and got out and walked back.

'Gee, it's Prince Charming!' Lynn said delightedly. 'Were you coming to see Tom? Briony thought maybe you wouldn't come today, being Sunday.'

Their eyes met.

'I thought Tom ought to have his injection in spite of ... of everything.'

"If it hadn't been for the puppy, he wouldn't have come," Briony thought. "He's right, of course. We ought not to see each other any more. Oh, but I'm glad, I'm glad you came!"

'We are going to the post-box, Robert, to post this letter to my Daddy.'

'I'll walk with you. Isn't it rather late to be out?'

'We're well wrapped up against the cold!' Briony said, surprised that her voice could be so casual. 'There's no need to come if

116

you're in a hurry, Robert.'

But he shook his head and walked along with them. In sight of the post-box, Lynn ran ahead. Robert took the opportunity to say:

'Briony, I know how you feel. But unless you want Elliot to take over the pup, I'll have to come every day till he's fit. I'll try not to see you if you'd rather it that way.'

'Yes! No – oh, Robert, I'm frightened! I've been telling myself nothing happened last night. Tell me it didn't! Tell me I have too vivid an imagination!'

'I can only answer for myself, Briony. As far as I'm concerned, it was all just as real when I woke up this morning as it was last night.'

'Then at least you slept.'

Briefly, they smiled.

'Only a little. I've been tramping the woods most of the afternoon, trying to tell myself not to be a fool, not to be a cad, not to be silly ... in fact, trying to tell myself it isn't true because it ought not to have happened. I think I convinced myself that I only imagined that to you ... then just now I saw your face, Briony. What a hell of a mess it all is! If only it were not so utterly hopeless!'

"We still have not said in words that we love each other," Briony thought with surprise. "Yet that is what we are talking about."

'You mustn't blame yourself for anything, Robert. It – it wasn't anything we could have helped. Our only hope was in never meeting each other. Now that it has happened ... we can only try to forget.'

'I've mailed it, Briony! Are we going home now?'

Lynn skipped along in front of them. Keeping their voices low, there was little chance that the child might overhear. Robert said suddenly:

'I suppose... there isn't a way out, Briony?'

She looked up at him, her face white in the gathering dusk. It was something she had not dared consider – a way out! No ... she would not be the one to let Charles down. Divorce was still a 'scandal' in Charles's world although commonplace enough. He would be made to feel small – cheated – let down. She couldn't do that to him in return for all his kindness to her. He would be, in any case, prejudiced against divorce ... a reminder of the Victorian upbringing of Mrs. Montague Stone! That would hurt Charles almost as much as her leaving him ... the mud that would be flung around the name of Montague Campbell Stone. She would try to explain this to Robert some time, when they could speak at length without fear of being overheard or interrupted. She would tell him, too, that *she* believed the marriage vows to be sacred ... up to a point anyway. Charles had never ill-treated her, been unfaithful to her, got drunk, behaved in a way that might excuse her leaving him. He had kept his side of the bargain and she would keep hers.

'Robert, there's only one way out, and I couldn't take it. I truly believe that it is impossible for two people – people like ourselves – to be happy at the expense of someone else's happiness. Does that sound trite?'

'It's merely a repetition of what I've been telling myself … of what I knew you would feel. Forget I mentioned it, Briony. It was just a last desperate attempt to hold on to … to hope, I suppose. Lynn's waiting for us to catch up. Briony, I must talk to you, just once before we finally say good-bye. There's so much I have to tell you … to explain … to ask. Please find an opportunity if you can. I won't take advantage … of our being alone to try to change your point of view. But I can't walk out of your life without knowing a little more of you … why this had to happen … if it really has happened.'

'Our guests go back to town tomorrow morning, except Lynn, of course. Charles will be going to town as usual. You could come to tea. But then Lynn would be there.'

'Couldn't you slip away this evening? Plead a headache – anything – and slip off for an hour? I'll have the car at the end of the drive ... we could drive off up the hill and park somewhere where we won't be seen.'

'It sounds as if we were fugitives!'

'I know – I know I'm asking you to do something underhand. But it's desperate measures, Briony. How else can we talk alone without people wondering what's going on? We have nothing to be guilty about – there will never be anything you need feel guilty about. Trust me, Briony.'

'I know I could trust you, Robert. I'm not sure that I could trust myself. I want to come ... I have a hundred things I want to say ... and to ask. Look – I'll try! I can't promise. If I fail to get away tonight, I'll find some other way. Can you be waiting between nine and ten? The others usually play Canasta then. I wouldn't be missed. There's just a chance, though, they won't feel up to playing tonight. But I'll try.'

'Briony, when Tom's better we can take him for walks, can't we?'

They turned their attention to the child.

As they went into the house they were met by Vanessa, coming down the wide staircase.

'Hi, folks!' she called down to them. 'Been out walking at this time of night?'

'Lynn and I went to post a letter. We met Robert on his way here to see the puppy, so he gave us a lift back. Are you feeling better, Vanessa?'

She looked very lovely and far from tired as she stood beside them, smiling up at Robert.

'Sure did enjoy my dancing last night,' she said. 'But I had too much champagne, all the same. How's your head, Robert?'

She ignored Briony and Lynn, having eyes only for the young man. Briony would have felt jealous had she not felt so angry with Vanessa for her rudeness.

'Come, Lynn, we'll take off our coats,' she said to the child. She did not look at Robert. The last person she wanted to 'suspect' was Vanessa Gough. Briony did not trust her and felt that it would be just Vanessa's idea of a mild form of amusement to make trouble between herself and Charles.

'Marion was looking for you, Binny!' Vanessa called after the child. 'She's pretty sore because she hasn't seen you all day, and since you're not going with her tomorrow she reckoned you could at least have spent a few hours with her.'

'Gee!' whispered Lynn, suddenly drawn and white. 'I'd better go find her right away, Briony.'

'I'll come with you,' Briony said quickly, seeing the fear in the child's face. Marion couldn't be too cruel with her words in front of her hostess!

She had intended to rejoin Robert upstairs with the puppy, but the ensuing scene between Lynn and her mother swept all other thoughts from her mind. By the time she escaped, Robert had gone. She knew then that, come what may, she would meet him that evening. She couldn't let him go without a word, not with things as they were at the present moment ... so much tacitly admitted, so little said.

Marion was alone in the drawing-room when Lynn, clasping Briony's hand tightly, went to see her mother. Marion looked up sharply.

'I declare, Binny, it's really too bad. You might have drowned in the lily pond for all I've seen of you since lunch. Just where have you been?'

Her voice was irritable and spiteful. Briony guessed that she was feeling the effects of the night before, and having no one else around to take it out on, had whistled for her small, defenceless daughter.

'Lynn has been with me all afternoon,' Briony answered for the child. 'We thought you were resting.'

'I should have thought you'll see enough of the kid these next weeks without having her tagging on to you all day. You spoil her. I think a kid of her age should remember she has a few duties to her mother ... or at least to show a little affection and respect. For God's sake, Belinda, have you lost your tongue?'

'No, Mommy. I'm sorry!'

Marion swung her legs off the sofa and stared hard at the shrinking child.

'For two pins I'd take you with me tomorrow, just to show you what I consider your behaviour to be; there's only one in a thousand kids of your age gets a chance to see Europe. It's costing your stepfather a pretty penny and quite a few headaches bringing you along with us. And this is how you repay us!'

Briony could feel the little hand in hers trembling violently and knew the child was not far from tears. She gave her a reassuring squeeze. Marion noticed it and said sharply:

'Step forward, Belinda, so I can see you when I'm talking to you. And speak up. Do you hear me?'

'Y-yes, Mommy!'

'What in the name of goodness is Briony going to think of American kids with you as an example! How I came to have a kid like you beats me. What you need is a good boarding school to knock some sense into you. It's your father's fault. He always spoilt you and fussed over you and now you're incapable of saying two reasonable words. Yes, Mommy! Is that all you can say?'

'N-n-no, Mommy. I mean, I'm s-sorry – I–'

'I'm sure she had no idea you were looking for her,' Briony broke in, forcing her voice to

123

keep a level tone. 'You had only to ring the bell for James or Nancy to come and fetch Lynn. She's been very good.'

She walked calmly across the room and tugged the bellrope. Within a few moments, James appeared.

'Would you please bring in some drinks, James? Dry Martini, Marion? I know it's a little early, but I think we could all do with a hair of the dog that bit us last night! Any idea where Charles is?'

'He disappeared with Gerald after lunch!' Marion said furiously. Briony had successfully spoilt the scene she had been working up to and diverted her irritation towards the absent, unflattering males.

'Be a dear, Lynn, and run and see if you can find them for me,' Briony said to the child. Lynn glanced briefly, fearfully, at her mother.

'Landsakes, child, do as you're told!' Marion barked at her. Lynn turned and all but ran out of the room.

Briony, still forcing herself to a casualness she was far from feeling, said:

'I'm really looking forward to Lynn's stay here with me, Marion. Of course, it's different for you, I realize. You'll have so much to do and see and it's never easy with children in hotels. But she'll keep me company and fill in a little of the many hours of spare time I have.'

Marion relaxed a little and sighed.

'I sometimes think I should send the kid back to her doting Poppa. She sure is a trial to me. Why couldn't she have a little personality ... charm ... like other people's kids?'

'I think she has great charm, Marion, and she's beautifully behaved. I think, if you'll excuse my saying so, it's just a question of your two temperaments being uncomplementary to each other. She quite possibly shows more personality to her father, whom I gather she resembles.'

'Spit image!' Marion said. 'He was just like a grown-up edition of Lynn ... mooning around, day-dreaming; I like a man to be a man. Now Gerald knows he's one hundred per cent male and so he wears the pants ... at least he thinks he does! But at least he acts masterfully. Binny's father ... well, you only had to disagree with him and he'd shut himself up in a room and refuse to argue. No temperament. Just sulks. Never could understand him. That's why I ran off with Gerald.'

Her good temper was returning now that she could talk to, or rather talk at, someone. She was a restless, self-centred woman who hated to be alone. Even Briony, whom she thought colourless and dull, was better than nobody.

'Don't you think, Marion, you might have had more fun on this trip if you'd left Lynn behind with her father?'

It was rather a presumptuous remark, Briony thought. What right had she, Briony, to interfere or make suggestions to another woman about her child? But she had guessed correctly that Marion would not take offence. She was only too willing to talk about herself, her life and its problems.

'I guess so! All the same, I have a duty to my child, and I'm not going to shirk it. Imagine what people would say of me!'

'People?' Briony asked as she handed Marion a Martini. 'What people? Surely your friends would know you too well to believe anything unpleasant of you. They would understand that you were doing what you thought best for Lynn. Other people don't matter, I imagine.'

Marion gave her an amused glance.

'Well, I daresay you've got something there. All the same, I haven't got quite your disregard for public opinion. Guess what I really need is a good Nannie to take the child off my hands.'

'But if you want her off your hands ... and as I believe you told me earlier her father would like to have her all the year round ... why put yourself to the expense and bother of a Nannie to care for the child? The answer seems simple enough. And Lynn could always come and stay with you for the odd week-end or so during her holidays. It's possible that she feels a little insecure with the constant change of school and home and this may well account for her "timidity".'

"I sound like a psychologist," Briony thought wryly. All the same, Marion had been listening to her and so far seemed unperturbed by Briony's remarks.

'Well, I'll surely consider it. I seem to recall a couple of the psychiatrists Binny saw last year saying much the same thing. Maybe it would be best. Still, I don't know if Lance would agree. All very well for him to make rash statements about wanting Binny all year round, but if it came to the point, would he? What about his clubs and his work and all the rest of the things I presume now occupy his day? He'd have to give up a lot for Binny and he may not want to. There's the expense, too. I contribute to Lynn's upkeep when she's with me. Of course, Lance makes me an allowance for her, but naturally it doesn't begin to meet the expenses. Lance isn't rich.'

"There's the line I can take with Lynn's father when I write," Briony thought. "Point out to him that if he can plead his cause strongly enough, Marion is weakening. Is it wrong of me to interfere? Surely this is something that ought to lie between Lynn's parents? Yet Marion is in very few senses a mother to Lynn – poor Lynn. I'll risk the consequences of interference, for the child's sake."

'Oh, well, I'd better go and change for dinner,' she said casually to Marion. Robert would undoubtedly have gone by now. She must find Lynn, too, and put her to bed. Marion had assumed that Briony was willing to this the night they arrived and subsequently 'handed over' all such maternal rights to Briony since then. In fact, she had barely addressed two words to Lynn until this evening! No wonder the child felt a world apart from a mother whose interest in her offspring was so casual and so uncertain that she did not know what mood she would find her in – or what care or interest might greet a chance attempt to get closer to Marion!

Lynn was waiting for Briony in her bedroom. She looked white and anxious and jumped to her feet as Briony came into the room.

'She isn't going to change her mind, Briony? I'm still to be allowed to stay with you?'

'Darling, of course!' Briony said soothingly. 'There's nothing to worry about. Mummy wasn't feeling too good after her late night – that's why she sounded a little cross.'

Lynn relaxed a trifle and sat down on the edge of her bed. But her eyes, large and thoughtful, were still anxious.

'I don't think it was just the late night.

Mommy often gets that-a-way. It's just her mood. Daddy said people have moods and can't help them and I shouldn't mind. But I do mind. It's just as if she hated me!'

Briony bit her lip.

'No, Lynn. No mother hates her child. Your Mummy wants to do what is best for you but sometimes she may be mistaken in what is best ... just as you might be mistaken when trying to decide whether Tom can have another piece of chocolate or not. Why, I have moods, too. And I expect you do. You're in a "thinking" mood right now!'

Lynn smiled.

'Yes – and I forgot to tell you, Briony, I have a message for you from Robert. He said that Tom was better and not to worry about him or anything, and that he'd come when he told you he would this afternoon.'

Briony felt the faint colour steal into her cheeks and turned quickly away from Lynn's searching gaze.

'Thank you,' she said briefly. 'It's bedtime now, Lynn. You get undressed, darling, and I'll go and run your bath.'

Twenty minutes later Lynn was tucked up in bed, soothed and sleepy. Briony went to her own room to change into a short dinner frock. Against her will, she found herself taking particular care as to her appearance. It was a subconscious action and when she realized that she was really making herself beautiful because of her promised assignation with Robert, she fought against it furiously. It was completely foreign to her nature to be conspiratorial, deceitful, underhand – and she hated herself bitterly for the indirect act of disloyalty to Charles.

"I'm not the type to be unfaithful to my husband!" she told herself, knowing that this stolen hour alone with Robert could never be repeated if she were to keep her self-respect, or her respect for Robert himself. "Oh, why, why, why did I have to meet him? Why should I have fallen in love with him? It isn't as if he's like Bob in any way. Why was I such a crazy fool as to believe that love died for always? I should never, never have married Charles. Yet I have not been un-happy with him until now!"

She gazed at her reflection with careful criticism. Her eyes, oddly like Lynn's eyes, were also thoughtful, introspective. She touched the red-gold hair above her forehead and wondered if she could ever be called beautiful. She had not considered the question since those brief months when Bob loved her. Somehow it had never seemed to matter with Charles. He seemed to admire her ... occasionally he told her she was 'jolly attractive' and 'knocked other women into a cocked hat', but beauty ... what did Robert see in her that had made him fall in love with her? *Was he in love with her?* Did he really know his own heart? Or was he, like many others, intrigued because it was the 'unobtainable'? It would be better for them both if he didn't love her. Then she need not have these painful, agonizing regrets that sought at the back of her mind for an outlet. But she would not allow herself to give way to her feelings. She must be strong tonight ... let Robert realize once and for all how hopeless it was for both of them; try to make him see that love could not grow unless it was nurtured, and if they really refused to allow themselves to think of 'what might have been', then once they had parted their love would – *must* – slowly starve to death.

"But I want life ... not a living death!" Briony cried in her heart. "I want love, to love and to be loved. I am alive again, and although it hurts I want to stay alive. Must I lose love twice in a lifetime?"

She heard the door of her bedroom open and forced the face in the mirror to be nothing but a face, reveal nothing of her thoughts, her panic, at Charles's approach.

'Well, m'dear! Nearly ready?'

'Almost,' Briony replied, surprised to find her voice so normal when inside she trembled. Already she knew the feeling of guilt! And yet only her thoughts were guilty.

'Dashed good week-end, what? You did splendidly, old thing. I think our guests have enjoyed themselves, don't you?'

'Yes, I'm sure they have,' Briony heard her voice answering. 'Do you think they will visit us again before they go to France?'

Charles sat down on the edge of the bed and lit a cigarette.

'Been trying to persuade them. Vanessa seems keen enough but Marion says they've masses they want to do in London. Gerald agrees with Marion, of course. Still, they may come. As a matter of fact, Gerald suggested we might go over to Paris with them for a week-end there. What do you think of the idea, old girl?'

'No!' The word erupted from her heart before she could stop it. It was a cry of one who has no wish to be taken hundreds of miles from the one she loved.

Charles looked at her in surprise.

'Why ever not? Thought you liked them. Thought you might enjoy a little breath of gay Paree, what?'

His questions gave Briony time to recover a little of the poise and calm that was naturally hers even under emotional stress.

'Perhaps you're right, Charles. I – I've only been to Paris once. I liked it very much. And I've nothing against the Martells or Vanessa. I suppose I'm just a little tired tonight. The thought of another week-end seemed a bit much.'

Charles laughed.

'See what you mean, of course. Got one hell of a hangover myself! Marion's in the dumps, too. Still, we'll have four weeks to recover before then, what? Might be fun. Jolly old Paree! Must say it could be fun in a party, too.'

"Oh, Charles, you're so young, so young! And you ten years older than I! Why have you never grown up?"

Softly she said:

'Remembering your bachelor days, Charles?'

'Whatever made you think – oh, I see! You mean because I said it could be fun in a party, too. I get it!' He laughed. 'Well, dash it all, old girl, I didn't know you in those days, did I? And Paris! Well, that's what a man goes to Paris for – *un peu d'amour!*' He gave the words an entirely English pronunciation.

'Some people go to eat!' Briony reminded him, gently teasing.

Charles looked uncomfortable.

'Dash it, Briony, I wasn't married – or even engaged!'

She reassured him quickly.

'I wasn't criticizing, Charles dear! Far be it from me to do that. I'm no moralist, as you know.'

Charles looked even more uncomfortable. He disliked being reminded of those unfortunate six months of her life when she had flung all caution, upbringing, reputation

133

aside in the name of love. He had told himself he would forget it ever happened and generally succeeded in doing so. It was hardly for Briony to remind him, as if she were not ashamed of admitting it, too! It had always been that way with Briony – when first she had told him about that fellow Bob; a chap would think that she didn't realize it was one of those things an unmarried girl just didn't do!

'I'm sorry, Charles,' Briony said, really contrite since she knew only too well how Charles felt about that period of her life and had correctly judged his train of thought. She turned round from her dressing-table and faced him, her eyes suddenly serious, questioning.

'Charles, have you ever – regretted our marriage? I mean, if you could go back to the day you proposed to me, would you do the same again, knowing what you do know now?'

Charles frowned.

'What d'you mean, knowing what I know now?'

'I only meant – knowing what our life would be like together?'

'Dash it all, old girl, what a confoundedly stupid question! Of course I would. Why ever not?'

Briony looked quickly away.

'I don't know. I just wondered. Lots of

men who've been married must suddenly – or at least sometimes – wish themselves free again.'

'But that's nonsense, my dear. Surely you don't doubt I'm as much in love with you as I ever was?'

"No, no, you've given me no cause to doubt it, Charles. But love ... have you never realized what you haven't had from me?" The words were unspoken, but Charles, oddly intuitive for about the first time in his life, said:

'Or did you mean have I doubted you? Look here, Briony, this is a queer sort of conversation to be having but since we've started it, then we might as well finish it. I knew you weren't "in love" with me when you married me – not the way you were with ... well, with that RAF chap. But I'm not a particularly romantic kind of chap, as you know. I knew you were fond of me and I imagined – I hope not wrongly – that you'd grow more fond of me as time went on. Well, that's more than enough for me. I know physical attraction isn't the same for a girl as a man ... that girls don't feel things so deeply and all that...' (talking of sex always embarrassed Charles!) '...but we've got along pretty well together in bed and out of bed, haven't we? What more can anyone ask of marriage?'

"Charles, Charles, how blind, how narrow, how inexperienced you must be! Do you not realize that a woman can feel every bit as much as a man feels, if she loves the man with whom she is to have such intimate contact? It isn't a purely animal instinct in a woman – it must be emotional, too. But if there is both, then she can know as great a delight in love as any man. You would know that if I had loved you instead of being an impassioned woman to whom you could make love. Sometimes I haven't wanted you to touch me ... but you haven't known that any more than you have realized what is lacking when you say we 'get on well in bed'. The phrase itself distresses me. But then I am ... always will be... romantic."

She turned back to her husband, angry with him, sorry for him, hating him and nearly loving him for his helpless childish ignorance which was not his fault – but hers!

'Dear Charles! Don't look so upset. I only wanted to hear you say you weren't sorry you married me ... that I might have failed you.'

'You could never do that, my dear,' Charles replied, reassured and complacent now.

"I could – how easily I could, Charles, but I won't – I never will 'fail you'. Not while I have will-power left to keep my vows. Till death us do part. But death is a long, long way off, and that is a different kind of death from dying of a broken heart. But hearts don't break. I believed mine broke when Bob died, and now I am heart-whole because I have lost my heart … never, never can I give it … but I've lost my heart to another Robert."

'There's the dinner-gong,' Briony said. 'Our guests will wonder what we've been up to!'

'Let 'em think the worst,' Charles said as he gave her his arm. 'Matter of fact, you look a picture, Briony. Wouldn't be difficult to make love to you even at this moment!'

His coarseness hardened her, his flattery made her feel guilty; his unspoken opinion which she knew so well that people only made love in bed, at night, with the lights out, all combined to give her an hysterical desire to laugh and cry at once. Steeling herself, she returned the pressure of his arm and went with him down the stairs to face the ordeal of food.

VII

An hour later Briony was in Robert's arms.

As she sat through dinner, listening to the others talk, she made her resolve to be firm with herself about Robert. Over coffee, while they discussed whether or not to play Canasta, she had felt the first weakening of resolve as fear claimed her that she might, after all, not be able to meet him. Running down the drive at half past eight, the night dark and cold, guilt that she might be seen and fear that Robert might not be there combined to make her so desperate that she was past clear thinking at all. Finally the relief of Robert's voice saying 'Briony, is that you?' drove all other thoughts from her mind. He opened his arms and she ran into them.

They had not kissed ... merely stood for a moment, blessedly close, each lost in painful awareness of the other. Robert too had been in a nightmare of anguish in case she could not – or would not – come. His own resolves to do nothing whatever that might make her regret this meeting were flung unconsciously aside as he saw her pale face and distraught eyes come towards him in the darkness.

He recovered first and said gently:

'Get into the car, Briony. We can't stand here.'

She obeyed him and in silence they drove away from the house, away from Briony's home, into the darkness. She closed her eyes, unwilling to know which road they took. For her this was to be an hour stolen from time itself. It must have no connection, no bearing on her everyday life; subsequently she could tell herself it had never happened and, in disbelieving it, forget.

Suddenly the car stopped and she heard Robert's voice:

'You can open your eyes now, darling. We're in the land of Nowhere.'

So he had guessed her thoughts!

She looked not at him, but out through the windscreen. They were on top of a hill, so close to the edge that it seemed as if they were in an aeroplane, detached from earthly ties. Bright moonlight flooded the distant fields and hedgerows below them, brightened the air around them. It was beautiful.

'Briony!'

It had had to happen. She knew it to be inevitable. This man who was so nearly a stranger to her, knew her innermost thoughts, understood her complex emotions, was sensitive to her every need. It was as if already they had been made part of one another and he knew her, she him, in the way that men and women who have long been lovers know and anticipate and understand without words the other's needs. So he knew now that she was afraid ... for herself, for him, of the power of their love.

'You mustn't be afraid, Briony. You have my word that you can trust me.'

She knew that he was not referring to the possibility that he might make love to her physically. He meant that he would not try to make her do anything she did not believe to be right – great or small though that action might be.

'I do love you!' she said softly, so softly that he barely heard the words. Still she had not looked at him. 'I have tried to believe it is not true. I have told myself that love … this kind of love … cannot happen twice. It has happened twice to me. I won't tell you about it, Robert, because it isn't important now. It's only importance is that it gives the reason why I married Charles. You see, the man I loved died. I thought that was the end. Now I know it wasn't.' She drew a breath and he waited for her to continue, as he knew she would.

'I've also told myself that one can't be truly in love with a man one doesn't know. But that doesn't apply to us, you see, because somehow we do know each other. In my heart I know all there is to know of you. I feel – yes, that's really what it is – I feel inside me what you will say, do, how you are thinking…'

'Then you know that I love you, Briony! This is the first time it has happened to me and I'm still a little stunned by it all. It's the inevitability of it that frightens me. It's just as if I were in a dream which wound its way on with my knowledge of what was going to happen but being quite powerless to control it. I knew from the first moment that you were a married woman. "So that's that," I told myself. "It's no good imagining what might have been." But telling myself, and knowing the facts, didn't make the slightest difference. I just went on falling ... falling ... and that in itself is untrue because I had fallen to the depths before I realized it had begun to happen. Briony, what you said just now – about knowing each other – it's true. I feel as though I've always known you, as if you were someone I have carried round in my heart, my thoughts, my dreams all my life ... suddenly come to life. Briony, how can I go on tomorrow, and all the to-morrows, as if you did not exist? Since I first saw you my life has become unreal... It is you now who are my life!'

He did not try to touch her but sat with his hands clenched on the steering wheel, staring out with unseeing eyes at the moonlit panorama before him.

Briony spoke softly, her face now turned towards him as her eyes studied his profile, etching his pictorial self on her memory, which must be all she would have to comfort her for the rest of her life.

'Oh, Robert! How wonderful it could have been! The things you've just told me ... they could have made me so deliriously happy. Now they hurt me because, however inadvertently, I know myself to be the cause of your suffering. What can I say? What can I do, Robert? Nothing in the world can help us, except the right to be together. And I'm a married woman. I *couldn't* ask Charles for a divorce. I couldn't, Robert.'

'Because he loves you?'

Briony bit her lip.

'Yes – in his way. It's perhaps a shallow emotion compared with what we feel, but it is at least real to Charles. He feels as much for me as he could ever feel for anyone. He isn't a person who is capable of any depth of feeling but there is one side of Charles which matters to him, I think, every bit as much as love can matter to others ... the question of his principles ... a kind of moral standard he has set himself and which he treasures unwittingly as perfection. It is really because of his mother. She was a real Victorian and Charles was brought up with a complete set of rules dividing right from wrong. Divorce for Charles is wrong, if it applies to himself. He's broad-minded enough to accept that others might and do get divorced, but not for himself. One just does not bring notoriety of that kind to the name of Montague Campbell Stone.'

Her voice was not so much bitter as matter-of-fact. It mattered so much that Robert should understand why she could not leave Charles. If he understood, it would be easier for him in the end.

'In a queer kind of way, I agree with Charles,' she continued. 'I don't mean because of the possible publicity, but on the

142

question of principle. I'm no moralist, but I have my own standards of what is right and wrong, even if they are not always – or often – synonymous with Charles's. I believe, Robert, that if two people make a bargain, and the marriage vows are in fact exchanged as promises, then one has no excuse for breaking them unless the other side has first done so. Had Charles been unfaithful to me, or were he cruel to me, if he got hopelessly drunk, if he were not to the best of his ability a good husband to me – then I might have reason to consider myself justified in breaking my side of the bargain. But, Robert, he is none of those things. He's a good husband. It isn't his fault that I have never and can never love him. He should not be made to suffer for my own selfish pleasures, especially since the whole of our marriage really was a mistake which I should have realized and which Charles could not possibly have known.'

'I don't altogether understand your last point, Briony. Charles was equally responsible for asking you to marry him as you were for accepting him.'

Briony shook her head.

'Charles has never really known me ... not the real me. I misrepresented myself to him. He imagines me to be quiet, thoughtful, very reserved, unemotional, cold. That was the woman he asked to marry him. That was the woman I had become since Bob had died. It really began then. I believed myself dead to all emotion for always after the grief of my loss had died away. My mother told me that one never really changes one's real self ... warned me that one day I might feel myself "alive" again. I thought it impossible. That was why I agreed to marry Charles. My life was over and done with – at least any hope of love in my life, so I believed. I felt I might be reasonably happy with Charles ... not quite so lonely ... and I thought I could make him happy. I think I've done so. He told me – this evening – that he had never regretted our marriage – that I fulfilled all his needs. I can't let him down now because I have started to live again. That must be my burden to carry, not his. And yours, Robert! That is why it hurts me most of all. You are suffering now because of me. I have it in my power to make you happy, but I will not because of something I believe. Do you think I'm desperately selfish?'

Robert turned and took both her hands in his own. For the moment, at least, passion was deadened by the utter seriousness of the discussion. So much that he had not entirely understood until now became clear to him. He knew, too, that Briony was perhaps the stronger of the two of them after all. If she had been willing to take her happiness at

Charles's expense, he would not have hesitated to encourage her! But he could not do this now for she had as good as told him that she could not be happy with him, Robert, at Charles's cost. If this were true, and he believed that she had considered what she was saying to him and was not speaking rashly or without a lot of forethought, then his own efforts to obtain his heart's desire were doomed before he began. He must lose the battle before he had been allowed to strike a blow! The pill was difficult to swallow. Only his love for the girl beside him kept the bitterness from his voice.

'It is because you are so unselfish that you take the view you do,' he told her. 'I love you for it, darling Briony, even while my heart fights against acceptance of what you say. Surely if Charles loves you he would wish you to have your freedom? No, don't answer that. It's because he would probably agree that you cannot ask him. I wish I could believe that he is capable of appreciating you ... and your sacrifice ... my enormous loss.'

'He could never do that because he could never understand the way we feel,' Briony replied truthfully. It was a bitter-sweet remark ... bitter in its revelation of Charles's 'type' ... sweet because of the innocent way in which she coupled her name with his own. We! To her they were already united. If only he could feel the same! Momentarily, at least, Briony had acquired a nun-like aura for him – she was untouchable. As a mere man, he was all too well aware of his urgent desire to possess her completely in every way – bodily, spiritually. To be united in thought, or in the name of love, even in the name of self-sacrifice, was not enough! But he could not tell her so and thereby add to her distress. The hopelessness of his position wrung a cry from his lips. It was as if he had touched a chord in her that brought every nerve in her body alive. Her arms went round his neck, her cheek pressed against his with fierce tenderness as she whispered:

'Robert – Robert! I love you so!'

He drew her closer against him and for the first time since they had met he kissed her. He had intended it to be a gentle touch of his lips on hers, but the contact of their bodies was too much for his self-control, and the kiss was as impassioned and pleading as that of any man in love.

Briony's response was instantaneous, intense as it was without reservation. Those almost forgotten desires that she had so wrongfully believed to have died with Bob pulsed now as fiercely as the beat of her heart. She knew, as she abandoned herself to Robert's embrace, that she loved this man truly, perhaps even more fully, since she was so much more mature, than she had ever loved before. Woman-like, her reasoning and self-control of a few minutes earlier, when she and Robert were apart, disappeared now in her desperate wish to know just once again the fulfilment of all that love and desire could mean. It was Robert ... the man who loved her ... who took control of the situation. He knew that if he did not soon release Briony from his arms they would be swept away inevitably beyond the realms of control; knew that he had promised her he would not force her to do anything she might regret and that because she trusted him he must be responsible for her actions. He had not bargained for the sweet completeness of her response and it took all his last vestiges of will-power to put her gently from him.

'It is because I love you too much to hurt you,' he said brokenly, seeing the sudden pain and anguish in her face.

His complete understanding of her, his desire to protect her both from himself and from herself, touched Briony to swift tears. It could have been so perfect; every new thing she discovered in Robert only proved to her how perfectly they were in tune with one another, how ideally they would have been matched, how perfectly mated. To say good-bye to him, knowing that there could be a different alternative, was almost too much to bear.

'Don't send me away from you, Robert.

Don't send me away!'

He cupped her chin in his hand and turned her to face him, the tears pouring down her cheeks.

'I could never do that, Briony! If ever you need me, or if ever you should change your mind, I will always be waiting, always. The decision for our parting has to lie with you. I will not ask you to do anything against your conscience. We could not be happy if you felt in any way guilty about ... about your husband. So long as you are completely certain, in your own mind, that it would affect him deeply, or hurt him, then there is nothing for us but to say good-bye. But if you do doubt it, then one word is enough for me, Briony. I swear to you now that there never will be ... never could be ... another woman in my life. I could never fall in love again. I'm yours whenever – if ever – you need me.'

Briony brushed the tears from her eyes and knew that she must try not to weaken at this last minute. Yet she could not resist voicing the cry of her heart.

'I said that once, Robert. But I fell in love again!'

'You were very young, my darling, when you loved the first time. I'm a good deal older and perhaps less susceptible because of it. I'd grown pretty used to being a bachelor and never imagined I'd want to

148

marry. Now I know differently – but since I can't marry the only girl in the world I can ever love, I repeat, *ever* love – I shall try to become a contented bachelor again and not think too deeply on how different my life might have been. Briony, if you could only know my thoughts! These last days I have imagined you as *my* wife ... imagined all the many, many things we would do together; I have imagined us now, and in the future, with children, with grandchildren, even! And always our life has been quite perfect because whatever we lost or gained, we always had our love. Do you think I could live those dreams with some other woman? Never!'

'I can never have children now!' Briony said suddenly, her voice calm and almost trance-like. 'I couldn't bear Charles's children now. And I had wanted a baby so much ... oh, Robert, am I being crazy? Tell me if I'm throwing away our happiness, robbing the children we might have had of their existence, for a stupid ideal. Don't let me throw so much away if I'm not thinking clearly. Am I right – or wrong?'

For a few long moments Robert was silent. When at last he spoke, he gave the opinion he hoped was unprejudiced, unbiased, and from his mind rather than his heart.

'I think you're wrong, my dearest. But how can I be sure that I'm saying that without my own desires influencing my view? I truly believe that if a marriage has gone wrong – really wrong – it is better ended. However unemotional your husband may be, Briony, surely he is capable of seeing that you are unhappy? That you have lost your placidity? That you are no longer willing to be an acquiescent wife, methodically permitting him his marital rights? However insensitive he may be, he *must find you changed.* Will you be happy then, even if he only half guesses at the truth? And you? Can you truly believe that you will be a good wife to him? He may not ask much, but are you willing to grant him what he does ask of you? You spoke just now of children. I presume that, in the past, Charles hasn't wanted children. But he may change his views. Are you going to give him the son or daughter he wants, or are you going to persist in the feeling you have just expressed – that you couldn't bear his children now? And if you have children, Briony, are you going to be able to love them as they deserve? Are you?'

Briony was staring at him from enormous, tragic eyes.

'Robert – stop! You're frightening me! I can go on being a good wife to Charles. I can! I don't think he'll ever ask me for a child now unless I re-open the subject. He's not – not a very paternal person. As to his state of mind – I'm sure he'll guess nothing, nothing. If only he will leave me alone for a little while, until I can forget a little how – how – Robert, I couldn't share his bed now. I'll have to find some reasonable excuse. I couldn't belong to anybody except you!'

Her words had stung him to a desperate jealousy and possessiveness which even her avowal that she could not be Charles's wife in the physical sense could not assuage. At the same time, he was appalled by the distress in her voice, her eyes, and all too well aware that he, by his words, had caused that distress.

'Don't worry about it now, Briony. Perhaps, after all, it will not be as I say. Perhaps everything will work itself out. Maybe in a little while you will begin to forget about me. It will be easier for you then.'

She clung to him again, weakened in her will as she had never for one instant believed she could be; as she had never for one instant imagined when she agreed to meet Robert this evening.

'I will never forget – never stop loving you!' she cried.

'Then, my dearest heart, if you feel that way, and continue to feel it, then Charles must set you free. And I shall be waiting. But meanwhile, because of your conscience, I think we ought to give up seeing each other. You need time to think about this. We've known each other such a short while – know so little of each other. It would not be right to throw over three years of marriage unless you were completely and absolutely certain that you were doing the right thing, and that you really were in love with me. No, don't say anything now. I, too, have known what it is to be infatuated – believed myself to be in love, and discovered that it was something else. You've been lonely in your life with Charles. Perhaps this is a sudden wish to escape from that loneliness. Or it may be simply that you've recovered from the shock of that other fellow's sudden death and are beginning to feel again and need an object to "feel" about. It may even be an unconscious form of escape from marriage with a man you don't love ... or your need for a child. I'm no psychologist, Briony, but I've seen so many people, and known myself to be mistaken when I imagined myself to be in love. It could be so with you.'

'Do *you* doubt *your* love for *me*, too?'

He laid his face against her hair and closed his eyes.

'You know the answer to that! How could I doubt such a thing? I love you, Briony, as I have never loved anyone in my life before. I feel inside me that you belong to me. I know your thoughts ... understand your heart. My great need for you is borne of my love for everything you are. If you were the ugliest woman in the world instead of the most beautiful, I still could not help loving *you*. But that does not alter what I have been saying, dear, darling child! I was perfectly happy with my life before I knew you – at least in a resigned sort of way. I had no *wish* to fall in love, no wish to marry or to have children. My life was really my work and that seemed enough. But you have been unhappy, lonely, thwarted, misunderstood, living an unnatural death in life against which your inner self has at last revolted. It may mean only the word "escape" to you which you confuse in your mind with love. You cannot prove it isn't so, Briony.'

'Prove it? No! But I feel it in every part of me!' she said. 'Even now, Robert, when you are trying to make it easier for me to do what I believe is right and are helping me to say good-bye to you, I love you for it. I know I would always love everything about you, that your decisions would be mine, your friends people whom I should like, your ideals my own. I *could* prove it, Robert, were the circumstances different. But what is the use of talking like this! In my heart I know I can't just walk out on Charles. I've got to go back and try to go on as if this hadn't happened. I daren't think of not succeeding because then all hope of peace of mind would be gone. I can't leave him, Robert.'

'I'm not going to say good-bye,' Robert stated calmly. 'It's too dramatic for one thing, and probably impossible under the circumstances for another. The puppy isn't well enough to do without his injections. I doubt very much if Elliot would take over from me at this stage even if I could think of a good reason for asking him to do so. And your husband might wonder at it, too. I'll have to come up to the house once or twice.'

'I'll try not to be around. No, I can't do that. If you are within reach, I must be with you. Robert, what shall I do? I'm so much weaker than I imagined myself to be. I don't think I could even successfully hide my emotions from Charles. Where shall I find the power to behave as if this – you and I – had never fallen in love? What am I going to do if Charles insists that I– If I'm to keep him in ignorance of my true feelings, then I shall have to find some good reason for refusing him that part of our married life.'

Robert looked at her with sudden pity. It seemed to him that Briony had set herself an unbearably difficult task, not only the task of putting her own desire and love out of her life, but of living a lie for the sake of the man she did not love, the husband she should never have married. Perhaps it was just as well he was, by all accounts, not very introspective or sensitive.

"I must try, at least," she thought, her heart quailing at the enormity of the problem before her. At least, for a little while, she had Lynn to keep her mind off herself. Lynn, whom she had asked to stay because she felt it might be good for the child, might turn out to be a god-sent blessing to her. If only there *had* been a child of her union with Charles! It would be so much easier to *know*, without a shadow of a doubt, where her duty lay.

"But I don't doubt it!" she told herself, angry that she should be questioning for one moment the inner conviction that marriage was and must be a holy state and a binding one. All the same, if Lynn had been her child, hers and Charles's, then this might never have happened.

'We've been here over an hour!' Robert's voice broke in on her thoughts. 'Might your absence be questioned, darling?'

Briony paled.

'Yes, yes, at any time. I'll have to go back, Robert. Oh, this is awful, terrible. It's our good-bye, isn't it? We shall never be alone like this together again. Robert, tell me I'm doing the right thing. Tell me that I'm not sacrificing our love for nothing?'

His arms went round her and held her tightly against him.

'My dearest love, I would not let you go if in my own heart I believed I had any right to claim you. You belong to another man and for as long as you do, then I must stay out of your life. I understand how you feel. I think you are probably right, too. I could almost wish that Charles beat you or was unfaithful to you; then I could be the gallant knight and rescue my faire ladye from the dragon.'

She smiled through her tears.

'I always thought the quotation so trite,' she whispered, 'but now I believe truly, that "I could not love thee dear so much..."'

'"Loved I not honour more,"' Robert finished for her. 'Oh, darling, don't be too lonely, too unhappy. Wherever you are, whatever you are doing, you can be sure that I am thinking of you, that I am with you in spirit.'

'And I with you, Robert!'

As he kissed her for the last time, anguish and glory mingled on their lips, passion momentarily deadened by the salt of Briony's tears. Desperately she fought for control, knowing that she must show no sign of crying when she returned to the house, to the life she had to live from now on. Already she was steeling herself to the task before her, and Robert knew that he had lost her without being able to lift a finger to turn her his way.

"I'll find some way to leave her alone!" he told himself with an inward groan as he touched his lips once more to the burnished red of her hair. "If necessary I'll take the puppy home with me and nurse it there until it's better. She'll understand. It will be easier for her ... for me, too, if we don't have to see each other again."

But the matter was taken out of his hands. Fate, for once, on the side of those who fought for what they believed to be right. When Briony reached home, it was to find a note propped up on her dressing-table, in Nancy's untidy scrawl:

Dear Madam,

The police foned during dinner and said not to worry you if you was eating, but they've found the owner of your Tom. They said as they'd come up tomorrow morning to see you bout it as the owner wants him back. He wasn't ill treated nor nothing but had got down a rabbit hole and they's searched everywhere, so if its a comfort, Ma'am, he'll be going to good hands. I thort as how I'd let you know so it woodn't be too much of a shock, like, tomorrow.

Yours respecfully,
Nancy

Kind Nancy to try to spare her feelings! But how cruel of Fate to claim the dog she loved in the same hour as it had taken her love from her, too!

The tears she had held in check during the

drive home, during the final desperate embrace and farewell to Robert, the race for the privacy of her room, were at last free to come as they wished. There was a tiny measure of comfort in their release and she sobbed unashamedly into the monogrammed pillow-case.

Charles, finding her there, took the letter that was clutched in her hand and, reading it, guessed only the smaller part of her reason for grief. With self-conscious tenderness he patted her gently on the shoulder and said:

'Dashed bad luck, old girl! Know how you felt about the poor little brute. Still, you must look on it the way Nancy says ... he'll be in good hands. Buck up, old thing. At least he won't be difficult to replace. The County's swarming with mongrels. Find you one myself tomorrow, and I won't make a fuss about your having a cross-breed; that's a promise. Now cheer up, old girl. Hate to see you like this, anyone would think your world had come to an end, what?'

"It has, it has!" Briony thought as she bit her lip to keep from crying aloud. "Oh, Charles, kind Charles, who means so well but understands so little!"

'Come on now, my dear! Here's my handkerchief. Shall I ask Cook to make you a cup of tea?'

Briony sat up and blew her nose like a

small girl. She was calmer now and there was a faint smile on her face as she said:

'Cook will long since have gone to bed, Charles. Anyway, I don't really want anything. I think I'll go to bed myself. I'm a little over-tired.'

'Good idea!' Charles said kindly. 'Matter of fact, we wondered where you'd gone when we finished our game. Never thought you might be up here. Well, I'll just go down for a night-cap and then I'll be up. Sure you'll be all right?'

Briony nodded quickly. At least tonight she could spare herself the further pain of finding excuses for her behaviour to Charles. When he came upstairs half an hour later, she feigned sleep. But as soon as her husband had closed his eyes, the tears ran down her cheeks silently and made a damp pool round the hand-embroidered initials of the man whose name she had taken for better or for worse until death did them part.

VIII

By lunch time the following day, Briony and Lynn were left alone in the house. Charles had departed about ten by car to London with Marion and Gerald and Vanessa. Lynn had carefully bade her mother a polite fare-well but, rather than appearing downcast by her absence, seemed to acquire new life as soon as Marion had vanished and a lessen-ing of tension that completely changed her docile exterior.

Only when the police had come with Tom's owner to take him away had the child become subdued and wept, although Briony, empty of tears now, remained dry-eyed. Tom's owner, a young farm labourer, had identified the dog at once, and even had Briony doubted his affection for the animal, Tom himself had wagged his tail and barked eagerly his welcome.

'I thought he'd become "my dog",' she told the man rather bitterly.

'Well, miss, it's as like as not he would have done, after a time. But these mongrels – well, they're faithful as no other kind of dog be. It's a case of being a "one-man dog" with Laddie here. Right worried I've been about him. Never thought to get in touch with the police like. Laddie'd gone a-rabbiting. Been searching ever since and about given up hope. Then someone in the pub was talking about a stray up at the big house and I wondered maybe it could be Laddie if he'd come across the hill and down this way. Soon as they described him, I reckoned on it being my Laddie all right.'

He fondled Tom's ears as he spoke and

looked uneasily from the policeman to Briony and the weeping child.

'Right sorry to have caused you this trouble, miss! I know as how you'd get fond of a dog, even in a short while, and him being ill, any time as your little girl 'ud like to come and see him, I'd be pleased for her to do so ... or yourself, miss ... and of course I'll settle with you whatever he's cost you.'

'No, please!' Briony had said. 'Let me do that. It's given me great pleasure and–' In spite of herself her voice broke. After all, it was Tom who had brought Robert into her life.

'Then I'm grateful to you, miss – I mean ma'am!' the man had said simply, realizing that she did not wish to be paid for her services to Tom. 'But for you he might have died. Did you have Mr. Elliot to him, I expect?'

'No! Mr. Baker. Mr. Elliot was away. As a matter of fact, I have great faith in Mr. Baker ... as a vet!'

Tom's owner smiled.

'Well, I'm right glad to hear you say that, ma'am. I know as how most people have Mr. Elliot, but we have Mr. Baker now on the farm. Real good sort he is, and knows his job, too. The animals all take to him, and you can trust an animal's instinct any time.'

'Tom – I mean Laddie – is still supposed to be having treatment ... injections,' Briony said. 'Maybe you would get in touch with Mr. Baker yourself and explain what has happened? That is, if you agree the dog still needs attention.'

'Oh, I can see as how he's still pretty sick! I'll ring Mr. Baker from the farm. And thank you again, ma'am.' He turned back to Lynn, who was still crying quietly. 'Now, now, miss. Don't you fret none. Your Mum'll let you come and see him, I'm sure. And there's other animals on the farm too. Maybe we'll let you ride Jake, our old horse.'

'It's not my little girl!' Briony said, putting an arm round Lynn's shoulder and smiling across at the man. 'Though I wish she were. She's just staying with me for a few weeks. If you really mean it, we'll come over to the farm one day next week, perhaps, when Tom's better. Then we can see the other animals and have that ride. Come on, darling, don't cry any more. You should be happy to know that Tom is happy because he's found his real master again.'

'B-but I'm n-not crying for me, B-Briony. It's for you. You loved him and now he's g-going.'

'We'll be pushing off, ma'am, and thank you kindly!' said the policeman, a fatherly man with children of his own. He guessed rightly that this little scene was only pro-longing discomfort for everyone. And a few minutes later they were gone. Lynn cheered

162

up a little when, by forcing a degree of gaiety in herself, Briony convinced the little girl that she did not really mind so much. But loss of the dog remained an added twist in her heart, though she tried her utmost not to think of the puppy or of Robert ... Robert, who might never come to the house again.

After lunch, Briony set herself the task of writing the letter to Lynn's father. At least it kept her mind off herself and she had hopes that it might eventually benefit the child who had been crying for *her!*

It was Lynn who brought the letter at tea time. She had been with Nancy in the kitchen, for Cook had the afternoon off, helping to get the tea, when the post had come. Nancy had given Lynn the letter to bring to Briony.

Looking up from her desk at the envelope Lynn held out to her, Briony knew instantly that it was from Robert. Afterwards, she wondered how she had known, for she had never had occasion to see his handwriting before. Yet she was sure ... so sure that she had waited for Lynn to disappear again before opening it.

My darling,
  I sat until dawn this morning writing you letters and tearing them up again, After all, what is there I can say that will help, or alter, the

situation in which we find ourselves? In the end, I found this poem I had once read, written by Alice Meynell, who must, I think, have composed it for us. I send it to you with my love and hope that it will comfort you as it comforts me to think that you feel this way, too.

Always,

Your Robert.

The poem, on a separate sheet, was titled 'Renouncement'. It read:

I must not think of thee! and, tired yet strong,
I shun the love that lurks in all delight…
The love of thee … and in the blue heaven's
    height,
And in the dearest passage of a song.
Oh, just beyond the sweetest thoughts that
    throng
This breast, the thought of thee waits hidden
    yet bright:
But it must never, never come in sight.
I must stop short of thee the whole day long.
But when sleep comes to close each difficult
    day,
When night gives pause to the long watch I
    keep,
And all my bonds I needs must loose apart,
Must doff my will as raiment laid away,…
With the first dream that comes with the first
    sleep,
I run, I run, I am gathered to thy heart.

Briony pressed the poem impulsively against her breast as if it were indeed Robert she held against her heart! For it was, in essence, the spirit of her love she held. Only Robert, who understood, could have found that poem, so exactly expressing her own emotions. Only Robert could have guessed her desperate need of reassurance that this written word from him would give. Only her true love could have known so surely that she needed one tangible, material object she could treasure always, the most priceless of all her possessions since they symbolized her lost love. Had he had some premonition that they would not see each other again? He could not have known when he wrote that letter that the puppy was to return to its owner.

Only then did the full force of this knowledge that she might never see Robert again ... *ever* ... hit her mind like a physical blow. She felt sick with the enormous sense of loss. Slowly doubts began to assail her. Was she being old-fashioned in her refusal to consider divorce? Was she throwing away the happiness of two people for the questionable happiness of one man who could not, by his very nature, feel things deeply? But that wasn't true! Charles did feel deeply, not in an emotional sense, but in a moral sense. Divorce, to him, must surely be as shameful a thing as it would have been to his mother. Briony could almost hear that rigid old lady saying in her dictatorial way: "Divorce? How disgraceful! Have the modern generation no sense of values, no awareness of their duty, no religion?"

Religion! Oddly enough, Briony had not considered her marriage in its religious light. She and Charles had been married in a church because Charles wished it so. But in making her vows she had felt no spiritual strengthening of her spirit, nor had she felt that the actual moment when they were pronounced man and wife had any Divine blessing. For her, all faith had been killed with Bob. How hard she had prayed in those days ... how earnestly and intimately she had pleaded with the Heavenly Powers to safeguard her love, to protect him and keep him safe! When he had been killed, it was as if it had been suddenly revealed to her that there was not, after all, another world, a God, a Christ, who controlled their lives. It was not so much that He had deserted her in her hour of need, but that He could not possibly exist. For she had had faith, unquenchable faith, and believed in her heart that nothing could happen to Bob, since she had herself given his safe keeping into all-powerful hands. Since that terrifying realization that she was alone in this world with only a cruel Fate or Luck guiding the way of her life, she had ceased to become an active member of her Church and had not even attended a service except her own wedding.

Once, when she first came to live in Charles's family home, the local vicar had called on her to ask if she would be attending the Sunday services. She had told him as kindly as she could that she was now an unbeliever, and while she was aware that he would have liked to know her reasons and perhaps discuss them with her, she had discouraged him by turning the conversation quickly to welfare work in which she was willing to participate. She did not wish to 'believe' again nor have to recount to a stranger the period of her life with Bob she had resolved to forget.

"Maybe I could be happier if I had some faith in a life hereafter!" she told herself now. "Maybe if I thought Robert and I would be together in the next world I could feel more resigned to being parted from him for the rest of my earthly life." But she could not believe. In any case, the mere fact that both the men she had loved would be in any 'heaven' that existed, and that this would place her in an impossible predicament if she were to be forced to choose between them, only made Heaven too complicated to be a paradise.

'Briony, what are you thinking of? You look so many hundreds and thousands of miles away. Are you grieving for Tom?'

Briony looked down at the pale little face raised to hers and realized with a shock that little Lynn must have been watching her for quite a time in thoughtful silence. The child was so quiet, so strangely adult in her sensitiveness to a mood, that one was apt to forget she was there!

'I was thinking about God ... and Heaven!' she said, putting an arm round the thin little shoulders. (How was it Lynn, who lived in the land of plenty, could be so thin?)

'God makes everything better, doesn't He?' the child was saying. 'Once my Daddy was very ill and I prayed and he got better. Daddy said it was probably my praying so hard and wanting him so much to get well that made him well again. Do you ever ask God for things, Briony?'

'I ... I used to do so!' Briony said awkwardly.

Lynn gave her a shy smile.

'You know, I prayed that I could stay here with you, Briony! Sometimes I'm very lucky, aren't I? I mean, God can't always answer prayers, can He?'

'Why not?' Briony heard herself asking harshly.

'Well, it must be pretty difficult, mustn't it? Suppose that man who took Tom away prayed to find him and you prayed that nobody found him, how is God to decide which prayer to answer? He can't answer both!'

Briony drew in her breath. How logical this child was ... how disconcerting with her direct approach to a problem!

'Of course, I've prayed and prayed to be allowed to go and live with Daddy for always, but God doesn't answer that one. I can't think why, because I'm practically certain Daddy prays it too, and I don't think Mummy would pray to keep me. I mean I don't think Mummy would be the sort of person who does pray, do you?'

'I'm afraid I'm not the sort of person either!' Briony said.

Lynn merely smiled.

'You just say that, Briony, but I don't believe it. Daddy doesn't say his prayers either, but I know he prays just the same because he always says "God bless you" when he says good night or when I'm going away. That's a prayer, isn't it?'

Briony nodded.

'Yes, I suppose it is, Lynn. You know, I started to write a letter to your Daddy to tell him all about you and I haven't finished it. Suppose you run and play with Nancy for a little while and then we'll walk down to the post together before bedtime.'

The child obediently ran off and Briony, putting all thought of herself out of her mind, continued with the difficult letter. It was difficult because she did not know the man to whom she was writing ... she had only Lynn's version of him: difficult, because she was not sure that she had any right to interfere in his private arrangements, or Marion's: difficult because she was afraid to say too much.

In the end her letter was, she thought, a fairly good compromise and might be posted without much fear of any harm done. It read:

Dear Mr. Wendover,

Your little daughter, Lynn, is staying with me for the next fortnight and I thought you might be pleased to have news of her. She has written herself, but you will no doubt be glad of another brief note to tell you she is well, and already a much-loved little girl.

She arrived here last Friday with her mother, stepfather and aunt to stay for a long week-end. London life did not appear to be suiting her very well so I suggested she should stay on with me until her mother went to France. Marion agreed to this arrangement as she has much to see and do in Town and it would be easier for her to make her plans without a small child to care for.

Having no children of my own, I have found myself becoming greatly attached to Lynn. She has such a sweet disposition and I am quite captivated by her strange mixture of youthfulness and sophistication. No, that is the wrong word. It is her quaint way of understanding a grown-up mind or mood ... so much so that she is really a perfect companion. While I believe, from what she has told me of her life with you and your close companionship with her, that this is partly the reason, I think it is also because she has, for the rest of the year, to live in a world of her own where she must fight her own battles and try to reason out the moods of the 'grown-ups' around her, She is, as you no doubt know, highly sensitive and at first very shy. But this shyness has quite vanished now that we are so fond of one another and she is a different person from the awkward little girl that seems uppermost in her mother's company.

I hope you will not object to the personal nature of my letter. I know you must be greatly attached to Lynn and possibly anxious about her welfare. She has not, after all, that placid, happy-go-lucky nature that will adjust itself easily to changes of atmosphere and company, and she loves you so dearly that separation from you is a constant misery which she tries hard and fairly successfully for one so young to conceal, since to mope would not please her mother. It would seem that a gayer, precocious child would appeal more to her mother, who I found so different from Lynn in temperament that it seemed difficult to reconcile the fact that they are mother and daughter.

Marion was discussing Lynn with me the other evening and felt that she had made a mistake in

171

bringing Lynn to Europe, both from the child's point of view and her own. She seemed worried, however, as to what her friends and social acquaintances in America might have thought of her if she had left the child with you. I couldn't help feeling what a pity it was that Lynn's happiness should be dependent on the possible unfavourable opinion of a few 'friends'. However, that is not really my affair and maybe nothing can be done about it, anyway.

I lead a very quiet life here in the country, and it has occurred to me that Marion might possibly agree to letting Lynn remain with me until the European trip is over and then pick her up on the way home. However, that has yet to be settled. If you care to write to Lynn at this address, I will forward the letter to her if she is not here in person to receive it. One of her great anxieties is that you will not know where to write to her if she is constantly moving around.

She is quite well physically, although I am hoping to fatten her up a little while she is here. Our English children seem so much plumper. At the rate Lynn is demolishing crumpets and butter, I think she is sure to put on weight!

Once again I ask you to forgive me if as a complete stranger to you, I have seemed to take too personal an interest in your little girl's welfare. Please excuse it on the grounds that I am so genuinely fond of her.

Yours very sincerely,
Briony Stone.

172

She found an airmail envelope and stamp and, collecting Lynn, went out to post the letter before she could change her mind. After all, she told herself bitterly as she slipped the envelope into the box, if this made Lynn's father, or more possibly her mother, a bitter enemy for life it did not matter very much. Nothing in the world mattered now that she had said good-bye to love for the second and last time.

IX

A week had passed since the end of the house party, the writing of her letter to Lynn's father and her final good-bye to Robert Baker. It had been a week of complete quiet and uneventfulness. If it had not been for Lynn's constant and strangely understanding company, Briony felt that she might have gone crazy.

Because of Lynn, she had forced herself to eat the meals Nancy served them in order to encourage the child to eat: because of Lynn, she had forced herself to go out for walks, even to the farm to see Tom, although she had been desperately anxious and at the same time afraid in case she might run into

Robert there. Because of Lynn, she had refused herself the comfort of tears at night in case the child should see tell-tale signs of her unhappiness next day. Because of Lynn, she carried on with her normal life as far as she was able, and even Charles failed to guess that there was anything unusual about her except a slight lack of cheerful good spirits, which he put down to the loss of her puppy.

Charles's very normality helped her a little to be 'normal' with him. When he put his arm round her shoulder, it was a gesture invariably accompanied by 'Had a good day, old girl?', so that it lost any trace of intimacy and was more of a brotherly nature, which she felt was the most she could bear from him at the moment. Fortunately for her, he had shown no wish for greater intimacies, and since he had twice been kept late in town entertaining business friends at his club, he had accepted her suggestion that he use his dressing-room so that he should not wake her if he were late home. Having the privacy of her own bedroom was an enormous relief to Briony and she could lie awake with the light on until the early hours reliving the few moments of ecstasy that were all she had to treasure of her lost love ... those and Robert's poem and letter. How often had she whispered to herself the last lines of the poem he had copied for her...

'With the first dream that comes with the first sleep, I run, I run, I am gathered to thy heart.'

She would close her eyes and try to visualize Robert as he might be at this moment, lying awake or asleep, thinking or dreaming of her. It was some small measure of comfort to believe that their thoughts might be joining them together to gainsay the cruel silence of the lonely days.

Then, suddenly, action took hold of her life. By one morning's post there came two fairly happy events and one wretched piece of news. Robert ... how her heart beat at the sight of his handwriting! ... how it had fallen in a hard, cold pain as she read the words ... Robert was going away.

I have been offered a job in a laboratory in California by a one-time American student friend of mine. Or rather, he has procured the offer of the job for me as he knew in our college days that I was interested in research, and when the post fell vacant remembered me.

Don't think I have not considered this question closely, and from all angles, my own dear love. To be separated from you by thousands of miles with no hope of seeing you, even glimpsing you from afar, is torture indeed. But I have realized in the last few days that I am not strong enough to bear the separation of only a few miles. I must put great distances between us if I am to play my part. Briony, my darling, what I am trying to say is that if I stay here, I shall weaken and come to see you on some trumped-up excuse, and that is wrong ... for you, for me and most of all for your husband.

This chance to take up research in the U.S.A. therefore seems the obvious solution to many things. In my present job I work fairly much without using my brain ... by that I mean most of the work is routine and automatic. I have, therefore, far, far too much time to think of you. In the laboratory, I shall be kept busy and can work myself to a pitch of exhaustion in which I trust I shall have little time for the bitter-sweet remembrances that haunt me now. We had such a little time together, went but to one place together, and yet your ghost haunts every corner of this place. You are in my room with me now, your sad little face raised anxiously to mine! You are in the country lanes with your beautiful red curls blowing with every spring breeze, you are in the trees, the sky, the car. I must get away.

Maybe you will haunt me just as truly in the great America! I know, without shadow of a doubt, that I can never forget. But to be so near and yet so very, very far ... do you understand, my dearest dear?

I am hoping perhaps wrongly but nevertheless desperately that we can see each other once more before I go. I must see you once again.

   For ever and ever,

     Your loving

       Robert.

When she had recovered from the first shock, Briony knew that, however unbearable the facts, Robert was right. She could understand so well since she suffered as he did the pain of a proximity which only a sense of duty made distant. She, too, had come many times to the point of weakening ... had found herself by the telephone, struggling not to ring his number just to hear his voice; had fought the desire to go again to the farm in the hope of seeing him on a visit to Tom. If it had not been for her conscious preoccupation with Lynn, she knew she might already have weakened in her resolve. There would be a finality in Robert's departure to America that might help her to accept the finality of her own decision.

"At least I shall see him again ... be in his arms once more!" she thought, her cheeks flushed with sudden colour. At least there would be this last meeting with him ... for nothing, nothing would prevent that. Wrong it might be ... weak, deceitful even! But surely Charles if he knew could not deny her this last goodbye, when it was for his sake that all this had transpired?

Her mind raced ahead, planning, alive once again as it had been numbed with pain all week. Charles had said he would be late home again on Wednesday. Nancy could be persuaded to stay late in order not to leave Lynn alone. She could meet Robert for several hours without fear of anyone knowing.

She reached for the telephone and dialled his number. It was not yet half past nine and she could reasonably hope that Robert had not left on his rounds so early. Lynn was breakfasting in the kitchen with Nancy ... a special treat as Nancy had persuaded Briony to have a tray in bed for once since she looked 'so washed out, ma'am, if you'll pardon the saying'.

Her heart pounded feverishly while the operator took the number and she heard it ring. Maybe he had gone out after all. Maybe...

'Hullo?'

'Robert, is that you?'

There was a second's silence and then Robert's voice saying:

'Briony! Then you have received my letter?'

She lay back on the pillows and closed her eyes. Like this, she might almost believe he was standing in the room with her.

'Yes!' she whispered and again: 'yes! I thought perhaps we could meet on Wednesday!' She recalled suddenly that the local operators had been known to listen-in on the lines and was suddenly cautious. 'I would suggest the same time and place.'

'I'll be there! Briony…'

'Yes?'

'You agree… that it's the best thing? I have to cable my reply by return. I'll have to decide one way or another today. I must be sure that you agree.'

'Oh, Robert, what can I say? I know you are right and yet … yet I would so dearly love to dissuade you.'

All her desperation and longing were in her voice regardless of listening ears.

'It's as I have felt!' she heard his reply. 'I've known I must accept and yet I hoped against hope you would ask me not to go. Crazy, isn't it?'

'There is another word for such emotions!'

'Oh, Briony … I couldn't have believed it would be so awful … this last week … it's been hell! I thought the world had come to an end when that chap rang me from his farm to say he had Tom and would I go there in future to treat the dog. I thought at first you'd arranged it so … then I knew you wouldn't have parted with the puppy unless you'd had to. My last hope of seeing you had gone and I was desperate. Now I can live again … for Wednesday.'

'As I shall, too!' she cried brokenly. 'Robert, if you accept the job, there's no going back. I'm frightened!'

'*Darling!* Don't feel that way about it.

Though there is no going back, I shall never cease to pray that we might yet go forward … that somehow, some time, you will find yourself free to come out and join me. Pray for that, too, Briony. Surely God will hear one of us?'

"Not me! Not me!" Briony thought, utterly wretched. "God, if there is a God, does not answer my prayers. And there *is* no answer to this one."

'Briony, are you there?'

'Yes, yes! I'm here!' she said, but the tears were flowing down her cheeks and her voice trembled.

'Briony! You mustn't cry! Oh, God, I can't stand this! I'm coming over now to see you…'

That sobered her.

'No, you can't do that, Robert! I'm all right, *really!* Don't worry about me. I'm really quite all right!'

'You don't sound it. Briony, I'll cable them no. I can't go and leave you like this. I shall worry myself to death out there not knowing what has happened to you … how you are!'

With all her heart she longed to abandon herself once and for always to his care … to a future of which she asked only to be allowed to be with him. But her hesitation was only of a second's duration and an instant later she heard herself telling him he must go ... that it was best for her as well as for himself ... the only possible action that would make this agony more easily bearable.

'You're absolutely sure you want to do this job, Robert? It isn't only because of me? Your career...'

'It's what I have most wanted to do. But, unfortunately, there has been no opportunity until now. I couldn't afford to remain idle waiting for a lab job in this country – certainly could not afford to go abroad in search of one. Research has always fascinated me. But, Briony, I wouldn't have dreamed of going ... not even for a moment ... if I had thought that by staying I could be with you.'

'I know that, Robert. I'm really glad ... if it means it is best this way for your career. I can bear your going if I know it's going to mean you will be happy in your work. Robert, I must ring off. I'll be there on Wednesday whatever happens. Good-bye until then.'

Two minutes later Lynn came dancing into the room, too excited to notice the expression on Briony's face.

She waved a letter in Briony's face and danced up and down the room.

'It's from Daddy!' she cried, her face aglow. 'Nancy helped me read it. He had your letter, Briony, and there's one in here from him to you.'

Briony forced herself for the hundredth time to put Robert from her mind and give her attention to the little girl who was obviously awaiting her eager reception of a letter that she felt must mean a lot to Briony, since it would have given her such a thrill!

Obediently, Briony took the letter and read it quickly.

Dear Mrs. Stone,

I cannot tell you how greatly I appreciate your very kind letter. Let me say this minute that nothing, however personal, could give me offence if I know ... and I do in this case ... that it is for my daughter's welfare. Lynn is all I have in the world and I love her very dearly. I know she returns this love but I have long believed that, being so sensitive, she is something of a chameleon, taking on the mood of the person with whom she is most in contact. I believed therefore that while she loved me to the exclusion of all else during her half-yearly visits to me, she also felt as deeply for her mother when she was with her.

I cannot think now how I can have been so blind to the truth. Marion ... I trust she is not a close friend of yours, or I am speaking out of turn ... has always been egoistical, self-centred, call it what you will. Her interests, desires, etc., come first. I supposed she might be different where her only child was concerned, but as she never had shown Lynn much attention even before our divorce, I suppose I have been attributing to her a nature which she never had. To believe that she did not love Lynn made her out to be so despicable a creature. And I once loved her! But enough of me. My main and only concern is for Lynn. Please, if you are able, write and tell me frankly if you think she is unhappy with her mother and would be happier spending the year with me. If it is the latter ... and I could not help but feel this was so after reading your tactful letter ... then I shall leave no stone unturned to get full custody of Lynn.

It is always difficult in American courts of law to take a child from its mother. I did not fight Marion's suggested half-yearly visits when our divorce was heard because this seemed to me to be a reasonably fair arrangement. After all, Marion had never and to my knowledge has never been cruel or neglectful to Lynn in its legal sense. How to go about getting full custody is a problem. But if you, Lynn's friend, tell me that you feel it for the best, I shall put the matter in the hands of my solicitor immediately. Deep in my heart I have often questioned whether or not Lynn was unhappy with Marion. But I wrote off these doubts as being a case of wishful thinking. You see, my life is completely empty and devoid of love and interest when Lynn is away and I so longed to keep her when it has been time to send her back to New York, I believed myself biased every time I began to wonder if Lynn's reluctance to leave me was purely temporary.

If you can spare the time ... and I believe you are the kind of person who will make time ... then write me again and tell me more fully what you advise me to do.

Tell Lynn I think of her always.

Yours very sincerely,
Lance Wendover.

Briony raised her eyes from the letter and met Lynn's expectant gaze. She knew she could not yet tell the child what her father had in mind, nor suggest it by so much as a hint. Yet she must say something to Lynn.

'It's a very, very nice letter!' she said at last. 'I think your Daddy is every bit as wonderful as you have told me, Lynn dear. Oh, and he said I was to tell you that he thinks of you all the time.'

Lynn sat down on the bed and clasped her hands together.

'Oh, I do wish you could meet him!' she said, starry-eyed. 'I know you'd be great friends. You'd like him just as much as you like Robert. He is just as much fun and ... well, he's swell!'

'Robert ... may be going to America!' Briony told the child. It was something, after all, to be able to talk about it. 'He might even be near where your Daddy lives ... in California.'

Lynn gazed at her wide-eyed.

'Briony! Just think, they could meet and Robert could tell Daddy all about us.'

She paused and, suddenly thoughtful, added:

'But, Briony, if Robert goes you'll be all alone!'

The unconscious perception of the remark left Briony breathless. After all, the child could know nothing. It was just that she believed Robert was her only friend. Certainly she had given the child no reason to suppose otherwise.

'It will be ... lonely,' she said as calmly as she could. 'It's always sad to lose a friend. But it's the best thing for Robert ... he's going to a good job out there, to do something he loves doing. We mustn't be sorry if he's going because it's best for his career.'

'No, I suppose not!' said Lynn, brightening. 'And it's so lovely out there, Briony. Everyone says California has the best climate in the world ... and the nicest people. I'd rather be there than anywhere else in the whole world.'

"Soon I shall echo that statement," Briony thought wryly. She was suddenly unable to bear the conversation any longer.

'I'll read my other letter,' she said. 'It's from London.'

'Why, that's my Mummy's handwriting,' Lynn said, glancing at the envelope. 'I wonder how she and Aunt Vanessa and Uncle Gerald are getting on.'

Marion's letter was full of detail as to their activities over the past week. Briony skipped the untidy paragraphs until she came to the news she wanted:

...As far as I am concerned, you're welcome to keep Lynn for the next two months. I've only realized this last week how much easier life is without the child tagging along. Naturally, we can't very well leave her alone in hotels and she's really not old enough to go to restaurants or bars. I guess I owe you a great deal for your kindness and Gerald joins me in saying that if ever we can repay you in any way, you have just to ask.

Tell Binny she's to behave herself properly and not be a nuisance to you.

Maybe we can all meet in town before we go to Paris. I know we would be glad to return your hospitality as well as enjoy seeing you and dear Charles again.

Grateful thanks.

Marion Martell.

'Oh, Lynn darling!' Briony cried. 'Mummy writes to say you can stay on here until they come back from Europe. Isn't that wonderful?'

Lynn let the glorious fact sink in and then, gasping, said:

'But how did she know I wanted to stay, Briony; did you write to her and not tell me?'

Briony smiled.

'I didn't want you to be disappointed if she said "no".'

'It's the most perfect surprise I've ever had!' Lynn whispered as she hugged Briony in her thin little arms. 'Oh, thank you, thank you! Isn't this the most wonderful day, Briony? A letter from Daddy and this news from Mummy all at once? It's like Christmas!'

"Except that I have heard that Robert is going away ... miles and miles away ... out of my life. Robert, Robert..."

'I'm happy for you, Lynn darling!' she murmured across the child's fair head. But the eyes that gazed into the hopeless future were filled with tears that could not be shed.

X

'Briony!'

'Oh, Robert!'

At last they were in each other's arms, locked in a timeless embrace that each had dreamed and longed for without ceasing.

'These two days have been like two years!' Briony cried. 'I thought Wednesday would

187

never come!'

He silenced her lips with kisses that were without guilt, for all he had no right to touch her. Yet in her presence he could never feel guilty. It was so absolutely 'right' that they should be like this, alone in the world. They had truly been created for one another by God. Surely the man-made law of marriage could not prevent this inner belief that they were already as one flesh?

Briony clung to him with the desperation that only imminent parting can lend. She could not forget, even for a moment, that he was so soon to go out of her life ... for always. As he held her against his heart, she knew the first real agony of temptation. If she could be wholly his ... just once to know the full perfect union that would be theirs and which she knew all too well he longed for too! If she could abandon herself for a short while ... only a short while in a whole lifetime ... to the desire to give him everything of herself! Adultery ... the word fought against her instincts... such a cold, horrible, sordid word! How impossible that anything she and Robert might do could be termed 'sordid' ... and yet that is how the world would consider it. It was in fact how she, herself, might consider such an act in retrospect. And yet ... she had once given herself to the man she loved ... to Bob. But she had not been a married woman then ... she had harmed no living soul by her months with Bob. Even the law did not raise the legal hand against such things ... nor the commandments. But both the law of God and of man forbade adultery...

'I can't bear it, Robert!' she cried. 'I want to be with you ... in every way ... for always!'

Robert was torn between his own natural desires and his wish to protect her ... from herself as much as from him. He fought for control and eventually mastered his emotions sufficiently to say:

'It mustn't happen this way, Briony. What is between us is too beautiful to spoil ... for a temporary satisfaction. One day ... I shall never cease to believe and pray for this ... we shall be together ... as it was meant for us to belong to one another. I know it will be so.'

'If I could only believe that! If I could only think that!'

'It must be ... else there is no reason for living!' Robert said quietly, taking her face in his hands and looking deep into her eyes. 'I know we cannot be parted for always ... it wasn't meant to be that way. I feel that we were intended for one another ... that it might even have been the reason for your ... your first love being killed ... so that in the end we should find each other.'

'But, Robert, why, if you think Fate has this intention for us, should I have married Charles?'

'My darling, I don't know! Perhaps Fate did not intend that you marry him. Perhaps you misinterpreted Fate when you decided to do so. We all have free wills with which to guide our lives. Maybe you were meant to marry him so that we could both learn to appreciate the vast treasure that was one day to be ours ... *is* to be ours. Briony, you must believe it, too. If we can think that, then anything is bearable. This separation ... it is of our bodies only. Our spirits are united for now and always.'

Briony lay back against his arm, exhausted in mind and body. She was so overcome by emotion that her mind would not work coherently. At last she said:

'If I were to ask Charles for a divorce–'

But he broke in quickly, saying:

'No, darling. That is not the way. I've thought about it for hours and hours and I know, now, that you are right. We cannot grab our own happiness with complete disregard for everything we have hitherto valued. We are Christians, and we are English. We are members of a community and we have always believed that we owe something to others. No one can be entirely selfish in this life and be happy.'

'But there is no other way ... no other way...!' Briony cried. 'You cannot tell me that Charles will die ... nor could either of us wish him dead. It's unthinkable. Only divorce can set me free.'

But there was another way, Robert thought grimly, silently. He could not tell Briony because he was afraid it might influence her future actions. But some day, if Charles were to find another woman ... come to Briony for the divorce... If the idea entered her mind, which it obviously had not yet done and he hoped never would ... then she might, however unconsciously, behave so that in fact she was throwing Charles into the act of unfaithfulness.

What Robert did not know ... and which was incidentally the reason why no such idea had occurred to Briony ... was that Charles was the most unlikely person in the world ever to consider another woman. He was perfectly content ... had he not said so to Briony only a few days ago? ... with his marriage, his wife! He was a steady-going, unemotional man with few demands on the opposite sex. Women were not sufficiently important to him for him to be the type to look around once he was happily married. No, Charles would always be a faithful husband by virtue of his very temperament and upbringing.

Robert, so different in make-up, could not envisage a man so utterly self-sufficient and insensitive. Faithful ... he could be that without any difficulty with the right woman ... but how could Charles be happy with a wife

191

who did not love him, had no natural desire for him, shared none of his interests as he shared none of hers? It seemed incredible to Robert that any man could be so blind to the truth. One day Charles must wake up to the truth. It must happen. His relationship with Briony had been made no worse by his, Robert's, effect on Briony's life. Their marriage had always been as incomplete and without foundation as it was now. It was true that Briony had admitted a new physical antagonism to Charles. But then that might have come any time. No woman of Briony's temperament and emotional make-up could remain an unfeeling automaton for years on end, submitting without the slightest emotion to her husband's love-making, neither abhorring nor desiring such contact.

Robert guessed correctly that circumstances had left Briony not a shell without substance, as she had believed, but with a hard protective shell round the warm, living substance which was herself. Sooner or later that true self would have broken down its self-made armour and then, since she had no love for Charles, she would have begun to find intimacy with him impossible. All that Robert had done, inadvertently, was to crack that shell and allow her to breathe again ... to be herself again.

He knew that he could take her now if he wished ... knew that she was too much in love with him, too desperate, to think with her head rather than her heart. But his desire for her was so small a part of his love for her that he knew it must be all or nothing. Neither could be the happier for this abandonment of their moral beliefs: neither would be any the better for it. They would have only guilty and frustrated afterthoughts which would harm rather than help them to bear the years of separation that lay ahead.

'Robert!' Her voice claimed him from his thoughts. 'Tell me something about yourself. I know so little of your life.'

She lay back against him, weary yet content to be there listening to his voice.

'There isn't a great deal to tell. I'm an only child ... my father was vicar of the parish and died when I was twelve. Fortunately for Mother, who had a tiny pension, I won a scholarship to a decent public school and again, fortunately, another scholarship to Cambridge.'

'So you're very clever?' Briony said, smiling a little. 'I know enough to be certain that people can't win scholarships by luck!'

He smiled back at her.

'Oh, well, I had to work hard because there was no alternative. If I'd failed to do well in exams, then it would have meant the end to my dreams of a brilliant future! After Cambridge, I got a job for two years as an assistant to a vet near home where I could see Mother fairly frequently. Then her health began to fail a bit and she went to live with her younger sister. I had been feeling pretty restricted by the work and decided to risk branching out on my own. That brought me here, to you.'

'To me! Robert, would it have been better for you ... for us both, if you hadn't come?'

'My darling, no! We would have gone through life missing the greatest of all experiences. We would have existed only ... not lived. It is always a good thing to live, even if one is unhappy.'

'I don't think life was meant to be very happy,' Briony said sadly. 'As a child I used to believe that when I grew up, everything would be perfect ... no discipline, no one to tell you not to do things you wished to do. I thought, "I can go anywhere in the world I wish and one day I shall fall in love and marry and have children and be the happiest woman in the world." That was the sum of my ambition.'

'Briony, you are only young. That can still happen. Don't lose your faith in the future just because you have had a few setbacks. One must work for happiness. It's not a tangible object one can grab.'

'I know! But there isn't any way I can work for happiness with you!' she whispered. 'I can do nothing. That is the most difficult thing in the world. I discovered that when Bob was killed. There wasn't anything I could do about it. You at least will have your work!'

'And you think that will compensate me?' Robert asked gently. 'If I had everything else in the world I had ever wanted, it could not spell happiness for me if I did not have you.'

She turned to him then and they clung to each other, not kissing but in silent misery. Already it had begun to seem as if they were being dragged one from the other ... not so much by Fate but by their own words.

'Tell me you love me!' Briony said, although she never doubted that he did. 'I love you so, Robert, I love you so.'

'Words cannot tell you all that I feel for you!' Robert cried. 'Love ... how small a word for all that is in my heart! You are my life, Briony, my heart, my dreams, myself.'

'Yes!' she whispered, comforted a little. 'I shall be a part of you, Robert. Wherever you go, whatever you do, my heart will go with yours. It will not really be me that goes on living here alone. I shall be with you ... in spirit.'

'If you were only coming with me!' Robert said, suddenly weak. 'If this were to be our honeymoon and the start of a new life ... together!'

Briony began to feel desperate. America suddenly seemed the other end of the world. Even the fact that one could fly there in ...

hours could not make it seem any nearer.

'Robert ... how long before you will come back to England? You will come back? I mean, there's your mother and your sister to visit.' She broke off, very near to tears. Robert held her tightly to him.

'My darling, the very first thing I shall do is tie up a certain amount of money so that I can be certain of my fare home ... at a moment's notice. Whatever happens ... whatever it may mean ... you have only to cable me and I'll come. As to a visit to England ... well, I suppose I shall get holidays and I can save up leave until I have a month or two and can come home. I'll write and tell you my plans, darling. There can surely be no harm in our corresponding ... as friends? Naturally I shall not be able to tell you all that is in my heart ... how much I am missing you. But I can give you the facts of my life out there.'

'Yes, yes!' cried Briony. This at least would give her something to live for ... Robert's letters. And she could write to him. They would not be love letters ... but at least they would be some contact between them.

'Oh, Robert!' she whispered. 'I cannot bear it!'

'It will come right in the end. Believe it, Briony. It must!' he told her, trying to bolster his own belief in their future. 'Now I'm going to take you home, darling. You look deathly tired, worn out, and this is not doing you any good. Kiss me once again, my love, my only love.'

She knew he was right ... that prolonging their parting was prolonging the agony of it all. But, nevertheless, she could not let him go yet. This might be the last time she ever felt his arms around her ... the last time she would feel his lips on hers, know the ecstasy and pain of her longing for him. She clung to him fiercely and passionately and knew that Robert, too, had abandoned himself to the intoxication of their love's force. Presently, however, he disentwined her arms and said breathlessly:

'No, darling, no! I am not made of steel! Don't let us give way to anything we might regret. I could not bear to think that you might hate me after I had gone for my weakness now. Come, my dearest heart. I'm going to take you home. There can be no more meetings like this. It is bad for you ... and we cannot, must not, forget Charles.'

The mention of her husband's name brought Briony to her senses as Robert had guessed it would. She was suddenly calm, utterly spent and all but drained of emotion. Only despair and a sudden loneliness remained. It was as if Robert had already left her. Once again they did not speak as they covered the few miles to Briony's home. Only when Robert stopped the car could they find words ... inadequate, hopeless whispers, as they spoke each other's name.

'Not good-bye ... adieu!' Robert said wretchedly, as thousands of other lovers must have said at parting. 'I love you, Briony!'

She ran quickly away into the darkness, tears that she had not wished him to see as his last picture of her now pouring freely down her cheeks. It was over – everything over and finished. Love was gone ... for ever, gone into the dreamless past. She could not hope, as Robert might do, for the future. It was not in her nature to wish any harm to Charles, who loved her in his own way, who was always kind to her. And divorce ... that, too, was impossible or almost so. Divorce, she knew, could bring her nothing but guilt and unhappiness.

'I'm doing the right thing!' she told herself, but there was no comfort in this knowledge of duty, loyalty to the man she had married. There was no comfort in the world except the feel of Robert's arm around her: and this was lost to her for always.

Alone once more in her bedroom, she lay tearless at last, in silent misery. Shortly before midnight she heard her husband's car drive up to the house and not long after, his footsteps went past her door.

"Poor Charles! Poor Charles!" she thought, for the first time forgetting her own pain. "He, as I must, lives without love. He may not suffer its loss as I do, since he has never known its depths of heaven and hell, but he is missing and always will miss the greatest of all emotions. Poor, poor Charles."

This feeling of pity for him helped her to consider the continuation of her life with him. At least she could try, in kindness and understanding, to make up to him for the love she could never feel for him. It must be her task to keep him from discovering the truth about her. In this way only could she repair the harm she had done him in marrying him knowing that she could only take and never be the one to give.

At long last she fell asleep while the man she loved sat wakeful at his window staring out across the dark fields towards the house he knew he must not see again.

XI

Charles returned from the telephone, his face unusually animated. He poured himself another cup of coffee and sat down opposite Briony.

'That was Marion ... long distance from Stockholm, of all places!' he said. 'Apparently they are not having too good a time there for some reason or another ... say it's very dull and they thought of coming back to England for the last ten days. Of course, I asked them to come here and Marion thought it was an excellent idea, especially as they'll have to collect Lynn anyway. You've no objections, my dear?'

'No, no, of course not,' Briony said listlessly. Perhaps a little company would help to ease the agony of trying to keep her own misery and loneliness from Charles. He would never know what effort it had cost her to be bright and cheerful when he came home at night. Six weeks had passed since Robert had left for America ... six weeks of alternate agony, despair, regret and desperation. Her days had been filled to the last minute with entertainments which she had planned for Lynn. Purposefully she had organized every hour of the child's day in order to prevent herself from having time to brood, to think. They had made day trips to Windsor Castle, Oxford, London. They had been to the circus, the cinema and she had even persuaded Charles to buy a television set. Anything to keep her from thinking – from having time to think. But when Lynn was in bed and the long evening lay ahead of her, Briony knew defeat in her game of escapism. Charles was not interested in the television set and his conversation made it impossible to concentrate herself on the programmes. In any case, she felt, to try and listen and deny him her company was in itself a failure in her attempt to put him first in her life and make him happy.

So she had smiled and talked and played a part, and only when it came for Charles and herself to depart to their separate rooms could she relax at last and suffer the mixed feelings of relief that she had shown her husband nothing of her heart, or the terror of the long hours of loneliness and thinking that lay ahead of her.

Oddly enough, Charles had shown no curiosity at the arrangement they had made about separate rooms. Briony had had a very severe attack of 'flu the day after her farewell to Robert, partly brought on by the germ itself, but mostly due to her exhaustion and the nervous tension she had undergone. It seemed reasonable that Briony should request the privacy of her room, if nothing else but to give Charles a reasonable night's sleep, for she was restless and said she was afraid she would disturb him. Although the 'flu had passed, she spoke the truth in saying she still slept badly and so Charles had remained in the dressing-room.

Once or twice Briony had asked herself if Charles had guessed anything. But she rejected the idea. He was as he had always been: bluff, hearty, mildly affectionate, completely devoid of introspection or of interest in what went on below the surface of life as he saw it.

Briony thanked God for Lynn. The child, sensitive without being aware of the facts, was an enormous comfort to her. She was merry, bright, talkative as if she understood that Briony wanted, needed distraction. She threw herself whole-heartedly into whatever jaunt Briony had arranged for them and the woman was able to derive a second-hand pleasure from Lynn's obvious enjoyment of the days.

More letters had passed between Briony and Lynn's father and he had stated his resolve not to let Lynn return to her mother after her next visit to him. Lynn was like a new child ... so completely different from the nervous, shy, hesitant little girl Marion had brought with her, that Briony found herself wondering what Marion would think of this alteration in her daughter. Perhaps Lynn would soon drop back into her other self when Marion reappeared on the scene. Briony hoped not, for the child had put on weight and was bright-eyed, rosy-cheeked and had lost the dark circles under her eyes. She was always happy and singing round the house.

'I shall miss Lynn when she goes!' she spoke her thoughts aloud.

Charles nodded his head absently.

'Eh? Yes, I s'pose you will. Have to think about having one of our own one of these days, what?'

A little while ago that remark would have thrilled her. She had longed so greatly for a child. Now she was horrified. The colour flared into her cheeks and her hands trembled.

'Not – not just yet!' She was surprised how casual her voice sounded. 'I – I've not been feeling too well lately.'

Charles frowned.

'As a matter of fact, I've noticed it, my dear. Ever since that 'flu, what? Sure you're not finding Lynn too much for you?'

'Oh no, no!' Briony cried. 'I love having her here, Charles. Anyway, she's old enough not to make a lot of work. She is company for me.'

'You need a change of air!' Charles said, after a moment. 'Must see what I can do about getting some leave. We might go abroad ... when the Martells have gone, I mean. Which reminds me, there's the Hunt Ball next week. We could all go to that. And I rather believe the point-to-point is on Saturday, too. Give them a gay time before they go back to the States, what?'

'Yes, of course!' Briony agreed. At least she could make Charles's friends welcome. It was a relief every time she could do anything for Charles.

There had been no word yet from Robert. She had not expected to hear very soon, for clearly he could not cable his safe arrival without arousing suspicion. For the same reason he could not write airmail ... or immediately. However, she watched every post and knew the first doubts that perhaps after all he would not write. Maybe he had thought better of it – maybe he thought it better for them both if they tried to forget each other; maybe he felt even a platonic letter with its underlying implications was unfair to Charles; maybe he had already begun to forget her in the excitement of a new world ... a new life and job!

But torture herself though she might, she clung still to the vow that he had made her ... *he would always love her*. Sooner or later he would write. The waiting was another agony to bear.

Five days later Marion, Vanessa and Gerald arrived. Lynn, who had been quietly dreading this invasion of the blissful privacy of her life with Briony, nevertheless bore up remarkably well under Marion's greeting. She did not stutter and dutifully kissed the proffered cheek.

'You look swell, Binny!' Marion said, as she divested herself of her mink coat and studied the child's face. 'Quite the little English rosebud. Why, you even sound English, too!'

Lynn looked at her mother shyly.

'I hope you've had a nice holiday; thank you for your post-cards!'

'I've got some nice *cadeaux* in my valises!' Marion said gaily. 'Hey, we don't call it "holiday" in the States, my girl. We say "vacation"!'

Vanessa and Gerald joined in the laughter at Lynn's expense, but the child seemed unperturbed.

'I expect I say "holiday" because Briony always calls it that,' she said.

'I'm just dying for a drink!' Vanessa said, glancing at Charles. 'We missed the comfort of your car ride down, you know. English trains are clean, I grant you, but oh, so chilly! I'm just frozen!'

'We'll soon get you warmed up!' said Charles. 'Matter of fact I had the car standing by, but you never let me know what boat and train you'd be on.'

'Oh, we came by air!' Vanessa said. 'Quicker.'

'But say, what didn't we pay on excess baggage!' Gerald broke in. 'I'm a ruined man, Charles. And duty! Still, I couldn't resist a good case of French champagne. We've brought it with us so you and your wife can see for yourselves what the *vin du Pays* really tastes like!'

Briony felt Lynn's hand slip into hers. Under cover of the strident American voices, she whispered:

'Can I go now, Briony? I want to finish *Black Bess* before bedtime.'

Briony looked at Marion but she seemed to have lost interest in her child already, in spite of the fact that it was nearly two months since she had seen her. Suddenly the American woman turned her head and saw the child's eyes on her.

'I'll come and say "good night" later, honey,' she said. 'Run along now. The adults want to talk.'

Lynn departed and Briony showed her guests into the sitting-room, where a huge fire blazed in the hearth. Her guests made themselves quickly at home, and before long James came in with the first bottle of champagne, duly sitting in a bucket of ice. Charles pulled the cork and although it was not long after half past five the drinking began in earnest.

Briony, sipping at her glass of champagne, felt suddenly deathly tired. So far, the wine had done nothing to lift her spirits, and the loud voices of Charles's friends and the superficial gaiety of their mood rasped her nerves. She tried to concentrate on Gerald's account of their travels, but her mind wandered. So short a while ago, on their last visit, these same people had been associated in her mind with her meeting with Robert. It was really the puppy who had brought about their meeting and yet she would always associate the house party and these three people with falling in love ... with

Robert. His absence seemed more acute than ever, although he could not fit in any more than she did with the present company or its mood.

As they opened the second bottle, Briony slipped away on the excuse that she was going to put Lynn to bed. Lynn was dancing about on the landing, obviously awaiting her coming. She held something long and white in her hand. Briony's heart leaped.

'A letter for you, Briony! ... and from America. It isn't Daddy's writing, so I think it must be from Robert. I wanted to come and tell you, but I knew you would want to read it the moment you got it and it's rude to read letters in front of people, isn't it?'

Briony took the letter and at one glance confirmed that it was from Robert. Colour flamed into her cheeks and, suddenly conscious of the waiting child, she slit the envelope and began to read aloud. Somehow, speaking the words Robert had written made it seem more real ... more as if he were here, beside them.

'Dear Briony,

I thought I would write and tell you my first impressions of America since you said you would be interested, especially California, Lynn's home State. Well, I arrived here three weeks ago after a very pleasant sea trip although I didn't strike up any friendships on board and was consequently rather solitary. [Robert's way of telling her that there had been no shipboard romance ... that he missed her.] *Of course, New York is incredible ... everything they say in books about it and just as magnificent as it seems on the films only more so since you see so much of it in one glance. I stayed only two days and came on here to California. The train ride here was an experience in itself. They are so much better equipped and staffed than our trains and far more comfortable for long journeys though rather warm!*

California is beautiful. No wonder Lynn loves it. I am living in the Lab. Professor's house. I meant to find digs but the Professor would not hear of it. They are most hospitable here and do everything to please you and make you comfortable and at home. But naturally, one is homesick in spite of all their kindness and attention [again meant as a private word for her, Briony wondered].

I find the work exacting but not too difficult and very, very interesting. To be truthful, I am so tired at night that I have little inclination for the parties that have been arranged to introduce me socially and I plead this as an excuse. The food, too, is first class and I've no doubt I'm putting on weight. I wish I could send you some of the steaks I've seen.

If Lynn is still with you, give her my love and tell her I shall call to see her father as soon as I can. I believe his house is only ten miles or so away from here.

England seems a very long way away as so much has happened, and travelling by sea, each mile seems a mile, or should I say each Knot seems a Knot. Much as I like America and the people and especially California, I am already thinking of my first visit home. There's nowhere quite like England however restricted our life there might be.

Will you be so good as to let me know when Lynn is likely to be coming here as I will make a point of seeing her. It will be a link from home. But perhaps her father will tell me. I assume it will not be for some months yet.

I hope you are all well and would be glad for any news you may have to relate. Do you happen to have heard how the new chap has settled down in my practice? I hope Tom is completely better by now.

My kind regards to yourself and family and friends.

As ever,

Yours,

Robert Baker.'

A platonic letter, but how skilfully Robert had contrived to show her that he still loved her, still missed her, thought of her, longed for news of her! "Oh, Robert, Robert, Robert! How can I have been so crazy as to let you go!"

Lynn was chattering gaily about Robert's

connection with her own home. She would write to Daddy immediately to tell him to call Robert on the phone ... and when she went for her six months to Daddy in two months' time she would see Robert often...

'Oh, I wish you could be there too, Briony. I wish you were married to my Daddy and lived with us always. I do love you so!'

Briony hugged the child to her, hot tears stinging her eyelids. It wasn't Lynn's father to whom she should be married, but Robert. Then she would be near at hand to see Lynn often. Oh, what a hopeless, desperate love this was! It was doomed as the love she had for Lynn, whom she might never see again.

Downstairs in the elegant lounge Vanessa was talking to Charles.

'Aren't you ever bored down here, Charles? I don't mean, of course, that I should be because I love country life, and with a home like this one could do so much entertaining. But I gathered from Briony that you scarcely see anyone from one year's end to the next ... except, of course, your shooting friends.'

Charles laughed indulgently.

'Oh, well, you know, I'm not as young as you are, Vanessa. I'm quite content to sit back at week-ends with occasional shooting parties from time to time. Naturally, we could entertain more, but ... well, to be perfectly frank, my wife doesn't care for the locals very much. Not her type. We soon found out when we were married that we didn't care for the same people. So we just didn't have anyone we both care to ask.'

'I suppose Marion and Gerald and I are hardly Briony's type!' Vanessa said with a rather hard laugh. 'I daresay she finds us very poor company.'

'Oh, I say, of course not!' Charles huffed. 'Why ever should you think so? She said she liked you very much!'

Vanessa gave an enigmatic smile.

'Well, naturally she wouldn't want to say she disliked us, since we're your friends. But a woman always knows if another woman dislikes her. Your wife is very polite, but I know she resents our being here. I felt it last time.'

'I really don't believe that, Vanessa!' Charles said truthfully. 'I'm sure you're imagining it. Why, she was positively radiant at that party we gave. I've never seen Briony so – so lit up.'

Vanessa's eyebrows lifted.

'I presume you don't intend that expression in the sense meaning tight. She drinks nothing, does she? Tell me, Charles, who was the rather attractive young man she danced with several times?'

Charles frowned, trying to recall Briony's partners. The veiled implication of Vanessa's remark escaped him, since he was never quick to get a point, however clearly it was made.

Vanessa tried again.

'Surely you noticed? They seemed to make the perfect pair. I danced with him once or twice myself till Briony took over from me and I must say he sure danced as well as he looked.'

'You don't mean young Baker, the vet?' Charles said. 'Oh, he's no one very much, someone Briony called in to see a dog she had which was ill. I believe she told me he'd gone to America ... got a job there. I say, Vanessa, did you take a fancy to the fellow, what?'

Vanessa smiled again.

'Oh, no, *I* didn't set my cap at him, Charles. He was far too busy with Briony, anyway. Poor boy was obviously head over heels. No, I much preferred to dance with you. It was a good party, wasn't it? I haven't enjoyed anything as much, although we've had lots of night life in Europe.'

Charles had finally taken Vanessa's point.

'Did you say Baker was in love with my wife?' he asked incredulously. 'Why, that's – that's unthinkable, Vanessa. Whatever made you say any such thing?'

Vanessa laughed lightly.

'Oh, don't take it to heart, Charles. It was clearly a case of calf love ... why, he couldn't be more than twenty-eight at the most –

Briony's age at a guess. She's hardly likely to take him seriously, do you think?'

'Take him seriously?' Charles repeated. 'Look here, Vanessa, just what do you mean? Did that fellow do anything – I mean, how do you know he was in love with Briony?'

'Just the way he looked at her when they were dancing. Of course, I could have been wrong, but it does seem rather strange he's pushed off to the States suddenly. Or did he always intend going? He didn't mention it to me when we were last here.'

Charles fidgeted awkwardly, thoroughly discomfited by the idea Vanessa had put into his mind. Not that he for one moment imagined Briony took the fellow seriously, but the cheek of it! Dash it all ... impudent young puppy!...

Vanessa handed him her empty champagne glass and at the same time patted his other hand with her own long, slender one.

'Don't brood about it, Charles. It spoils your handsome forehead when you crease it up like that!'

Charles grinned sheepishly. It was always flattering when a girl as stunning as Vanessa paid him compliments, however her eyes might tease as she did so. He liked Vanessa. She was smart and sophisticated and a chap would be proud to be seen with her. What's more, she was always cheerful and friendly ... rather as a man might be. She'd make a good companion.

Unexpectedly, Charles found himself criticizing Briony. Why must she always wear those tweed skirts and twin sets, as she called them? Why couldn't she be smart, like those two American women? Of course, she could look lovely ... as she did the night of that dance, for instance. Then there wasn't a woman in the room to touch her. That was why it was so irritating to see her looking almost shabbily ordinary next day.

Of course, English women didn't care about their appearances the way American women did, Charles recalled having heard on one occasion. All the same, it was wrong that they shouldn't care. Dressing themselves up was in a way a compliment to a man. Now Briony never asked him what he liked to see her in ... or whether he liked her hair style.

His irritation with her gave way to a sudden affection. Good old Briony ... she was at least always the same – or rather, she never let him down by appearing in anything outrageous or ultra-fashionable. He could count on her not to look ridiculous, whatever the occasion. As a matter of fact, Briony was still something of a schoolgirl, he told himself, feeling very much older and more sophisticated himself. Strange little thing, really: moody and quiet ... but very sweet.

He looked round the room and realized

that she wasn't there and his irritation returned. She was probably playing some fool game with that child when her place was here with her guests. Briony would have to try and grow up. It wasn't good enough if people like Vanessa thought her evasiveness was really dislike or at least rude

Briony chose that moment to appear. She had changed from her skirt and jersey into a smart cocktail dress and was carefully made up. Her face was pale but her large eyes were unnaturally bright. She no longer looked the schoolgirl of Charles's imagination. She was as sophisticated as the other women. Charles felt a stir of pride. He realized nothing of the effort it had cost her to put Robert's letter away and dress up for the part she had to play tonight as Charles's wife, and hostess to his guests.

'Oh, Briony, dear!' Vanessa said with her drawl even more exaggerated. 'We were just talking about that perfectly swell party you gave last time we were here. Charles tells me your boy friend has gone to the States.'

Briony, taken completely unaware, was unable to control the angry red colour that flared into her cheeks. For one ghastly moment she believed that somehow Vanessa had guessed her secret. Then she rejected the idea as she told herself that 'boy friend' could mean merely 'partner' and nothing more. The colour left her and she felt icy cold.

'I suppose you must mean Robert Baker, the vet! Yes, he had a rather interesting job offered to him out there. He left a few weeks ago.'

Her voice was calm, too carefully casual to deceive Vanessa. But Charles, who had noticed her blush with a strange discomfort, was vaguely reassured.

'Vanessa was saying young Baker was smitten by your charms, my dear!' he said with a half-laugh. 'Never noticed it myself. Was he a conquest?'

"I can't stand this," Briony told herself, knowing at the same time that she must somehow talk her way out of this unbearable conversation. Her eyes went to the American woman and seeing the cool, amused expression on her face, she knew that she hated Vanessa. It could only have been Vanessa who had started this subject. Certainly Charles had had no suspicions of Robert. And to what end?

'What makes you think so?' she heard her own voice, deadly quiet. 'I think he only danced twice with me all evening and he must have had many more dances with you.'

'Oh, did you notice?' Vanessa replied with an implication that Briony certainly did not miss. 'But that was before you came on the scene. After that be never danced with anyone else.'

'Really?' Briony asked. 'Oh, well, perhaps

216

we tired him out between us. I'm sorry he isn't here to entertain you this time, Vanessa! We've no very handsome young men to introduce you to, have we, Charles?'

It was the first shot scored against Vanessa and she derived some satisfaction from it. But Vanessa was not long in finding a reply.

'I'm perfectly content with present company,' she said smoothly. 'You're always so busy looking after Binny that I have Charles practically to myself.'

"Is she trying to make me jealous, or what?" Briony asked herself as she purposefully moved away and spoke to Marion. "What is Vanessa's game? Is it just a wish to put things wrong between Charles and myself? Or is there a motive?" Somehow with Vanessa one could not help but suspect her of a motive for whatever she did. But what motive? What could she, Vanessa, gain even if she succeeded in arousing Charles's suspicions about her affair with Robert?

'My dear!' Marion was saying. 'I'm just *so* grateful to you for looking after Binny all these weeks. You can't imagine how much easier life is without the child.' She bent closer to Briony and said, 'You know, Gerald is frightfully good to her, but it isn't *his* child, and well – well, naturally he'd rather have me to himself.'

'But you're hardly alone with Vanessa around!' Briony said spitefully, and was amazed at herself for the remark,

'Oh, Van! She's different. She knows when to make herself scarce, and she's so amusing. I can't think why she hasn't married again. Of course, I understand her enjoying her freedom ... and I know she won't marry unless she finds someone with plenty of money. And she's quite right. I said the same, and I'm really *fond* of Gerald. Wasn't I just too lucky to find a man I liked who had money, too? And I guess that goes for you too, Briony, dear.'

Briony bit her lip.

'Yes, I suppose Charles is ... rich ... though that wasn't the reason I married him,' she said quietly. 'He was in the Army at the time and when I agreed – accepted his proposal – I didn't know he had any private means.'

'Well, what a pleasant surprise!' Marion said. She was not being catty. Somehow Marion was never that – as was her sister, Briony thought. She might be selfish and sometimes cruel to Lynn, but it sprang from an inherently stupid nature and lack of character. Marion was just a spoilt, good-natured, over-indulged woman with nothing more to her than exactly what she revealed in her disconnected and superficial conversation. There were no ulterior motives.

Because, of the two sisters, she suddenly found herself liking Marion so much the better, Briony relaxed and became for the moment friendly.

'You know, I can't help feeling that it would be much better if you let Lynn stay all the year round with her father … just let her visit you occasionally, Marion. I hope you don't mind my talking like this?'

'Why, no, indeed not!' Marion said. She sighed. 'I dare say you're right. Binny does get me so vexed sometimes and I'm sure it isn't good for my nerves. I really must write to Lance when I get back and suggest something of the sort. In any case, I'd rather choose *when* I'm to have Binny on a visit. As it is, I just have to take her when her six months with her father is up, and it isn't at all convenient. It's very sweet of you, dear, to take such an interest in Binny. I'm sure she's grateful, and I certainly am. Oh, well, I'd better go and say good night to her and then I'll take a shower – I mean a bath – and change for dinner. It's good to be in a house again. I just hate hotels!'

"It's going to be all right for Lynn," Briony thought triumphantly. "A letter from Lynn's father now will just about settle the point. Marion just hasn't time for the child."

She looked across the room and saw Vanessa's eyes on her. There was a look on her whole face that made Briony turn suddenly cold. It was almost as if she could feel the venom in that glance as an actual physical danger. But what harm could Vanessa do to her? None, that Briony was aware of. At worst, she could probe into her feelings for Robert, of which she would betray nothing at all. She could have no proof of those stolen meetings, for they had been seen by no one. And even if she had, what could be proved from the fact that she had gone twice for a drive alone with Robert? Charles at worst could be made suspicious, unhappy, but there was no proof. And if Briony could possibly help it, she told herself with determination, Vanessa would get no chance to upset Charles.

'Well, old girl,' Charles said, walking over to her, 'what about another little nip of champagne? Do you good, what?'

Knowing Vanessa's eyes were on her, she deliberately placed her arm in Charles's and held out her empty glass.

XII

Briony sat by Lynn's bedside and studied the flushed little face with anxious eyes. All day Lynn had been complaining she had felt sick ... that she had the stomach-ache. But Briony had, until now, been firmly convinced that the child was imagining these symptoms, as children will, because she did not wish to leave tomorrow. The Martells and Vanessa were catching an early train to Southampton, where they were booked on the *Queen Mary* for their return across the Atlantic.

For three days Lynn had begged Briony to ask Marion to leave her here. She had overcome Briony's refusal to do so since there would be no one to take Lynn home when she did go. After all, in another eight weeks she would be off to California to stay with her father.

'I could fly alone. Lots of kids do, Briony. The stewardess takes care of them. Oh, please ask her, Briony, *please*. I just can't go to New York and face two whole months there. I want to stay with you. Please let me, Briony, please!'

But Briony had refused to approach Marion on the subject. After all, she had already kept Lynn the best part of three months and Marion would not want her bookings altered even if she did not particularly care whether the child was with her or not. The parting had to be made sooner or later. Much as she herself dreaded it, much as she longed to keep Lynn longer for her own sake as well as the little girl's, she dared not interfere further with Lynn's life.

'Don't you want me any longer, Briony? Is that why you won't ask Mommy?'

'You know that isn't so, darling. You have

221

grown to be like my own daughter. I'd sooner part with anyone in the world than you. But you have to go sooner or later and it wouldn't be fair to Mummy to upset all her arrangements at this time. You know, she lost a great deal of money cancelling bookings over Europe when she went without you, and it costs a great deal of money to fly to America.'

'But Uncle Gerald has plenty of money,' the child had pleaded.

'That isn't the point, darling,' Briony had said gently. 'You have a certain duty to consider your mother just as she has to consider you, her child. She was very kind to let you stay here with me so long. Now you must do what will please her.'

Lynn had not argued further but Briony had frequently found her crying and Nancy reported that she had eaten nothing. Certainly she hadn't looked well these last few days but Briony, knowing how children could make themselves ill when they wished to further their own ends, pretended not to notice, much as she longed to hug Lynn and hold her close and tell her how desperately she, too, hated the thought of their imminent parting.

Now, for the first time, she began to wonder if Lynn really was ill. On an impulse she went along to the bathroom and found the thermometer. Lynn's temperature was a hundred and two. Aghast, Briony went immediately to Marion.

'I think we should call in the doctor!' she said.

'Oh, Heaven forbid she's got some infectious disease *now!*' Marion cried in annoyance. 'It would be just like Binny to get measles or something at the last minute. They'll never let her on board. Oh, blast the child. Yes! do call the doctor, Briony. No point not knowing the worst, I suppose.'

Briony felt her heart harden against this mother whose first thought must always be for herself. Then she forgot Marion as she went to telephone old Dr. Stains.

Within twenty minutes the doctor had arrived, and by that time Lynn had started vomiting. Before she took the doctor to Lynn's room, she told him what she herself had believed until now to be wrong with the child, explaining also that this was the reason she had taken little notice of the fact that Lynn had been pleading illness for the last few days. But she need not have done so. Within five minutes the doctor closed the door of Lynn's room behind them and said to Briony:

'Acute appendicitis. She'll have to be operated on immediately, tonight if possible. I'll make arrangements with the hospital. Let's hope I can get an emergency bed. May I use your phone?'

It took Briony a few moments to register the fact that Lynn was really ill. Then her hands went to her cheeks as she realized how wrongly she had judged poor little Lynn. She pulled herself together quickly, knowing this was no time for remorse, and showed the doctor to Charles's study. While he was telephoning, she went to Marion and reported the facts.

'I thought you'd be sure to want to speak to Dr. Stains before he goes and make whatever arrangements you think best,' she said. 'I'm so sorry, Marion. Lynn has been saying she wasn't well, but I thought nothing of it.'

'Of all the—' Marion broke off and bit her lip. 'Well, I'm not going to cancel our *Queen Mary* bookings. I had a ghastly job getting them and we had to come over in the *Charlotte*, as you know.'

'You'd be most welcome to stay here if you want to, Marion. You know that,' Briony said, helpless in the face of Marion's callousness. Surely no mother could leave her child at such a time! Marion couldn't do it ... not even Marion.

But Marion's mind never wavered.

'I'm just not going to alter those bookings. Gerald and I have been set on travelling in the *Queen Mary* and we may not have another chance for years. Perhaps Van would stay and keep an eye on Lynn and bring her

224

over later.'

'No!' Briony said sharply. She didn't want to be left *à deux* with Vanessa. She added quickly: 'Surely that isn't necessary, Marion. I will naturally look after Lynn ... just as if you were over in Europe when this had happened. I'd enjoy doing it. She can come back here and convalesce.'

Marion looked at Briony hopefully and gratefully.

'Well, that sure is kind, Briony, and I'd appreciate it. All the same, who'd bring Lynn to New York? She can hardly travel alone.'

Briony remembered Lynn's own suggestion.

'Suppose she flew? Lots of children do ... the stewardess looks after them and they never seem to mind.'

The discussion continued long after Lynn, accompanied by Briony, had been taken in an ambulance to the Cottage Hospital. Marion had reluctantly offered to go with Lynn but the child had continually asked for Briony and in the end Marion had confessed to a horror of hospitals and antiseptic smells, which she 'guessed Lynn knew about', so it was Briony who went.

It was past eleven when finally Briony returned home ... alone in a taxi. She was very tired but her news was good. She had waited at the hospital until the operation had taken place and been reported completely successful. Lynn was still under the anaesthetic when she left and Briony would go again first thing in the morning.

What Briony did not tell the four people facing her was Lynn's whispered words as they prepared her for the operation, of the smile on the child's face as she said:

'I can't go to New York now, can I, Briony?'

She had been perfectly content.

'What a mercy that's over and done with!' Marion broke the silence. 'Thanks a lot, Briony, for going. I guess you all think I'm a pretty bad mother but I just can't stand the smell in hospitals. It's a psychosis of mine, I suppose. I'll have to get a psycho-analyst find out the reason for me one of these days. Well, at least we can go tomorrow with a clear conscience. Binny's okay.'

'Do tell Briony what we've fixed up!' Vanessa said in her brittle voice. 'Come on, Charles, you surprise her.'

Briony looked at the row of faces and lastly at Charles. He grinned at her.

'Marion felt she was so much in your debt, Briony, for what you've done for Lynn, that she suggested this as a kind of – well, repayment. I'm agreeable and I'm sure you will be. We were only saying the other day that you needed a holiday.'

'But what ... exactly what are you talking

about?' Briony asked, some queer inner sense warning her that what was to come would be, if not a shock, then a surprise at least.

'Well, my dear, we're off to America. I'm paying our passage out by boat and we take young Lynn with us. Then we stay a couple of months in New York as Marion's and Gerald's guests. Pretty good idea, what? Always wanted to see America. Well, old girl, what say?'

There was only one thought in Briony's mind – one thought that could not be spoken aloud. So she remained silent while in her heart that voice cried:

"I shall be near Robert ... nearer Robert. I might, even see Robert again!"

Lynn was back once more in her 'own' bedroom, convalescing. Ten days had passed since her operation, which had been highly successful, and the doctor had said she might get up next day.

Briony sat by her bedside, her hands still holding the book she had been reading to the child, although many minutes had passed since Lynn had dropped asleep.

Briony was wondering whether she should give Lynn an inkling of the news in her father's latest letter. Perhaps not, she decided, for many things could yet go wrong. But Lance Wendover's letter had been jubilant and every line gave confidence in the success of his attempts to get full custody of his little daughter.

…My solicitor tells me that I have every chance now that Marion has actually left Lynn in your care. How ungrateful and ungracious that sounds, knowing as I do how wonderfully kind you are to Lynn and how fond of her, too. Still, you will know what I mean. It would seem to any jury or judge a very unnatural and unfeeling mother to leave a child the instant after such an operation, and on top of parking her on you for two months.

Of course, I am fully aware that the latter arrangement was made at Lynn's request and your own and it may not be altogether playing the game to stress this fact of Marion's disinterest in Lynn. All the same, if necessary I shall do so since it is ultimately for Lynn's good. It seems pretty certain, however, from all you have told me of Marion's behaviour and state of mind, that it is unlikely she will contest the issue and it need never therefore be fought in court. I have, of course, made it quite clear in my letter to her that I shall fight every inch of the way if she opposes me. If she is prepared to be reasonable then I will give her a written guarantee, should my word not suffice, that Lynn may visit her whenever the child wishes and as often as they both desire it.

Once again I am hopelessly in your debt … for

the two cables you so kindly sent me regarding Lynn's condition. Had you reported anything but a perfect recovery I would have flown over immediately. Now, however, it seems scarcely necessary nor practical since you will so soon be on your way over the Atlantic.

Dare I hope that during your visit to the States you and your husband would pay us a visit? I would so welcome the opportunity of thanking you in person and to show you a little of California. Perhaps it could be arranged that you bring Lynn home? I leave this question entirely in your hands as you may have other plans or wish to remain with Marion and Vanessa in New York.

By the way, I met a friend of yours the other day, a very decent young fellow by the name of Baker. He dropped in to see me and I was more than glad to have first-hand news of Lynn and I'm afraid I must have bored him with my questions. I naturally enquired about you and he confirmed my own opinion of you by saying you were the most charming, kind and sympathetic person he had ever met. I have arranged to take him up to the mountains next week-end. Since he is a friend of yours, then he is also a friend of mine, and I have told him to consider my home his also while he is over here.

I am writing under separate cover to Lynn as I know how much a letter of one's own means to a child of her age! Please be good enough to buy her anything she might need to amuse her or

*benefit her health and I will mail a cheque to
await you in New York to the value of fifty
dollars.*

*My renewed thanks and I terminate this letter
with every hope that I shall be able to thank you
in person before very long.*

Yours most sincerely,
Lance Wendover.

The news of Robert, however brief, tore at
her heart. Robert's compliments to herself
touched her deeply, for she could understand how difficult it must have been for him
not to betray his real feelings and yet say nice
things about her! It was good to know that
Robert had a friend ... someone to take him
out of himself ... help him to forget.

But the possibility of her taking Lynn to
California, with or without Charles, was a
hopeless one. After that first instinctive joy
at the thought of being nearer Robert, perhaps even seeing him again, she had come
to her senses. What avail that Robert should
take a job in America in order to put the
Atlantic between them if she were to meet
him out there and reopen the old longings?
They had agreed they could not live at close
quarters and hide their love. Neither could
bear the strain of proximity. And since they
had agreed to part, then she must keep her
side of the bargain.

Desperately she had sought for arguments

against the trip to America. But Marion, Vanessa ... even Gerald had laughed her tentative refusals aside.

'Of course you'll come, honey! Why, in New York we can give you as good a time as you can get anywhere in the world. We'd feed you up, too.'

'You could do with a few man-size steaks, Briony. You're thinner than Vanessa!'

And from Charles she had a puzzled frown.

'But what have you got against going, Briony, eh? You agreed you'd like a holiday. Well, what's wrong with America?'

'Nothing, nothing!' Briony said weakly. 'But surely it will mean you being away from the office for longer than you intended, Charles?'

Charles laughed.

'Well, old girl, they can spare me. You've no need to worry your little head about that! As a matter of fact I can look into one or two of our export markets and kill two birds with one stone.'

What excuse could she give? There had been no valid reason why she shouldn't jump at the opportunity.

Later that night, Charles had come into her bedroom and questioned her rather oddly.

'Look here, Briony, what's behind all this? I mean, don't you *like* my friends?'

231

Briony had looked at him, standing awkwardly at the end of her bed, his face a little red and angry. She considered his remark and said:

'Well, that isn't the real reason, Charles. Anyway, I do quite like Marion and Gerald – or at least I don't dislike them. I can't pretend to be fond of them. You know how I feel about Marion's behaviour to Lynn.'

Charles looked even more annoyed.

'And what have you got against Vanessa? She's always charming to you and you're nothing but rude to her.'

Briony checked her surprise. Was Charles trying to pick a quarrel? This conversation was so unusual that she was momentarily taken aback.

'Rude to her? When?' she asked. 'I've always tried to conceal from her the fact that I didn't like her. After all, she is my guest, however I may personally feel about her.'

'That's just it!' Charles said, striking the bed with his fist. 'She told me you didn't like her and I didn't believe it. You obviously haven't concealed your feelings very well.'

'I'm sorry, Charles!' Briony said wearily. 'I don't think Vanessa likes me, you know. It's a mutual antipathy. In her way, she's shown me her dislike just as she seems to have guessed mine.'

'That's nonsense!' Charles broke in

rudely. 'Vanessa likes you very much. 'She's told me so. I think you're being very unfair to her ... catty.'

Briony was still too surprised to be angry. It was so unlike Charles to have a post mortem on their friends or anything else. He was usually the most casual onlooker and seldom seemed to be aware of Briony's reaction to the guests of the moment or of theirs to her.

'I'm sorry if she knows it,' she said at last. 'But surely it is hardly important, Charles? They leave tomorrow morning and she and I will no doubt never meet again. You can't *make* yourself like people, you know.'

'Since we are going to New York as Gerald's guests, we shall undoubtedly be seeing Vanessa again. She lives with them, you know. I must ask you to try to be more polite, Briony. However much you may not like her – and I can't see why, myself – then at least remember your manners.'

Briony felt her irritation rising.

'Surely if you can't trust me to behave ... and since I feel this way about Vanessa, it would be best if we chose to go elsewhere for our holiday?'

'Certainly not!' Charles retorted with asperity. 'It was damn decent of Gerald and Marion to invite us and I'm not going to hurt their feelings by refusing. Besides, I'd like to go to America.'

Briony bit her lip.

'Then why don't you go alone, Charles? I'll be quite all right here by myself.'

Charles's face suffused an angry red.

'Look here, Briony, let's get this straight once and for all. Are you or are you not my wife? If you are – and I can't help feeling sometimes that you forget the fact – then you have a certain duty to me. I've never failed in my duty to you, have I?'

She shook her head, knowing herself beaten. What Charles had unwittingly said was all too true. She had 'forgotten' she was Charles's wife ... had never loved him or given him what other wives gave their husbands. She had denied him much and he had never denied her anything.

'Then, dash it all, Briony, why can't you come along and be *gay*? You're always so confoundedly gloomy these days. Oh, you laugh from time to time, no doubt for my benefit. But I'm not a blind man, you know. I've seen you go off into those day-dreams of yours and anyone would think you were imagining a funeral! You creep around the house like a ghost! What's the matter with you, old girl?'

How could she tell him? Part of her longed to confess ... to tell him everything, to beg his understanding and the chance to begin again ... to do better in future. But how could she? It would be relieving her own heart at the expense of his. She remained silent, her eyes on the hands folded in front of her like those of a child who is being reprimanded.

'I know you haven't been too fit lately,' Charles's voice droned on. 'That's why I jumped at this suggestion of Vanessa's to take a good long holiday abroad. It's just what you need to pick you up. Then you go and trump up a lot of excuses to stay at home! It's plain silly!'

'Yes! I'm sorry, Charles. Maybe it will do me good. I shall enjoy a sea trip at all events ... and ... well, I should enjoy seeing New York. Perhaps because I haven't been too well, the thought of a long journey rather scared me–' She broke off, hating herself for the lie. How willingly, how joyfully she would have undertaken the journey if she had been free to go to Robert! She hated herself and yet how could she be different when there was no control to be found over one's heart?

Charles unbent a little.

'Well, I'm glad you see sense at last. And do try to be more decent to Vanessa. I'd like you to be friends, you know.'

'I'll try,' Briony said, wondering why Charles wished such a friendship. Obviously Vanessa had been playing up to Charles, twisting him round her finger as any moderately clever woman could do, since

Charles was still so immature, so much a schoolboy at heart.

Perhaps she had underestimated Charles's sensitivity? Maybe he had been depressed by her own low spirits without knowing just why. Vanessa, brittle, gay, sophisticated, no doubt made him feel on top of the world again.

After Charles had left her with a perfunctory kiss on the cheek, she lay awake wondering why Vanessa bothered. Perhaps her woman's vanity made her the same with every man... Vanessa was obviously used to having men admire her and run after her. No doubt it was second nature to her to try to attract every man she came in contact with! At any rate, she hadn't been entirely unsuccessful with the unimpressionable Charles, from all accounts. He liked her ... enough to quarrel about her.

Thinking back on the evening as she sat by Lynn's bedside, Briony felt a sudden twinge of awareness which had not struck her hitherto. Could Vanessa be trying to attract Charles *for a purpose?* Could she be in love with him? She rejected the last idea. Surely Charles, decent, kind, nice though he was, was far too ordinary and unsophisticated for the mature Vanessa! Was she merely trying to cause trouble between herself and Charles for the fun of it? To see Briony jealous, hurt, worried? No, Vanessa couldn't be bothered to waste her time unless it was for some ulterior motive; of that Briony was convinced. Then what motive?

'I'm imagining things!' Briony told herself sharply. After all, she had no facts to substantiate her instinctive feeling. Nor could she find any motive.

She looked down at Lynn and as she did so the child stirred and opened her eyes. She smiled sleepily.

'Oh, Briony, did I go to sleep in the middle of the story! How awful of me!'

'It's the best thing in the world for you, darling!' Briony said instantly, forgetting her own feelings. 'Just what you need to make you strong and well again.'

'I had such a funny dream ... about Robert!' Lynn said, stretching her arms and yawning. 'I dreamt you and Daddy and Robert and I were all living on an island ... just like in the story you were reading, Briony. It was such a lovely dream. We were all terribly happy and we didn't mind whether a ship came for us or not – to rescue us, I mean. I suppose if it hadn't been a dream and we were there we would have wanted to get away. What do you think, Briony?'

"I'd have been willing to stay there for eternity!" Briony thought; but aloud she said:

'Well, I don't know. Suppose you had your

appendicitis trouble on the island! There'd be no kind doctor to send you to hospital or clever surgeons to operate and make you well again.'

Lynn laughed.

'Well, couldn't Robert have operated on me? He said he often had to operate on dogs and cats, and sometimes horses, too. You could have been the nurse and Daddy the doctor.'

"If we could but live our dreams!" Briony thought. "If dreaming could become reality and reality but a dream!"

'Briony, how many days before we go? I'm *so* glad you're coming, too. It'll all be such fun with you. Will you and I share a cabin or will you be with Uncle Charles?'

"I daresay we could arrange to be together!" Briony thought with sudden relief in the suggestion. The thought of the intimacy of life in a small cabin shared with Charles left her trembling She must try somehow to calm her feelings. Sooner or later Charles would expect her to behave like any other wife and she would have no argument to put forward that would spare his feelings. Yet the longer it was postponed, the more she dreaded the thought. Soon there would not be Lynn's protective presence. Then...

'Briony, do you think Daddy and Robert have met yet? Robert said in that letter that he was going to call on Daddy.'

Briony hastily fetched Lance Wendover's letter and read the paragraph concerning Robert to her. The child did not question her on the rest of the letter. She understood even at her age that it was nice to keep certain bits to yourself, though she seldom concealed anything from Briony.

'It's only the thought that I shall so soon be home with Daddy that makes me happy again,' Lynn said quietly.

'But you are not unhappy, darling?'

'Only because it'll soon be time to say good-bye to you, Briony. It's nearly always nearly time to say good-bye to someone I love.'

Briony longed to tell her then that the good-byes were nearly ended ... that soon she would be with her beloved father for always... Lucky, lucky little Lynn, for whom there would be a happy ending, however much she had suffered in the past!

XIII

Robert sat smoking his pipe, staring with unseeing eyes at the glorious panorama that lay before him. Lance Wendover had brought him up here on the Sierra Nevada ranges, from where there were some incredibly beautiful and striking views of the whole State of California. It had been a long drive and for the most part they had been silent except when Lance had pointed out some place or feature of interest.

Now, having eaten from an enormous picnic hamper and drunk a quantity of quite agreeable American canned beer, they had stretched themselves out on their backs and started talking.

Somehow the conversation had become personal. Robert was not quite certain how it had happened. He looked over at the man beside him, ten years his senior and yet, in the casual American clothes, looking more like Robert's idea of a college kid! Yet Wendover was not young in his manner. He, too, had suffered, and hard. Telling Robert of his early years with Marion, it had been easy to see how desperately he had been hurt and disillusioned.

Naturally enough, the talk turned to Robert and, the next minute, Robert found himself confiding in Lance the hopelessness of his love for Briony.

'I can't think what made me tell you all that!' he said at last. 'I've not talked to another living soul about her. Perhaps I just needed to get it off my chest!'

The older man smiled.

'I guess this will surprise you ... but I

kinda jumped to a conclusion about you and this girl. Maybe because of the way you looked when you first told me about her that afternoon we met, remember? It isn't as easy to keep the way you feel out of your eyes as it is out the conversation, if you know what I mean.'

'Oh, blast!' Robert said with a very English intonation. 'I had hoped I had myself under control. Apparently I've failed.'

'Well, I wouldn't say that. You see, I've been through plenty myself, so I recognize it in others. You chose your words to describe this Briony very carefully, you know ... too carefully. You'd have been more complimentary – or, rather, more effusive – about a girl who didn't mean anything to you.'

'But we aren't, as a race, very effusive!' Robert argued.

'Taking that into account, you hesitated too long and picked your adjectives. What was it you said? "Charming, kind, sympathetic". Now I think if you had asked me what I thought she was like just from her letters, I'd have said: "surely the kindest woman I've ever met ... beautiful to look at ... very sweet and I'm very fond of her indeed!" Doesn't that sound more natural?'

Robert laughed in spite of himself.

'Well, maybe you're right. It doesn't much matter since you know now anyway. She is the most wonderful girl in the world ...

241

literally. I know there will never be anyone else. She set too high a standard.'

Lance considered the remark. From another man he might have argued the subject, pointing out that those words had often been spoken before and sooner or later the fellow did find another girl and fall in love again. But this young Englishman ... he was somehow different. There was a strange quality in him that made Lance believe those words. Robert would be consistent in his love – just as he would be in his work. It seemed a crying shame that the girl he loved should be married.

'In the States, we don't take such a serious view of divorce,' he said at last. 'I guess in England it means more. You're more old-fashioned than we are. I'm not saying it should or shouldn't be so. Is it quite out of the question?'

'I think I would willingly be divorced if it lay in my hands!' Robert said thoughtfully. 'But that isn't really the issue. It really means that Briony would be divorcing her husband. I do in a way agree with her that it's easier to be the "wronged" that the "wronging" party. No one can be glad to hurt someone who has never done them any harm. This husband of hers ... well, he's in love with her and he's kind to her and all that. And, of course, he doesn't know about "us".'

'But surely he must have guessed ... if his wife isn't in love with him any longer?' Lance asked curiously.

'No! Briony never did love him. She married him on the rebound from a wartime affair. The chap died. She thought that was the end and as her husband was pressing her to marry him, she finally agreed. Then *we* met. It couldn't have been avoided ... what happened. We were really meant for each other. We fought against it until it was hopeless. When we talked about it there seemed nothing else we could do but say good-bye. Briony will never tell Charles. He isn't the type of person to look below the surface so he won't probe too deeply. She'll convince him if she intends to do so and I know she does. If she were different, it might be easier for her to ask him for her freedom. But she's too kind, too decent to make him suffer.'

'So you two suffer instead? Seems kinda crazy to me! Still, if that's the way she wants it, I suppose you've no right to step in. I guess I did the wrong thing, Robert. I wrote asking her to visit me – perhaps bring Lynn out next month. You heard they were coming to America, I suppose?'

Robert sat up and stared down at Lance. His heart was beating furiously and his hand clenched the stem of his pipe.

'No, no I hadn't heard! I haven't had a letter for weeks ... only one in answer to mine. How do you know? Are you sure?'

'Poor devil!' Lance said, grinning. 'You've got it bad! I'd have broken it more gently if I'd thought you didn't know. It was arranged pretty much on the spur of the moment, when Lynn got ill. Marion didn't care to cancel her plans for the child and it seems they arranged that your Briony and her husband would take a vacation and bring Lynn to New York when she was better. They'll be there as Marion's guests for a couple of months.'

'In New York!' Robert echoed. Then his heart and his hopes fell. What use in counting the miles to New York? What use in dreaming and planning when they had already parted ways? When he had himself taken this job in the States to be far away from her?

With his whole heart he longed to take the next train to the great capital and be there to greet Briony when she arrived. But even as he saw her in his imagination walking down the gang-plank towards him, he knew how crazy he was to have such dreams. He must not see her. If she did come here to bring Lynn to her father, then he himself would have to go away.

'I'm sorry, Robert,' Lance said gently. 'It's a helluva life, ain't it? Still, I think if I were you I wouldn't give up all hope.'

He – Robert – had said those same words to Briony, and yet what hope was there? It seemed such a remote chance that Charles might ever ask Briony for a divorce. How could he want to be rid of a girl like Briony? How could he ever find a woman more beautiful, more desirable, as a wife?

'Will you ever marry again?' he asked Lance abruptly.

The older man shrugged his shoulders.

'I might ... if I can find the right gal. But it will have to be the right person for Lynn, too. She means more to me than anything in the world. I guess I'd like other kids, too, maybe. I'm a great believer in large families. Still, it isn't every girl wants kids and I'm not too well off financially, so I haven't much to offer in the way of luxuries.'

Robert grimaced.

'You can say that! Why, your house is perfect. I imagine your kitchen is any woman's dream. Certainly any English woman's. You should go to England and find an English girl. She'd be satisfied easily enough with all those labour-saving devices and so much sun!'

'Maybe I will, at that !' Lance said. Then changing the subject: 'Do you ever do any mountain-climbing, Robert? It's a hobby of mine when I can find the time. I go up Mount Witney. It's well over 14,000 feet, you know, and one of the highest mountains in America. Not that I go up that far! I'm more or less an amateur at the game. Still, it's fun. Ever tried it?'

Robert shook his head. Although he had always loved mountains and had been for several holidays to Switzerland and France and Austria, it had always been to ski.

'You'll get plenty of ski-ing in the winter!' Lance told him. 'Most of the kids here ski before they walk, practically.'

Robert nodded.

'Maybe I'll find time. I keep pretty busy at the lab., you know. Thank the lord the work is interesting enough. It keeps my mind off myself. Look here, Lance, I don't want to stand in the way of anything that might be best for Lynn. And Briony should see California. When you next write, tell her I'll be away for a couple of months – anywhere you can think of. I shan't, of course, but I don't think she'll come if she knows I'm nearby. I have a feeling she'd be happier here than in New York. The sophisticated life, as well as the tempo at which you Americans live in the great city, will tire her out. A week or two here would do her good. Will you do that for me?'

'Sure I will!' Lance agreed willingly enough. 'Seems a shame, though. However, that's your affair. Well, we'd better be starting home. Now we will say farewell to the beautiful Sierra Nevada ranges and wend our way–'

Robert's laughter broke the 'travelogue'

246

quotation and the two men, better friends now that they knew a little of each other, began to retrace their steps to the road where they had left the car.

Charles had been morose and unusually edgy until at last the time came for them to board the *Normandie*. Briony, tactfully trying to find out the cause, found herself echoing his irritability and feelings were strained. On board, however, Charles took a new lease of life ... or rather good spirits. He joined Lynn in even the most childish deck games and at night, when the child was in bed, insisted that Briony should dress up and join in the various amusements, bridge, whist drives, dances. With an effort he little guessed, Briony tried to be gay and hide her own unhappiness and the acute fatigue that she had felt so often of late. The sea air during the day had her tired out by Lynn's bedtime and she would dearly love to have joined Lynn in the cabin they shared. Lynn, herself, was gay enough. Fully recovered from her operation and both rested and fattened by her convalescence, she was eagerly looking forward to 'showing Briony America'. She talked continually about the letter she had had from 'Daddy' asking Briony to visit him and bring Lynn back with her. Briony found it hard to make excuses and knew that there were none any more than there was a valid reason why she should not go, since Lance Wendover had clearly stated in his letter to Lynn that Robert was going away for two months. He had not stated any reason, whether it was work or pleasure, but she had been unable to prevent herself wondering if Robert had known of Lance's invitation and arranged to be away for both their sakes.

In the end she capitulated.

'Provided Marion ... Mummy agrees!' she said at last. 'And, of course, we'll have to see what Uncle Charles says, too. He may not want to come.'

Charles, when broached, looked uncomfortable.

'Dash it all, Briony, how can we just walk out on Marion and Gerald and push off for a couple of weeks to her ex-husband? It's out of the question.'

'But, Charles, someone presumably has to take Lynn back to California. I think Lynn told me once that either Marion or Vanessa went with her. So if we don't go, they will have to. I don't think you need worry about Marion's feelings regarding her ex-husband. They are quite friendly. She'll probably be grateful to us for relieving her of a job she doesn't particularly enjoy.'

'Haven't you done enough for that child?' Charles asked with a return of his edginess. 'You're always fussing over her. Anyone would think she was your own brat!'

Briony bit her lip.

'I wish she were, Charles. Still, there's no reason why you should go if you don't wish. I thought you might be glad to see more of America than just New York. I'd like to go. I'm told California is beautiful.'

'You're a queer woman, Briony. Not long ago you didn't want to come to America at all. Now you want to see the whole forty-nine States!'

Briony softened. After all, it must be difficult for Charles to understand her changes of mood when he didn't know the cause. She felt a sudden deep pity for him ... a kind of remorse for her own selfishness.

'I won't go if you'd rather I didn't!' she said on the impulse. 'I'm quite happy to stay with you, Charles!'

He looked at her for a minute or two and then turned away from her.

'Nonsense! If you want to go, then do so. But I prefer to stay in New York with my friends.'

She looked at him anxiously.

'But, Charles, I don't want to go unless you come too: or at least unless I'm quite sure that you don't mind my going!'

'Mind?' Charles asked quietly. 'No, I don't mind. Now don't let's argue about it, old girl, what?'

She could not fathom what lay behind his words ... if anything. It seemed as if she no longer understood him. Only one possible cause for his unusual behaviour occurred to her ... that he might know of Robert's friendship with Lance and somehow or other be suspicious of her own feelings towards Robert. Could Vanessa have guessed and put those suspicions in his mind?

She said casually:

'By the way, Charles, you remember the young vet who looked after my puppy? Robert Baker.'

Charles looked up quickly:

'Yes! Why?'

'Well, he lives quite near Lynn's home. I don't think we shall see him though. Lynn told me her father had written to say Ro – Mr. Baker was going to be away for a couple of months.'

'Vanessa thought that fellow was in love with you!' Charles said suddenly, so unexpectedly that Briony almost jumped. 'Any truth in it?'

She could not lie directly. She said:

'Yes! I think he was, Charles. I think that was why he left the district.'

'Sensible thing to do!' Charles said approvingly. 'No good chasing another man's wife, what? Still, can't exactly blame him. Did the same myself, didn't I?'

She looked at him puzzled.

'You fell in love with me, Charles, but I wasn't married!'

'Huh!' It was an indescribable exclamation but it had an undertone of sarcasm. 'No, not actually married. Still, you were in love with the R.A.F. chap, weren't you? Always have been, eh?'

She was aghast that Charles should have brought up this subject for the first time in their married life ... and now, of all times. It seemed suddenly as if he, who had always been so easily understandable and predictable to her, had suddenly become a stranger; a frightening stranger. Had he, after all, been far more sensitive and aware of her innermost thoughts and feelings than she had ever imagined him to be? Had she underrated his own ability to feel things? Was their marriage, from his point of view and in spite of his protests to the contrary, really a failure *for them both?*

It opened an entirely new line to Briony and one which caused her not a little uneasiness. Believing Charles's emotional demands to be all but non-existent, she had made no effort to share of herself; no effort to give him the intimate companionship that she had never for a moment thought he required of her.

What was Charles really like ... underneath that very familiar exterior? Was he, as she had been, wearing a shell to hide his real inner self? She found it hard to credit, even now. Only one possible explanation occurred to her that might have caused her to misjudge him and one which his peculiar remark about her always having been in love with Bob would confirm – namely that because he had known when he married her she *was* still in love with Bob's memory, he had for her sake made few demands on her; had believed, perhaps, that in time she would forget and begin to care deeply about him.

"How terribly selfish I have been if this is the case!" Briony thought in an agony of remorse. "How unfair to Charles! I always believed I was giving him everything he required of me. But never, never have I given him love ... the closeness of love. I've never even tried to pretend I cared deeply. He knew I was fond of him ... knew that in an odd, grateful kind of way I did love him. But not as a woman *can* love a man, with every thought, nerve, action!"

It could never have been so! she told herself, admitting the truth. However much Charles might have shown her he needed her love, she could never have given him *herself*. But she might have given him more tenderness, more understanding, more thought.

'Bob has been nothing but a memory to me for a long while now,' she told him gently.

Charles gave her another searching glance.

'I wouldn't have guessed that, old girl, unless you had told me. I believed you still cared. Well, I won't ask you if, when you stopped loving him, you began to love the man you had married. I think I'd rather not know your reply. Don't think I'm blaming you, old girl. I daresay no one is to blame.'

Briony, white and strained, put out her hand to Charles in a gesture which was almost an appeal.

'Charles, do you regret our marriage? I asked you that not long ago and you said that you did not ... in any way. Have you changed your mind?'

Charles did not meet her eyes.

'No, of course not, old girl. Still, I sometimes think that *you* might have been happier if I hadn't married you. We – we haven't a great deal in common, have we? Makes things harder. Our friends, for instance. But we haven't made a bad try, have we? No one could say our marriage had been a failure!'

'No, no!' Briony cried. There was something so odd about Charles's behaviour, his very expression of thoughts which he had never brought into the open before. It was as if she were seeing before her a very lonely and unhappy person whom she longed to console. 'You've done so very much for me, Charles, and – I have been happy. I thought you were, too.'

'Quite true!' Charles replied, his hand reaching for the door. 'Still, I do realize that there's more in marriage than just being content. Now what about a drink before we dine, old girl? Could do with a quick one myself.'

She knew that he wished to discontinue the conversation, and forbore to question him further. Nevertheless, she longed, now that for the time they had spoken a little of what lay in their hearts, to try to get a little closer to him ... to understand him ... to get below the surface of this new Charles she did not know.

Slowly, thoughtfully, she began to change into an evening dress; within half an hour she went down to the first-class passengers' saloon to find the old bluff, hearty Charles, and knew that the momentary flash of insight he had afforded her was not to be repeated. Anxious and confused, she forced herself to play her part as his gay young wife, and all the time she wondered if he were playing a part too.

XIV

As the train neared California, Lynn's excitement grew to bursting point. Briony made every effort to distract the child's attention by insisting that Lynn point out landmarks. But even while the child obediently did so, Briony knew her mind was really on the coming meeting with her father.

Only a week had passed since they had docked in New York and been swept away by Marion and Gerald and Vanessa to the smart 'apartment' where luxuries seemed commonplace and the ordinary extra-ordinary! Marion had a full programme awaiting them – luncheons, cocktails, dinners with each of their friends, who had all demanded to meet the English couple. American hospitality at its best and yet so completely exhausting that within forty-eight hours Briony felt herself a nervous wreck. Squeezed into spare half-hours, they were taken to see the famous buildings and places of interest and Briony was further forced on a long and tiring 'shopping tour'. Even while she was grateful to Charles's friends for planning this 'amusing holiday' for them, she knew that she could not stand the strain for long; knew, too, that it was completely foreign to her nature. Essentially she was a 'country girl' who loved the quiet serenity of life in the country. She had outgrown the need of hot music, exotic night-clubs, dancing till the early hours. It seemed to her that Marion and their friends were all behaving like young girls just out of school. They were unable to enjoy a quiet evening at home. Even in the apartment, the radio or television blared incessantly.

No wonder, she thought, that Lynn was fast losing the shipboard tan she had acquired and had begun to look tired and drawn again.

'No wonder,' she added wryly, 'that Marion finds it difficult having Lynn to stay for six months.' There was always the problem of what was to be done with the child, who would 'baby mind' at night when they were out. Lynn, it seemed, was placed entirely in the care of the maid and only saw her mother for brief moments in the day.

A long letter from Lance Wendover put an end to the situation. In it he told his former wife that he thought it better that Lynn should make her home with him all the year round ... that she should occasionally visit her mother for the odd week in the holidays when it was convenient to Marion; that he would be entirely responsible for her upkeep, education, upbringing. He had tried to reconcile himself to living without Lynn when the divorce broke up their home, but after long and careful thought and in four years of experience he felt that the solution they had arranged at the time as to how Lynn should be 'shared' was utterly wrong for the child and unsatisfactory for them both. Would Marion agree to letting the child return to him? If so, they could arrange things quietly between their solicitors and no trouble would ensue.

Marion took the letter to Briony and remained silent while it was being read. When Briony looked up, trying to conceal the flicker of conscience that told her she was partly responsible for this, Marion said:

'You know, honey, this letter is almost a relief. I think maybe Lance is right and it would be best for Binny to go back to him. I really lead such a busy social life these days – I haven't the time to give the child. I suppose Lance could take the matter to court if he chose and there'd be a lot of nasty publicity if I fought him. But then, no doubt, the same result would ensue, or alternatively I would be given full custody of Binny and that wouldn't suit me either! What do you, think, Briony? You can tell me the truth. After all, you must know Binny pretty well now. I do want to do what's best for her.'

It only needed Briony's confirmation of Lance's letter to settle the point in Marion's mind. Deep in her heart she knew that she wasn't being fair to the child; deep in her heart she knew that 'Binny' would have a better and more settled life with the father who adored her. Within half an hour she had become so reconciled to the thought of her freedom from material commitments that she was suggesting to Briony they might skip the last of the six months in New

York and send Lynn home immediately.

'The only problem is who will take her?' Marion sighed. 'Last time Van went with her and it's really my job, but I can't leave New York now.'

'Let me go, Marion,' Briony said eagerly. 'I want to see California, and Lynn's father wrote asking me to visit him when he heard I had been caring for Lynn. I would enjoy the trip and it would save you going.'

Marion was delighted with the suggestion. A telegram was despatched to Lance that evening and bookings made for the following Saturday morning. And now, even before Lynn could really believe the full import of all that had happened in forty-eight hours, they were within a few miles of what to her meant 'home'.

Charles had stuck to his point and refused to accompany them. He did weaken sufficiently to say that if Briony was nervous travelling so many miles alone on a strange continent he would do so, but she said she did not mind in the least, which was true enough.

'Van is taking me to the theatre tonight,' he told her a trifle sheepishly, almost guiltily, as he saw them off at the station. 'Wish you were going to be with us.'

'Nonsense, Charles!' she had teased him. 'Two's company, you know!'

But Charles had given her no answering

smile and had fidgeted uncomfortably with the luggage as if there were something he still wished to say to her.

Lynn, however, made private conversation between them rather difficult. For a long time after they had steamed out of the station Briony had pondered the question of Charles's behaviour. He had been gay enough since they had arrived in New York, fitting in with all the arrangements, and, as far as Briony could judge with her new uncertainty of him, enjoying every moment as much as the others were doing. Only when he turned and met Briony's gaze did his cheerful grin fade and his forehead crease in a slight frown.

"Maybe he's glad to be rid of me!" she told herself wryly. "Perhaps I spoil his fun because I can't enjoy myself as much as he can with the superficialities. Vanessa can always make him laugh. I have never done so."

But as the miles took them further and further from New York and Charles, and nearer and nearer to California, Robert and Lance, Lynn's spirits began to sore and Briony felt her own heart lifting. It would have been impossible anyway, not to be infected by Lynn's obvious radiance.

Her good spirits faded, however, when they arrived at the station nearest Lynn's home town and there was no sign of Lance waiting for them on the platform.

'He must have guessed which train we'd be on!' Lynn said. 'What did Mummy say in her telegram, Briony?'

'Darling, it doesn't matter!' Briony had said consolingly. 'Daddy will be waiting at home, I'm sure. Look, is that someone you know? He seems to recognize you?'

'Oh, it's Forbes, Daddy's houseman!' Lynn cried, all her good spirits restored. 'I expect Daddy sent him to meet us. Hi! Forbes. It's us.'

'We received your telegram, Miss Lynn,' the man said, smiling. 'But your Dad had gone off for the week-end climbing, or else he'd have been here himself to meet you, I know. He didn't say just where he was going or I'd have contacted him. It's a shame ... but we expect him back later tonight,' he added, seeing Lynn's face crumple with disappointment.

'Oh, well, only a few more hours to wait!' Briony said, being as practical as she could. 'That'll mean a chance for you to show me round, Lynn darling, before Daddy gets home.'

Lynn brightened again as they climbed into the waiting cab.

'I want you to see the skating rink,' she said. 'And we'll go get ourselves a soda in my favourite drug store. And, Briony, you will come and see my school, won't you? It's a swell place. Miles nicer than my New York school!' She hugged her long, thin, legs. 'Oh, I'm so glad I can stay here all the year round. I'm certain sure it's your doing, Briony, even if you won't say as much! You know, I love you very next best in the world to Daddy, Briony! Even he doesn't understand what I'm thinking and feeling just as well as you do!'

Briony was to remember those words and to thank God for them some hours later when the first ghastly inkling of tragedy marred the expectant happiness and the radiance of the sunny Californian day.

She and Lynn were returning from the town for tea when Briony saw the man Forbes come across the gravel driveway towards them. His face was chalk-white and he glanced continually from her to the child.

'Could I have a word with you, Mrs. Stone?'

'Run in, darling, and get yourself tidied up for tea!' Briony said. 'I'll be in in a moment.'

The man looked grateful, and as soon as Lynn was out of earshot he said:

'I don't know how to break the news. It sure has come as a terrible shock to me, Mrs. Stone.'

'I can see that,' Briony said, trying to still the fear in her own heart. 'Tell me, has something happened to Mr. Wendover?'

'An accident, madam. A terrible accident ... and at such a time. Little Miss Lynn, what will she do? How are we going to tell her?'

'He's not ... dead?' Briony asked, aghast.

The man shook his head.

'No – no ... but they don't expect him to live more than a few hours. He fell while out climbing early this morning and was brought down on a stretcher and rushed to hospital. They couldn't even operate ... it would have been no use. They give him twenty-four hours to live at the most. He – he's asked to see *you*, Mrs. Stone! Of course, the hospital didn't know who you were or where to contact you, so they telephoned me. Fortunately you had arrived here so I had no trouble identifying you and telling them you were close at hand. I said I'd call them back as soon as you came in. What shall we do, madam?'

Briony forced herself to keep control of her jangling nerves. What a terrible, terrible thing this was to have happened at such a time ... just when all was coming right for Lance and his daughter at last! Just when Lynn had, unknown to him, arrived home for good! How could she tell the child? How could Fate allow a little child like Lynn to suffer such a ghastly loss at such a time! It was unbearable to think about. She must at all costs keep this from Lynn for a little while longer.

'I'll telephone the hospital now,' she said, surprised at the coolness of her voice, seeing a look of relief on the face of the man, who had not known how to cope with the situation. 'I'd better go to a call-box or Miss Lynn might overhear. Tell her I've gone back to buy something I need which I had forgotten to pack. Give her tea. I won't be long.'

Forbes nodded and gave Briony instructions to find the nearest call-box and the number of the hospital. Then he went back to the house and Briony ran quickly down the street.

The doctor to whom she spoke eventually at the Nevada General Hospital was concise and calming, even while his words confirmed her worst fears.

'There's no hope at all, Mrs. Stone,' he answered her question. 'It's a matter of hours only. I've been with Mr. Wendover this last half-hour and he's worrying about his daughter. He wants to talk with you about her. Can you get out here?'

'I don't know how far it is!' Briony said. 'I've only just arrived today from New York. Could you give me instructions?'

Three hours – in a fast, hired car. She must hurry. Meanwhile, what was to be done with Lynn?

'I don't think the child should accompany you,' the doctor said immediately, without

263

hesitation. 'She's bound to be pretty upset and that will naturally upset Mr. Wendover. It might be easier for her, too, if, as he tells me, they haven't seen each other for five months. That can be quite a time in a child's life. Come alone, and come quickly!'

What could she do with Lynn? Forbes was in no state to hide his agitation and, in any case, what excuse could Briony give Lynn that would explain her absence for the next six, eight, ten hours?

She glanced down at the directory and suddenly an idea occurred to her. If she could contact Robert ... the only person she knew in the locality, maybe he would find a solution. He would advise her what to do with Lynn. If only he were there! But he had told Lance Wendover he would be away for two months. Was it true? "Oh, pray God he's there!" Briony thought desperately.

Within a very short time an efficient operator had given her the telephone number of the Professor's house. A minute or two later a woman with an Irish-American voice told her that Mr. Baker would be at the laboratory right now and if she cared to call him up there the number was... So he hadn't gone away after all!

Feverishly Briony struggled with dimes and nickels, and at last was put through to the laboratory.

No, she was told. Mr. Baker was not on

vacation. She would fetch him right away!

It seemed hours to Briony as she waited with beating heart before at last she heard Robert's voice ... that calm, deep, hesitant voice she loved better than any in the world.

'Yes? Robert Baker speaking? Who is it, please?'

She caught her breath.

'Robert, it's me, Briony! Oh, my dear, I'm in such a muddle. I need your help, Robert. Have I surprised you? Didn't they tell you it was me calling you?'

'No! No, they just said a lady wanted me on the phone. I didn't know who it would be. Briony! I can hardly believe it is you. But you're in trouble. What's happened? What can I do?'

She was very nearly crying when at last she had told him as briefly as she could what had transpired. The news had been a shock in itself and added to the tension of hearing Robert's voice and the need above all for haste, she felt her nerves jangling.

'You're not to worry about Lynn,' Robert said after a moment's silence. 'I'll take care of her. Don't go home, Briony, unless you have to ... I mean, back to the house. I'll drive straight there in my car now and have some suitable explanation for Lynn. I'll stay with her till you get back. Meanwhile, telephone Wickers ... they're a reliable taxi-hire firm. I've used them often before I got my car. Tell them you're a friend of mine and that it's a matter of life and death. They'll take you to the hospital and wait till ... till you want to come back. My dear ... I wish I could come with you!'

'So do I,' Briony whispered. 'But I can't leave Lynn alone. I'd better ring off, Robert. I'll see you – later. Thank you ... for being such a help. Don't let Lynn guess the truth – not yet!'

'I won't,' Robert promised. A moment later she was alone again. It was as if a strong comforting arm had been withdrawn from her shoulder.

On the long drive to the hospital Briony was left no chance to dwell on her thoughts, not the least important of which was the fact that Robert hadn't gone away after all. Somehow in her heart she had *known* he would be there and her own feeling of being closer to him as the train drew into the station of the little Californian town had not misled her. Knowing that she would not – dare not – come if he were there, Robert had told Lance he would be away in the hope that this information would reach Briony. To them both just the thought of proximity was as exciting as it was dangerous, as longed for as it must be avoided.

Now Fate had taken matters out of their hands. Knowing no one else in the vicinity whom she could trust or confide in, she had

had no alternative but to try to contact him, for Lynn's sake. Poor darling Lynn. This would be a mortal blow to her. Briony did not dare to think what the child's reactions might be ... nor dare to look ahead to the future. All she could see for Lynn was a life with Marion that must inevitably mean unhappiness and perhaps lead to a complete change in the child's personality and character.

But no sooner than these thoughts had sped through her head in a matter of seconds than the young cab-driver had opened a friendly conversation. He plied Briony with questions about England ... about the British way of life, politics, the rationing system, the police force and so on until the distance grew behind them and they began to approach the more hilly environment of the Sierra Nevada ranges.

'You're the second Britisher I ever met!' he was saying to her. 'Your pal, Mr. Baker, was the first ... swell guy! I kinda fancy your countrymen, I guess. I hoped to get to England one time but the doggone war ended before I was old enough to quit high school.'

For a moment Briony did not reply. When she did it was to ask how much further they had to go.

'Sixty miles, I guess,' she was told. 'Say, you told me it was a matter of life and death... Sure hope it isn't so bad when you get there!'

Briony reacted to the friendliness and kindness of the driver and within a moment or two she had told him the little she knew about Lance Wendover's accident and the serious consequences.

'Say! That's bad!' he exclaimed, his face screwed up in a frown. 'I know Mr. Wendover quite well – swell guy ... gee, I sure feel sorry for his kid. There was a divorce some time ago, wasn't there? I guess little Lynn will go back to her Momma!'

Briony was silent, but her heart cried out against the very thought of Lynn's spending the rest of her life with Marion. In giving way to Lance's demand to have full custody of Lynn, Marion had shown how little she cared about the child, how little time she had for her. It had shown up so clearly ever since Briony had first laid eyes on them when they had arrived ... how many months ago it seemed now! ... at their country house; and most of all when Lynn had her operation.

"I can't let her go!" she thought violently. "I'll look after her myself. Charles and I will give her a home and I'll give her all the love that Marion can never be bothered to feel and which her poor father will no longer be able to supply. Poor man! How worried he must be about leaving his little daughter!"

An hour later Briony was taken by a white-coated doctor to the cool, shaded room where Lynn's father lay. Looking down at the heavily bandaged face and hands, Briony felt the uselessness of words. It was too late to make the conventional remark that she 'hoped he would soon be better'. The doctor had already informed her that she had come none too soon. He had also said that Lance Wendover was in some pain but had refused more than the mildest drugs because he wished to retain his full faculties for talking to Mrs. Stone when she came.

'Mr. Wendover, here is Mrs. Stone to see you!'

The man opened his eyes and Briony saw with a tiny shock that they were the exact replica of Lynn's eyes. They searched her face slowly, and seeming to approve of what they saw, they crinkled into a smile which once again brought Lynn into the room with them.

'I knew you'd come,' he said in a whisper. 'Doctor, I'd like to talk alone with Mrs. Stone. She can ring the bell if I need you.'

The doctor hesitated and, seeing him pause, Lance said with an attempted grin:

'We all know I've only got a little while. Let me have these last hours as I wish!'

The doctor looked at Briony, who nodded reassuringly. She would ring at the slightest change in Lance's condition.

When they were alone she sat down by his bedside and said:

'It's about Lynn you want to talk, Mr. Wendover?'

He nodded his head, grateful for her understanding.

'You know that she's now at your home? We sent you a wire but Forbes didn't have a forwarding address to say we were arriving this morning. Marion finally gave in, you know. Lynn was to come home for good.'

Again he nodded his head.

'I guessed as much when they told me you were coming. I knew they hadn't had time to contact you in New York, and Forbes told the doctor you were out for a walk with Lynn. It – it's a cruel trick of Fate, isn't it, dragging me off just when I'd won the battle!'

Briony bit her lip. It was ironical and tragic. There was nothing she could say to comfort him except:

'Mr. Wendover, you haven't lost the battle entirely. Marion agreed to part with Lynn. That much is in Lynn's favour, for I don't honestly believe she can ever be a happy, normal little girl in her mother's care.'

'Then what is to happen to her when – when I go?'

Briony leaned forward, her face alight with eagerness.

'I'll give her a home ... she loves me

already, and I love her just as if she were my own child. It would be the most wonderful thing for me and I'd spend my life trying to make her happy.'

Lance Wendover relaxed so that the tension went out of his face.

'If you knew how I had prayed that you would say those words. In my heart I knew you would suggest it, but I hardly dared to hope. I had only the picture of you that I had imagined from your letters – and Lynn's. I knew she loved you dearly from the way she wrote about you. Then when I first saw you just now I felt that my picture of you was complete ... that your living face confirmed my thoughts of you. There's only one thing, Mrs. Stone. What about your husband? Would he be willing? Of course, I shall make my will leaving everything to Lynn on trust, and there would be no question of you having to support Lynn. There should be enough with my life insurance to see her through the next ten years and more. But does he care for her, too? You so seldom mentioned him ... nor Lynn. She only spoke of – of Robert Baker.'

He was watching her closely now for he knew that Robert loved her and that she had turned him down to stay with her husband from a sense of duty. Her private life was her own affair but this time it involved Lynn, too. No child was happy in a broken home.

If only he could die knowing that Briony was going to divorce her husband and marry young Robert Baker! Then he would be utterly confident that happiness would lie in that home and love encircle his own dearly loved daughter.

'You – you've met Robert?' Briony said stupidly. 'Yes, I know you have. You wrote and told me. Mr. Wendover, how much do you know? I feel I must be entirely honest with you at – at such a time. You know that I'm in love with Robert?'

The older man nodded.

'And that he loves you. I know too that you have resolved never to see each other again because of your husband.'

It was Briony's turn to nod her head. She tried hesitantly to explain to this man why she could not leave Charles.

'You can trust him, Mr. Wendover! He would never undertake a job and throw his hand in half way. If – if he agrees that we can adopt Lynn, then he will do his best to be a good father to her. I can swear that much.'

'You say ... if? Then it is not certain that he will want her?'

Briony could not bear to leave this dying man in any doubt and yet even for his sake she could not lie to him. Until now, she had not thought what Charles's reactions might be to making a permanent home for Lynn. He had been agreeable enough about having her to stay for a long period and yet on the boat coming over he had shown ... was it jealousy of Lynn? Called her 'a brat' and implied Briony was more interested in Lynn than in himself.

What would Charles think of the idea? Would he leave it to her as he might well do? Or would he turn stubborn and difficult and refuse to allow it? His co-operation would be vital if they were to adopt Lynn legally. They would both be required in court to state their desire to have the child. And Marion's agreement would have to be sought again, too.

Suppose Charles did refuse? What would she do?

Suddenly she knew. If Charles should refuse something of such importance to her, then it would mean that in reality their marriage was a farce. True understanding of a loved one meant to share to a certain extent their most ardent feelings. Briony loved Lynn dearly and Charles surely could love her, too – if not for the child's sake, then for hers. He could have no reason for denying her what she wished. He had refused her a child of her own in the early years of her marriage for reasons that were his own. She had not argued with him about it. If he wanted children in the future she would not deny them to him. But if he could not give her a sound reason why they should not give a home to the little girl she so much wanted to adopt, then she knew that their marriage was well and truly finished. If, however, he showed understanding and love, she would grow close to him again; otherwise they must inevitably drift apart in an ever-growing gap of misunderstanding.

'If he doesn't want Lynn, then I'll leave him!' she told Lance Wendover. 'Then I'll marry Robert when I'm free. I know he would want Lynn. He loves her as I do.'

Lance Wendover forbore to say what lay in his mind now ... that he hoped with all the failing strength in his heart that her husband would object to Lynn. He could not voice those thoughts any more than he had the right to interfere between a man and his wife even for his little daughter's sake.

'I'd like to see my solicitor now,' he said, his voice growing weaker. 'I believe he's waiting to see me. I had to speak to you first and I'd be glad if you'd stay a while longer. I'm going to make my will ... and I must write to Marion, too. You'll stay?'

'Of course!'

The next half hour was almost as much an agony for Briony as for the man whom she could see was dying slowly while he struggled for the last remnants of strength to safeguard his daughter's future. His will left everything in trust for Lynn until she came of age. He nominated Mrs. Briony Stone as guardian in his place and clearly stated that it was his dying wish that Lynn should make her home with Briony, who had stated her willingness to have the child. If his former wife tried to take Lynn back, then he had instructed his solicitor to take the matter to court, where, with evidence he had himself compiled at an earlier date and which documents lay in his solicitor's keeping, they were to fight Marion through every court, and a certain sum of money had to be set aside for this purpose. He stated further that it was his wish, and Mrs. Stone's desire, that she adopt his daughter legally as her own.

This done he signed and two doctors signed as witnesses that he was in his right mind and fully capable of understanding what he had written; further, that he was under no duress by Mrs. Stone or any other party at the time.

Then he dictated a last letter to Marion explaining what was in his will and asking her to grant him this last request being what he truly believed to be best both for their daughter and for her.

He began a last paragraph but to the waiting solicitor, to Briony and the two doctors in the room, it was obvious that he could never finish what he wished to say. His voice grew weaker and became indistinct and his head fell back against the pillows.

'A few minutes more,' one of the doctors said, feeling his pulse. 'He's worn himself out, poor fellow.'

But Lance Wendover made one last effort, opening his eyes and searching the faces for Briony.

'My ... dearest ... love ... to Lynn,' he whispered. Two minutes later he died.

XV

It was dark when Briony reached home – Lynn's home – to find Robert waiting on the doorstep at the sound of the taxi's approach. He took her arm and, nodding to the driver as he gave him a handsome tip, drew her inside the house to the softly lit lounge.

'Lynn has been asleep a couple of hours and Forbes has gone off duty,' he told her. 'There's a tray here with sandwiches and a thermos of coffee. Sit down, darling. You look exhausted.'

The unconscious endearment roused her from the numbed apathy that had all but drugged her since she had seen Lynn's father for the first and last time. Except to tell the cab driver that Mr. Wendover had died a few minutes earlier, Briony had not spoken for the last three hours and was grateful for the silence and unspoken sympathy of the young American. Now, alone with Robert, hearing his beloved voice, feeling his quiet understanding and love, she felt the tension leaving her and the tears of fatigue and worry well into her eyes.

'It – it was awful!' she whispered. Then his arms were round her and she was crying on his shoulder – knowing the blessed relief of those tears and the sharing of the burden that lay on her shoulders.

When she was calm again, Robert made her eat a little and drink some of the hot coffee before he allowed her to tell him what had happened. He listened in silence while she recounted all that had passed. When at last he spoke, it was with such loving gentleness that Briony felt she could bear anything if she only had Robert beside her to help.

'I'm terribly sorry about Lance. I only met him three times but we got to know one another pretty well. And I liked him a lot. I'm glad you were able to put his mind at rest – about Lynn. I told her you'd had some very bad news and wanted to be alone. Of course, she asked me where you'd gone and what the bad news was, and why couldn't you have told her yourself, along with a dozen other quite natural questions. I countered the lot by telling her that she must try to be very grown-up and not ask questions just yet. She accepted that once I had reassured her you would be coming back later in the evening but she nearly broke my nerve when she suggested that maybe you and her father would arrive home about the same time.

'She talked of him incessantly! Of course, she was quite pleased and excited to see me and I tried to divert her attention by talking a lot about Tom and the walks we had in England and so on. We went out to tea and I thought of a "movie" but didn't know what time you would be back, so we came home and played cards instead. Finally I could see she was pretty tired so I put her to bed, and read to her till she dropped off. At least tomorrow she will be well rested and better able physically to stand the shock this will be to her.'

'You'll be here when I tell her?' Briony asked him.

'Whenever you need me, you know that,' Robert said quietly, searching for and holding her hand.

Briony drew in her breath. This wonder of seeing Robert again, of having him near, hearing his voice, was almost too wonderful to believe, and yet the tragedy that surrounded them made anything but quiet expressions of their love impossible. This

278

was no time to think or talk of themselves. Yet they, too, were involved because of Briony's words to Lance Wendover.

It was Robert who drew attention to that part of her story.

'Perhaps I shouldn't be the one to say this,' he told her gently. 'But I think you let yourself be carried away by the moment, darling. I don't think you should have committed yourself so completely.'

Briony stared at him aghast.

'But, Robert, why? You mean, saying I would have Lynn ... at all costs?'

'Briony, *dearest*, can't you see how difficult it is for me to say this to you? If you make Lynn a condition of your continuing your marriage to Charles, I must be the gainer if your husband does not want you to have her. That being so, it's very difficult for me to talk impartially. You see, I'd give anything in the world to think there was even a remote chance that you might soon be free to marry *me*. But I must be impartial because I think at all costs you will want to be fair to Lance Wendover, to Lynn *and to your husband*. Not least of all to him, either. Your first consideration should be for him.'

'But Robert, if he loves me at all, he couldn't refuse ... why, what would happen to Lynn?'

'She'd probably go back to her mother,' Robert said softly. 'And I have a feeling,

Briony, that that is where your husband, and most men no doubt unless they were psychologists or doctors or something, would agree with him. Marion has never been cruel to Lynn – not actively – nor, I presume, can anyone prove she's neglected her – in a criminal sense, anyway. I rather doubt, from the little I know of your husband, that he really understands children very well. What is more, he likes Marion, doesn't he? I don't think, if I judge him right, that he is going to look at this from the same point of view as you do.'

'But Robert, there can't be any question as to whether or not I have Lynn. I must have her. I'm certain I can help her to get over this shock and, in time, settle down happily with me. If I'm not there ... and I'm the only person in the world she loves ... now that Lance is dead ... what is she not going to suffer?'

'Will your husband see that? And Briony, suppose he really has no fondness for the child ... suppose he really feels that it would be having a third and unwelcome stranger in his household, can you force him to take her? It isn't every man who would be agreeable to adopting a seven-year-old girl who bore no relation to himself at all.'

Briony stared at Robert wide-eyed.

'You mean you'd hesitate, if you were in Charles's shoes?'

'No!' Robert said firmly. 'But I love Lynn ... and I'd know that you and I could be happy however many children we adopted and however many diversions we had. But you see, the position is not the same for your husband. At least, I cannot believe that it is. I cannot believe that he is so short-sighted that he truly believes you love him and that your marriage is a perfectly happy one in every respect. He must doubt – and there lies the snag.'

Briony was silent. It was true that Charles was not after all as complacent as she had imagined. He had made no demur about having Lynn staying but he had known that it was only for a short period ... not a permanent arrangement. *Would he refuse to 'adopt' her?* If so, was she willing to break her promise, rightly or wrongly made, to Lance Wendover? Betray Lynn's trust in her by leaving her to a mother who neither understood nor cared for her? Was she to give up everything for the man she had married without loving in order to remedy her own conscience about his happiness? Had she not given up enough when she gave up Robert for his sake?

Briony stared at Robert from stricken eyes. She had felt grief at Lance Wendover's going for Lynn's sake, but the depth of the tragedy so far as the child was involved had not been plumbed since she had been convinced in her own heart that Lynn would, in time, learn to forget or, if not entirely to forget, to remember happily the father she had loved so dearly and lost. *Lynn would be happy* with her, of that she was certain. And she had never until now doubted that this would be the ultimate solution. Robert had made her face the situation unemotionally and what he had said she knew now to be true ... she could not force Charles to take on another man's child unless he were willing, and it was more than likely that he would not be willing. Moreover, it would not be fair to threaten him with divorce if he did not comply with her wishes. It was really an emotional blackmail she had contemplated. 'Either we have Lynn or I go!' That was wrong, as she could see now. Yet, surely, *surely* Charles must understand that she could not abandon Lynn? Most of all at a time like this in the child's life?

She said as much to Robert.

'I'm sure he would not refuse you having Lynn to stay for a while until other arrangements were made for her!' was Robert's reply. 'But Briony, why torture yourself with these unanswerable questions? I don't see how you can prejudge your husband's reactions. Don't worry yourself until the worst happens.'

'Then I must find out *now!*' Briony cried,

colour flaring into her cheeks as she rose impulsively to her feet. 'In any case I must telephone Marion and give her the news. I *must* know how Charles will react before I can tackle Lynn tomorrow. If I can only tell her that she is to live with me now that her father is dead!'

'Do you know the number?' Robert asked practically, realizing that Briony would be unable to sleep that night if this question of Lynn's future were still unresolved.

Within five minutes Briony was speaking to Marion. She made no attempt to speak to Vanessa first in order that she could break the news more gently to Lance's ex-wife. After all, Marion cared little, if anything, for Lance.

In fact, as was natural, the news did come as a shock. But Marion was more incredulous than upset.

'It can't have happened – it just can't!' she reiterated.

'I'm afraid it's true!' Briony told her. 'I went to the hospital myself, Marion, as Lance wished to talk to me about Lynn's future.'

'Binny! Oh, lord! The child will be suicidal!' Marion cried over the wire. 'I just don't know what to say, Briony. I can still scarcely credit it!'

'I told Lance I would like to adopt Lynn – have her to live with me always!' Briony plunged right into it. After all, there was no point in avoiding issues that would have to be faced sooner or later. 'He was very anxious that Lynn should lead a settled life and he knows you enjoy travel and haven't the same opportunity as I have to give Lynn a quiet home life.' Urgency lent her tact. 'He wrote to you about it himself, Marion.'

'This is too ghastly!' Marion said, a trifle hysterically. 'Poor Lance. As to Binny ... well, as you know, I'd quite resigned myself to parting with her since she was so keen to live with her father. All the same, I can't expect you to take on my duties, Briony. That wouldn't be fair.'

So Lynn was only a 'duty' to her mother.

'It's what I would most like for myself!' Briony said carefully. 'As you know, we have no children of our own and I'm devoted to Lynn. I would have missed her terribly when we said "good-bye". Please let me have her, Marion. I'd do everything in the world to make up to her for this tragedy in her young life. And I think she'd like to live with me.' It was the nearest she dared come to suggesting that Lynn would not want to live with Marion.

There was a moment of silence and then Marion said:

'Well, we'll have to discuss this more carefully, I suppose, but as far as I'm concerned, I'm willing to let Binny do as she wishes. If she wants to live with you, then that's okay by me. I don't stand in her way ... not after that. I feel ... well, kinda guilty ... I mean, these last six months she might have been with Lance.'

'You couldn't have known what would happen, Marion. All the same, I truly believe that I can understand her sufficiently well now to help her through what is bound to be a very tricky time. She'll be very unhappy and possibly rather difficult. It would be a strain for you with Gerald to consider as well.'

'And what about Charles?' Marion asked curiously. 'Won't he object?'

Briony bit her lip and was glad Marion could not see her expression.

'I sincerely hope Charles will feel as I do. I'd like very much to speak to him now. Could you ask him to come to the 'phone, Marion?'

'Gee, I'm sorry. He's gone out somewhere or other with Vanessa. To a theatre, I think. They'll be back before long, I imagine. Shall I ask him to call you back?'

'Yes – yes, please!' Briony said slowly. 'No matter how late it is, I'd like to speak to him tonight. You see, I'll have to tell Lynn in the morning. She doesn't know yet.'

'I guess it's really my duty to do that,' Marion said reluctantly. 'I'd better come over and help fix things up.'

'I ... I can manage ... unless you want to come,' Briony said quickly.

'You remember Mr. Baker ... well, he's living near here and he has promised to see to ... to most things for me ... for Lance. He ... he stated that he wanted a very quiet funeral with the minimum of people there ... for Lynn's sake, I think. So unless you feel personally that you'd like to be there, then I don't honestly believe it's necessary.'

'Well, if you're sure,' Marion said, glad of the excuse Briony had afforded her. 'Funerals are so frightfully depressing, and if Lance didn't want a fuss ... well, I'm not one to deny him his last wishes... As to Binny, well, I daresay you'll be far better with her than I could be. I just don't understand my own child. I'm very grateful to you, Briony, and it seems too bad you should have walked into all this trouble on your vacation...'

A moment or two later Briony had replaced the receiver and turned back to Robert.

'Charles is out at a theatre with Vanessa,' she told him. 'I've got to wait till he gets back before I can ask him. Oh, Robert!'

His arms opened to receive her. Then, and only then, did she realize the full impact of being with Robert again ... feeling his arms round her just as surely as she felt the comfort of his love encompassing her mind.

The magnitude of her own love for him came near to overwhelming her. Soon, too soon no doubt, there would be another heart-breaking parting to be faced. But not yet. Not yet! For this short interlude in life which Fate had afforded them, in spite of their own intentions to the contrary, they were together again. Let them draw what comfort they could from each other's presence.

'It's just as if I had been reprieved from a living death!' Briony whispered. 'Oh, Robert, dearest, if you knew how my secret heart has longed for this!'

He drew her gently down beside him on the settee and kissed her yet again ... without passion but with tenderness and all the pent-up longing that lay in his heart.

'I guess we make a pretty handsome couple!' Vanessa said, laughing, as she pressed a little closer against the man in whose arms she was dancing.

The lights were as in many other night-clubs, carefully dimmed. A small negro band played its soft, stirring rhythm to inflame more than their dancing feet.

Charles drew Vanessa even closer in a sudden unbridled desire for the slender woman whom even he had realized was being as seductive as she could be. Ever since he had first set eyes on her, he had known and fought against, this gripping desire of his body for hers. How many times had he reminded himself in the past that he was a married man – that he loved Briony, that she was sweet and good and everything a man wanted for a wife! Yes, he had told himself these things but he had known in his heart that Briony had not, after all, been quite everything to him. Until he had come up against Vanessa's casual, controlled, but fiery appeal, he had not known what it could mean to long, day and night, to possess a body for its own suggestive beauty.

He was not such a fool that he had not known Vanessa was his for the taking. No man could have been blind to the invitation of her eyes, her every gesture, when they were alone together. He had known, too, that she was aware of the feelings she aroused in him. But until this moment he had never by word or deed admitted her power over him. After all, he had told himself bitterly, once he weakened in his resolve to be faithful to the wife he respected ... and loved, there would be no going back.

He wondered whether Briony had suspected there was something between himself and Vanessa these past months. Nothing, of course, that she could complain of. But surely she must have wondered why he had kept to his dressing-room, where, during her bout of 'flu, he had been relegated? Surely she had wondered why he had not even visited her for an occasional night since she had recovered?

The truth ... and he could face it now ... was that since he had lain awake at night craving for the feel of Vanessa in his arms, he had lost all trace of physical love for his wife! He had been shocked by his feelings as greatly as he had been afraid of them. Most of all, he was afraid of the power Vanessa had over him. Many was the time when they were in Europe that he had considered flying out to Paris, Venice, Copenhagen ... throwing caution to the winds and taking Vanessa off somewhere where they could be alone together!

But he had not done so. The rigid standards of behaviour that he laid down for others he could not lightly throw over himself. A man just was not unfaithful to his wife if he wished to retain his self-respect. Certainly he did not deceive her behind her back, slipping off abroad pretending he was on business, and coming back to her as if nothing at all had happened. No, that was not his way! He reminded himself of the fact again as his whole being trembled at the feel of Vanessa's body pressed against his while they danced slowly and languorously round the tiny floor.

'Well, Charles?'

He stared down at the slightly smiling face

turned to him and felt a moment's swift anger. No woman had any right to tempt a man as this woman was tempting him.

'You're a witch, Vanessa!' he said huskily. 'You should be burned at the stake!'

She laughed into his eyes.

'But, my dear, you would be the one to suffer if you did that.'

'Meaning?'

'Meaning that you will not find peace that way! You want me, Charles, just as I want you. Until you've had what you want, you will have no rest!'

'Damn you!' Charles said softly. It was acknowledgment of the truth of her words.

'But why?' Vanessa said calmly. 'Why not take what you want, my dear?'

Charles met her look, his own face flushed.

'You know why, Vanessa. I'm married. It wouldn't be fair to Briony.'

'Oh, stuff!' Vanessa said calmly. 'At this moment, she's probably lying in young Robert's arms. Or if she isn't, she's wishing she were. She's no more in love with you than you are with her.'

'That's not true!' Charles argued. 'I do love her. She's my wife!'

'Oh yes, you're married to her. But alas, dear boy, marriage does not automatically guarantee love, does it? You thought you loved her when you married her ... maybe you did. But not now... No, not now. You love me now, Charles. Why not admit it?'

'Damn you, Vanessa!' the man said again, his voice hoarse and shaken. 'I need you ... you know that!'

'We need each other,' Vanessa said in that same calm voice. 'It's funny really ... that I should need you, too. I dare say most people would wonder why. You're no glamour boy. But you have something else, Charles. You have a deep-down, well-concealed passion that could answer my own. We both knew that the first time we looked at one another, didn't we?'

'Yes, yes!' he all but groaned. 'But we're different in this much, Vanessa. If I took you away for a night, a week ... it wouldn't be enough. I'd want you more than ever. If I let go the reins, I'm lost.'

'Then let's get lost together!' Vanessa said, her eyes smiling. There was something feline about her expression. She knew her power, knew herself and she knew the man she had to deal with. She wanted him ... and she would have him and his terms would end up the same as hers ... marriage. She knew quite well that there might be other men who could equally well satisfy her physical needs ... but they hadn't Charles's money ... his position. She was in her thirties now and not so many years ahead of her lay 'middle age' with its accompanying loss of looks ... power. Marriage now ... with Charles ...

would give her security, comfort and all the powers she needed, for she would always be able to twist Charles round her little finger. Saturated though he may be with tradition and prejudice, she knew only too well that a clever woman could be greater even than these provided she never gave quite everything of herself to the man who was in love with her.

'And ... Briony?' she heard his voice.

'My dear old thing, you know in your heart that she doesn't love you. You might as well face facts. I'm pretty well ready to swear that she's in love with that young vet. Why, you've discovered yourself that he's in love with her and ran away to California because of it. Now do you honestly believe that if – and I repeat, *if* – Briony cared not a fig for him and told him so, there would have been any need to run away?'

The answer to that question was so enlightening that when it sank into Charles's mind he felt as if he had been stunned with a sudden revelation. He paused in his dancing and it was Vanessa who half dragged him across the floor back to their table.

'Then you think *she* loves *him?*' he asked almost stupidly.

'Don't you? Why, they are as ideally matched as you and I!'

Vanessa's voice was still flippant but it had a note of sincerity. Had it suited her books, she would not have hesitated to do her best to take Charles from Briony even if Briony had been in love with him. 'Charity begins at home' was her motto for living. However, in this case, she did not for a moment believe Briony cared. Never once had Briony shown the least jealousy of Vanessa. Many was the hour Vanessa had spent alone with Charles or as a foursome with Marion and Gerald, and Briony simply hadn't noticed ... or cared. A woman in love would have suspected even where there was no need for suspicion, shown jealousy. No, Briony did not love her Charles ... so there was no reason why she, Vanessa, should not have him except that Charles was not the kind of person to take to divorce too easily. That was one of the prejudices she would overcome. But she never doubted she could. Not once she had had the chance to show Charles just what marriage with her could mean.

'Let's go get ourselves some coffee at my place!' she said to Charles. 'It's too noisy here for discussions of this kind.'

'Your place? You mean Marion's flat ... apartment?'

Vanessa laughed.

'No, honey, I don't mean Marion's apartment! My place is my own very private hide-out. Only my very nearest and dearest friends know of it. It's a tiny pent-house, flatlet you'd call it, way up on the top floor of a block not very far from here. I keep it going because I like occasionally to have a break from Marion and Gerald. It gives me complete independence when I want it. You can see most of New York from the window and that's quite a sight at night. We might even watch the dawn break!'

She was laughing at him and yet none knew better than the man beside her what she intended him to understand by that remark. If he went with her now, then they would certainly not be watching the first light steal across the sky.

'Still worried? Don't you trust me, Charles?'

'I don't trust myself!' he cried, fighting his weakening resolve.

'Then I'll do the trusting for us both,' Vanessa said easily. 'Come, Charles, or else the sun will be up before we even get there and that *would* be a shame.'

She stood up slowly, gracefully, the skin-tight silver lamé dress with its high collar and deeply slit bodice revealing every beautiful and desirable line of her body. She laid her hand lightly on his shoulder and he felt the touch of her finger-tip against his cheek. Slowly, he turned his head and looked into her eyes, and from that moment knew himself lost.

XVI

Briony had barely been awake a few moments when Lynn came running into her bedroom in her little pink dressing-gown and moccasins and flung herself onto the eiderdown beside her. Briony had waited up until four in the morning in the hope that Charles might still telephone her. If it had not been for Robert's company, she would soon have become a complete nervous wreck by that prolonged and useless wait. It was he who had at last said, sensibly enough:

'You really should get some rest, darling. I'd better stay the night, I think. There's a spare room leading off this room. If I sleep there, I'm bound to hear the telephone and I can easily wake you. You look utterly exhausted, poor sweet.'

'But *why* hasn't he telephoned?' Briony asked desperately. 'He can't still be out at this time of the night!'

'In New York, night life can go on until breakfast-time,' Robert told her grimly. 'Anyway, maybe he can't get a line. The long-distance calls are often ages coming through. You *must* get some sleep, Briony.'

She had known he was right. She was so tired she could not even argue when Robert went to fetch her a hot-water bottle and make a last cup of tea, which he brought her in bed.

'I suppose I ought not to be in here!' he said with a glance round her bedroom. 'However, I'm acting in a purely medical capacity for the moment.'

She had smiled at him from large, violet-shadowed eyes.

'Oh, Robert, nice as you would be as a doctor, I'd rather have you as just you!'

He had come to her then, pulled her roughly into his arms and showering the white, strained face with fierce, protective kisses. More than anything in the world, he wanted to spare her pain and anxiety and worry. Yet he could do none of these things. Only by showing her how deeply he cared could he lend her a little strength. Or so she had told him. In fact he wondered if the knowledge of his love for and his need of her was not just one burden more for her to carry ... one further worry.

Such doubts had finally brought him to release her from his embrace and leave her alone ... to sleep. In his own room, he could not do likewise, for his whole body was aflame with longing for the girl upstairs and with faint hopes that he scarcely yet dared to admit that maybe in the end she might yet be his ... his wife to love and to cherish.

Briony had slept deeply ... too deeply, she now realized, as she opened her eyes and took in the little figure curled up on the bed beside her. She should have waked hours ago and tried to call Charles again. Now she must face Lynn's questions... and the ghastly fact that she must now tell her the truth about her father without yet knowing if she could offer the child her love and her home as a compensation.

'Briony? Forbes says Uncle Robert is asleep in Daddy's study. Is that true? Why did he stay the night? You never came and said "good night" to me when you got back. Briony, where did you rush off to yesterday? I just don't understand what it's all about!'

As the questions poured out of the trembling lips, Briony felt her own hands reach out for the child and draw her close.

'I'm glad you came to see me. There's lots of things I want to talk to you about,' she said gently. 'Things I want to ask you, too, before I answer *your* questions.'

'Yes, Briony?'

How could she bear to be the one to turn that small trusting little face into a mask of misery? How could she soften the unalterable facts? Silently, Briony prayed for help ... any help that would enable her to say the awful things she must say, but in the right way.

'Lynn, darling, do you remember once before we talked about how it felt loving people? How sometimes it could hurt?'

The fair head nodded, the blue eyes wide and searching Briony's own.

'Well, I want to ask you something else. Suppose you love someone very dearly ... me, for instance–'

'Oh, I do, I do!' Lynn interrupted impulsively, hugging Briony.

'Yes, darling! Well, suppose you knew that it was possible for me to stay here always ... be with you always, that would make you happy?'

'Briony, you know it would! It would be *heaven*–'

'Yes, but suppose I knew I would be happier somewhere else... a long way away perhaps, where I would never see you at all ... somewhere which I thought "heaven". Do you think that if I left the choice to you, you would love me enough to say to me, "You go where you will be happy, Briony. I want you to be happy before I want myself to be happy"?'

Lynn frowned.

'But why couldn't you be happy here with me, Briony? Don't *you* love *me*?'

'Darling, of course! I'm just taking you and me as an example. It might be anyone you love very much. I want to know if you understand that really loving someone can make you want them to be happy even although it may make you unhappy to say good-bye to them.'

The little face was serious, thoughtful, a little torn with indecision.

'Well, I do understand what you mean, Briony. But why can't people who love each other be together?'

'Because life ... God, whom you believe in, darling ... doesn't always want the same thing you do. But He is always right even although you may not understand that now. Maybe one day, years and years hence, you will suddenly say to yourself: "Oh, now I understand why God did this. Now I see what was His purpose!"'

'But Briony, what has God done? I mean, I guess I just don't understand what you are talking about. Is God going to take someone away that I – Briony!'

She broke off, her face suddenly tensed and drained of colour.

'Briony, Mommy isn't going to make me go back? She hasn't broken her promise to let me stay with Daddy for always?'

Briony bit her lip.

'No, Mummy hasn't broken her promise. But ... Lynn, try to be brave about it, darling ... I'm afraid it isn't going to be possible for you to live with Daddy now.'

'Not *now?* But why? When can we be together? What's happened?'

'You will be together one day ... many, many, many years hence. Then no one and nothing will be able to part you – ever. But now ... well, Daddy has had to go to a place very far away from you, darling. He didn't want to leave you but he had no choice. What you must remember as more import-ant than anything else is that the place he has gone to is the most wonderful of all places, Lynn. He'll never be lonely ... or unhappy ... or worried ... or ill. Everything will always be perfect for him now. If you love him, you must be glad for him that he has gone ... even although you are lonely without him.'

'Gone? Where has he gone, Briony? Why can't I go, too?'

'Because God didn't want you to go ... not yet, Lynn. He wants you to live and learn to be happy, my darling.'

The word 'live' had immediately brought its opposite into the little girl's mind and in that instant she knew the truth. Briony saw the eyes widen a little as if in disbelief and then with an agonized cry the words of denial poured out.

'It isn't true! He's coming back! He'll be here today! It isn't true, is it? You're just frightening me! I don't believe it! Daddy can't be–'

'Daddy has gone to Heaven,' Briony said as calmly as she could. 'He's happier than he has ever been before and you must try to be glad of that for him. Don't be sorry for yourself, Lynn, dearest. Be glad for him.'

The tears came then, the child's frantic sobs mingling with hysterical words that tried to refute the truth she was slowly beginning to accept. Holding the shivering little body in her arms, rocking her to and fro as if she held a baby, murmuring soothing words, Briony suffered the child's pain and fright and shock just as deeply as if it were her own. Lynn was closer, dearer to her than anyone in the world. She had felt all the greatest of maternal emotions for this little girl and she knew that although Lynn was not a child 'of her body' she was none the, less the child 'of her spirit'. If necessary she would give up anything and everything for Lynn's happiness. It didn't matter now if Charles refused to permit Lynn's adoption. If he refused, Briony would leave him and have Lynn herself. It didn't matter if Robert said it was 'wrong' ... that her first duty lay to Charles. In her own heart she felt that her one and only duty now was to Lynn. She would give up Robert, too, if divorce from Charles would jeopardize her chances of getting a court order to adopt Lynn.

For the first time in her life Briony knew the meaning of complete selflessness. She would deny herself anything in the world to ensure Lynn's happiness.

The child was suffering now from shock and was in no state to listen ... or even care ... if Briony were to talk of their future together. That could wait. Now she must get the little girl to bed and give her a sedative ... call the doctor.

But it was Robert who carried Lynn back to her room and tucked her into bed. Briony, watching him in surprise and tenderness, saw that it was he who first began to calm the child and who, while he talked to her softly, gently, of his friendship with her father, soothed the hair from the hot little forehead and dried the tears from the cheeks.

'You know, Lynn, your Daddy and I were great friends, even although we hadn't known each other very long. I admired him a lot. I think he was a wonderful person. He was brave, too. He showed me where he used to go mountain-climbing and I knew I'd have been afraid. But he wasn't. He was brave. He told me you were very brave, too. That when you were a little girl you had often fallen down and you never cried however much it hurt. I can see now that he was absolutely right about you. You are being brave. Of course, you're quite grown up now so that it makes it easier, doesn't it? I mean, when you're older you can think about things sensibly. You can say to yourself, "Oh, I've hurt myself much worse than that before now and the pain soon wears off, so I won't cry about it." Or you can say, "Being without someone I love very much is terribly hard to bear but I can bear it because I'm my father's daughter and he wants me to be happy and not to grieve. And time will make it better because awful things – no matter how awful – never seem quite so bad a little while after they have happened." Or you can say, "I'm feeling lonely now because I know I shan't see my Daddy again – but I'm not really all alone. I have Briony, who loves me very very much, and Uncle Robert, who'll look after me and be a real uncle to me whenever I want him and he'll take me out for treats just as he did yesterday. We'll go to—"'

'Robert, she's asleep!'

The man whom she had never loved so much as she loved him now, rose slowly and turned towards her.

'Poor kid,' he whispered. 'Poor little kid. Fancy having to grow up when you're only seven!'

'In some ways, Robert, she grew up years ago. Thank you, darling. You were sweet with her.'

Briefly their eyes met. Then Robert drew her outside the room and closed the door behind him.

'Maybe you'd better telephone New York again,' he said. 'I'll find Forbes and tell him we'd like coffee. When you've finished, I'll ring the doctor and he can see Lynn when she wakes. Things won't be easy for a while. Will you be able to – to stay?'

'I shall stay for as long as Lynn needs me!' Briony said firmly. 'In fact, I shall never leave her now, Robert.'

For a long moment he did not speak. Then he said quietly:

'No, I suppose not. I think I knew you'd say that all along. I just felt I had to point out to you that – that–'

'That I ought to put Charles first? Well, I did once, Robert, when I let you go. That was because it was a question of my duty against my happiness. But this time it is a question of my duty to Charles and my duty to a little girl who has no one in the world to love her but me.'

'I love her,' Robert said quietly.

'I know, I know,' Briony whispered, tears stinging her eyes. 'I just didn't dare say "us"!'

She left him and went to the telephone. She had just given the operator the number when the girl said:

'New York is on the line calling you. Will you take the call, please?'

A moment later, she heard Charles's voice.

'I say, Briony, that you? Marion's just told me the news. Pretty ghastly, what? Dashed sorry! Ruined your holiday, eh?'

Briony almost smiled in her turmoil of

emotions. As if she were even considering how this affected her *holiday!* It was ironic in a way.

'Did Marion tell you anything else?' she asked hesitantly. 'I mean, have you spoken to her about – about Lynn?'

There was a pause, then Charles said:

'As a matter of fact, I didn't get in till pretty late last night. Went to a party ... er ... Marion asleep when I got in. Rather late. She woke me up and told me Wendover had been killed in a mountaineering accident. Anything happened to the child, then?'

'No. I mean, naturally she's terribly shocked and unhappy. I saw Lance Wendover before he died. Charles, I offered to look after Lynn. I – I promised.'

'Well, of course, old girl. Naturally. Stay on as long as you think it's necessary. Funeral and all that.'

She fought a rising hysteria.

'But Charles, I don't mean just for a while, I mean, I said I'd give her a home now she hasn't got one. Marion agreed to part with her and you know she doesn't really care for children ... even Lynn. She said last night that she's quite willing for me ... for us to adopt Lynn if you agree.'

'Adopt Lynn? I say, old girl, you mustn't let your feelings run away with you and all that. Dashed sorry for the kid, naturally. Still, I don't see how we can *adopt* her ... not

305

just now, anyway.'

'Why not *"just now"*?' Briony asked. 'Surely now is the time to do it?'

There was another pause which continued so long that Briony asked:

'Charles, are you there? Have we been cut off?'

'No. I'm here, I mean. Look here, old girl, we can't very well discuss this over the telephone. Fact of the matter is, I think we should talk things over. Everything.'

'Well, of course we'll have to discuss it,' Briony said. 'All the same, I would be glad if you could let me have some idea how you're going to take this, Charles. I'd like to be able to tell Lynn not to worry about the future. She loves me and I think if I can promise her she can be with me always, she'll get over this more quickly. Please, Charles! Lance Wendover has left sufficient means to support her entirely. It won't really affect you or your life at all. And you know how happy it has made me having Lynn to stay.'

There was another pause while Charles fought with a tangle of emotions utterly foreign to him. First and foremost he was feeling wretchedly guilty about the previous night with Vanessa. Secondly, he was perfectly well aware when he left Vanessa in the early hours of the morning that he would return, however remorseful he might feel about Briony at that moment. He knew that, for once, his personal desires out-weighed the moral standards by which he had lived. *He could not give up Vanessa.* At the same time, hearing Briony's voice ... his wife's voice ... he felt an unutterable cad and knew himself incapable of a life of deception. Sooner or later, Briony must be told the truth. Then what?

'Charles! Are you there?'

'Yes, yes! Look here, Briony, I must see you. Can't you fly back to New York for a few hours? I must talk to you.'

'But, Charles, I can't leave Lynn *now!*'

'Oh, blast the child!' Charles said in desperation. 'I didn't mean that. Look here, Briony, surely we can leave the whole question of her future till things have calmed down a bit ... till we know where we are?'

'But I do know where I am!' Briony said, aware for the first time that there was something peculiar about Charles – his conversation, his tone of voice, which had nothing to do with the long-distance telephone. 'Can't you fly out here, Charles? As you say, a few hours would suffice to talk this over. It's very important to me – vitally so. Surely you can understand that?'

'But I can't–' He broke off, realizing how he had nearly betrayed himself by saying he could not leave Vanessa. Another rush of guilt assailed him, and feeling himself on the defence, he turned angrily to the attack.

307

'Look here, Briony, I won't be rushed into anything we might both regret. You can't force me to give you an answer. This whole business wants thinking over very carefully. We'll talk it over when you get back to New York.'

'I may not come back, Charles,' Briony said slowly, carefully. 'I cannot leave Lynn at a time like, this,' she appealed to him again for understanding. 'Surely you see that? The child is suffering from shock. She has no one but me.'

'All right, all right!' Charles said furiously. 'I'm not asking you to leave her, am I?'

'Charles, why can't you come here? It would be the best thing in many ways.'

'Surely there's someone to see to things for you?' Charles said, purposefully evasive. 'Wendover must have had some friends, neighbours, relatives? They'll see to the funeral and that kind of thing.'

'Mr. Baker is here and taking care of those details,' Briony said weakly. 'But he can't decide what is to be done with Lynn, Charles. That's up to you.'

'Baker? The vet? Then Vanessa was right!' The words slipped out before he could stop them.

'Vanessa right? About what, Charles?'

'That fellow's in love with you!' Charles said accusingly, again on the defensive. 'Shouldn't be surprised if he wasn't the reason you were so keen to go to California! Don't deny it!'

Briony felt ice-cold.

'I wasn't denying it, Charles, but I will do so now. I truly believed Robert was away. You have no possible reason to make such accusations.'

'Then you deny he's in love with you?'

'No, I don't deny that!' Briony said, feeling the tide whirl her off her feet, destroying her equilibrium. 'I already told you that was true. But there's no reason for you to doubt his integrity. He's helping me to cope with things here. If you'd come with me, I wouldn't have had to ask his help.'

Again, Charles's conscience pricked. It was true that Briony had asked him to go with her to California; true that he had refused and that his real reason for refusing was that he did not want to let Vanessa out of his sight!

'Then if he's being so helpful, what do you need me for?' he asked petulantly.

'Oh, Charles – to discuss Lynn's future – *our* future!' Briony said desperately. Why was Charles being so obtuse? So aggressive?

'Maybe you should discuss that with Mr. Baker, what?'

She felt her nerves jangling.

'Exactly what does that remark mean, Charles?'

'Do you deny you're in love with him?'

309

It was a direct question which took her unawares. Even as she framed an evasive reply, Briony sensed that it was Vanessa who had put the idea into Charles's head.

'Surely this isn't the time to discuss things of this nature?' she said. 'It's Lynn I'm thinking about now, Charles!'

'Well, I'm not! I'm thinking about us. Let's have an answer to my question, Briony. Are you in love with that fellow?'

She laughed, a high, bitter laugh.

'If you insist, Charles, the answer is yes! But I have no intention of doing anything about it and you have no single reason to be jealous or to worry about what I'm doing here with Robert. I am not the kind of person to deceive you behind your back.'

Unknowingly, the shaft went home. Charles's face flushed a dark red.

'So you *are* in love with him?' he said at last.

'Yes, yes, yes!' Briony all but shouted in her distraught state of mind. 'But it has nothing to do with the present situation, Charles. We already agreed to – to say good-bye to each other. Robert doesn't want to break up our marriage any more than I do. Please, Charles, take the next plane out here and let's talk this over calmly. It's impossible to continue the conversation on the phone.'

'I quite agree,' Charles said, his voice suddenly quiet, the voice she remembered.

'I'm sorry I – I failed to understand, old girl. You won't hold it against me?'

She felt suddenly near to tears. This was the Charles she had married ... of whom she was genuinely fond. If he could only see his way now to letting her keep Lynn ... everything could still come right between them. She'd never see Robert again ... never let herself think of him. She would devote her life to Charles and Lynn ... to making them one happy family.

'No, of course I won't, Charles. It'll be all right. Don't worry. Robert won't be here when you come. We'll talk everything over alone and sort it all out.'

'Yes. Well, we'd better put an end to this call. We've had nearly half an hour I should think. I'm sorry, Briony – about last night, I mean. If I'd known – I mean – I'd have telephoned you last night if I'd known... Well, good-bye, old girl.'

'What plane–' Briony began when the sudden hum on the wire told her that Charles had cut off. She sat down weakly on the chair in the hall and tried to gather her wits. What a confused and hopeless conversation it had been! If she had known how it would turn out, she would have written to him ... no, cabled him to catch the next plane. But that wouldn't have helped. Sooner or later he would have asked her about Robert. Vanessa had been putting suggestions into his mind... suspicions; he would have had to question her in the end. And he would have discovered that Robert had been here. Now, perhaps, he would be bitter and in blaming her about her love for Robert, feel unwilling to make a fresh start with Lynn as a third.

'Coffee's ready, Briony!'

She looked up and saw him standing there, staring down at her with a tenderness shining from his eyes. He saw her face and quickly reached for and caught hold of her hand.

'Well?'

'He's flying out here to talk it over!' Briony said.

'Then there's a chance he'll agree?'

'I – I suppose there's a chance. But, Robert, he knows about us – that we love each other, I mean. He asked me outright – just now.'

'How peculiar!' Robert said thoughtfully, 'I mean, it's an odd time to start questioning your wife about her feelings, isn't it?'

'I think Vanessa – he was out with her last night – I think she's been putting ideas in his head and getting him thoroughly suspicious. Why, Robert? Why? What can she have to gain by splitting up our marriage?'

'If that's what she *is* trying to do. Maybe she's the type who likes to throw a little fat on the fire just to liven things up.'

'Yes, she might well do that!' Briony admitted. 'I never liked her, Robert, and I don't think she liked me. Marion's different. She isn't consciously "nasty". She's just self-assured and self-centred and consequently she's cruel because she's thoughtless of others. But I think Vanessa is aware of everything she does ... calculating. I'm afraid!'

'She can't harm you, darling. Don't worry about her. It's between you and your husband and I don't think she can interfere over a thing like this. Anyway, why should she care whether you and Charles "adopt" Lynn or not?'

'No, I suppose not,' Briony said. 'All the same, I have a queer feeling that Vanessa is up to something. Oh, Robert, what would I do without you? You've been so marvellously comforting!'

'And the coffee will be even more so!' Robert said comfortingly. 'Now go and drink it, Briony, and try to eat something – even if it's only a little toast. You'll need your strength, you know. I'll telephone the doctor – Forbes gave me his number – and explain what's happened. I suppose it will be all round the town before long. We'll have to expect a stream of sympathizers and friends and possibly reporters, too. Lance was pretty popular locally and quite well known in the district.'

'Robert, I forgot to tell you. I promised

Charles I'd be alone – I mean, he seemed worried about you being here. I told him you wouldn't be–' She broke off unhappily.

'I understand,' Robert said quietly. 'There'll be lots for me to arrange outside the house in any case. And I must get back to the lab, and explain why I've taken a few days off! I'll telephone you later this evening, darling – just to make sure you are all right!'

Robert – dear, unselfish Robert, who could understand that she must deny herself even the comfort of his company and support for the sake of Lynn and Lynn's future.

'I love you so much!' she whispered.

'But no more than I love you!' he replied with a faint enigmatic smile. 'Now go and have your coffee, darling, before it gets cold!'

The house was quiet when Lynn woke in the late morning. She opened her eyes and stared up at the sunlight dancing through a chink in the curtains on to the ceiling. This was her room – her own room that meant she was home. Nowhere else in the world would ever be 'home' so much as this room which she had had ever since she was born. Here Daddy would come and say 'good night' to her ... tell her stories ... help her with her homework. This room held all the happiest memories of her life. No bedroom she had ever slept in when she stayed with her mother had the same happy, personal, homely feeling of this one.

Now Daddy would never come to kiss her good night again. He was gone ... to a place called Heaven, where God lived and everyone was always happy. She supposed he was dead because only dead people went to Heaven. But the word itself meant very little to her, since she had never seen death except occasionally a dead fly or a mouse and this bore no possible association in her mind with what had happened to her father.

What had happened to him? she wondered, her whole body aching with a pain that she could not define. Forbes had said Daddy had gone mountain-climbing. Yesterday Uncle Robert had talked about mountain-climbing. What had he been saying? That it was a dangerous sport but that lots of people loved it beyond all other activities. Could Daddy have fallen down a mountain and hurt himself so badly he was dead? *What had happened to him?* She must know.

'Briony, Briony!' her voice shrilled out, and she was herself frightened by the fear it held. *'Briony!'*

A moment later Briony was beside her, holding her hand tightly. Briony was so warm and sweet and comforting. With Briony near you, you couldn't really be afraid. You could trust her. She would tell you the truth and you would know it was the truth. She would explain things you didn't understand.

'Tell me what happened!' she commanded, her voice calmer and the fear gone from her eyes.

Briony told her as sparingly as she could the details of Lance's accident. She told the little girl more fully of her own meeting with him and how he had talked so much about her, Lynn; how anxious he was that she should be happy and not grieve about him; how she herself had promised to take care of her always.

'Then *you* aren't going to leave me, too?'

'No, darling, no!' Briony renewed that promise with a conviction that filled her heart with its 'rightness'. 'I'll never leave you, my precious, as long as you need me.'

'Then we'll be together always?' Lynn asked, still not trusting her ears.

'Always!' Briony promised.

Lynn was quiet. It seemed the child was beyond tears ... that the sobs which had racked her earlier had drained her of the childish relief of crying.

'Why didn't you take me with you yesterday?' she asked suddenly. 'You knew Daddy was in hospital, didn't you? When you left, I mean. Why did you leave me behind?'

Here was an accusation which Briony had anticipated and was ready to deal with.

'Daddy didn't want you to remember things like hospitals and doctors and nurses when you think of him, darling. He wanted you to remember all the lovely times you had together here in this house and on outings together. Then you would have only happy memories.'

'I'll never be happy without Daddy!' Lynn said, her voice breaking. 'I love him better than anyone in the world ... better than you or ... or anybody. I want him to come back. I don't want him to be dead. I want him to come back!'

As the thin little voice rose hysterically, Briony was more than grateful to hear the door open and see the doctor come in. He was a middle-aged, kindly-looking man whom she trusted immediately. He nodded to her briefly and, taking the hint, she left him alone with Lynn.

As she waited for him in the sunny living-room that was filled with the personality of the man who would never return to it, Briony tried to think coherently about the future, immediate and distant. Presently, no doubt, Charles would be here. Robert had telephoned the airport and learned that there was only one plane arriving during the afternoon which Charles could reasonably have caught. He had been unable to discover if his name was on the passenger list but Briony assumed he would arrive then. She must try to be calm and unemotional with him – not to be irritated by his disinterest in Lynn as a person. She must try to put right out of her mind all thought of Robert, and yet even now she found her thoughts turning involuntarily to him.

How wonderfully kind and understanding he had been! What a tower of strength and sympathy! How sweet he had been with Lynn too!

"Oh, Robert, darling Robert!" she thought desperately. "This afternoon I shall be fighting to repair the breach that threatens my marriage with Charles, and if I succeed, it means I will have, once more, to say good-bye to you and to love. Better that we had never had the good fortune ... or misfortune ... to meet again."

Yet how precious were the memories of these last twenty-four hours! Robert had shown another side of himself to the man she had discovered in England. Then he had been the vet, and later, the passionate, adoring yet considerate lover. Now he had shown himself as he might have been as her husband ... selfless, capable, calm, yet giving her of his own inner strength by the quiet undemanding offering of his love.

He had gone now ... back to the laboratory to explain why he had been absent and to request a few days' leave. He would later return to his digs to be available should she need him again.

He had known, just as she had known herself, that it was more than probable that they would not be able to see each other again... at least only formally at the funeral and such occasions. It was to be presumed that Charles would stay for a few days at least, and once it was agreed that they would make a fresh start to their marriage, with the addition of Lynn to help them, then she intended to do nothing that would place the future in jeopardy. Robert's good-bye to her an hour ago had been all too brief, yet pregnant with all the things still unsaid between them. Holding her two hands tightly in his own, staring down into her large, tired eyes, he had said:

'Try to take care of yourself, my darling. And if it is any comfort, remember that I love you now and always!'

He had touched her lips once briefly with his own and before she could speak, he was gone.

As Robert had foretold, the telephone calls, telegrams and messages of sympathy began to pour in as the news filtered out that Lance Wendover was dead. It seemed he had a hundred friends in town and many married couples asked anxiously after Lynn. Replying as best she could to the strangers with whom she talked, Briony let them believe for the moment what they automatically assumed ...

that the little girl would go back to live in New York with her mother. It was the obvious solution to people who did not know Marion or the relationship she had with her child; who knew nothing of the child's feelings towards her two parents or the unsuitability of the life Marion led for a child of Lynn's years.

The afternoon passed swiftly enough. The doctor had given Lynn a strong sedative and she was again sleeping after Briony had assured her firmly that she would not be going back to live with Marion; that she, Briony, would be staying with her, or if she went away, Lynn would accompany her. Sleep was the best possible antidote to shock, from which the child was naturally suffering, the doctor had said. As soon as possible, it was advisable that she went away. He, too, had presumed that Marion would shortly be calling to fetch her daughter back to New York. He had promised to call again first thing next morning and Briony was not to hesitate to ring him if she needed him.

Tea time passed between phone calls and visitors, and Briony, glancing at the clock, realized that Charles's plane must be late or else he was not on it. She waited a further half hour and then rang the airport. She learned then that Charles had not been on the plane and the next one was not due until 9 p.m.

Replacing the receiver Briony debated whether or not to telephone Charles again. The waiting was playing on her nerves and she felt keyed up for a situation that she could not explain. Some inner sense was warning that the next hours were to decide not only Lynn's future but her own. If only Charles would come so that they could have everything out in the open and decide what to do!

But Charles was not coming. Immediately after his telephone call to Briony, he had taken a cab round to Vanessa's pent-house flat. Vanessa was still in bed, looking even lovelier and more desirable than he last remembered her – how many hours ago was it? But this time he had no intention of making love to her. He was far too per-plexed, confused, distraught. He wanted to talk.

Sensing his mood with a clever, feminine intuition, Vanessa 'fixed' him some coffee, and listened in silence while he gave her the details of his call to Briony. She was too clever to show her own satisfaction at that account.

'Then she has only confirmed your sus-picions!' she said at last, artfully attributing those suspicions to him rather than to herself and, at the same time, exonerating herself from any possible repercussions. 'What are you going to do about it, Charles?'

'Dash it all, Vanessa, what can I do? She admits this fellow Baker is in love with her. She admits she's in love with him. But she's sworn there has never been anything between them and that there never will be. She wants to make a fresh start and – and keep Lynn.'

'Binny? What has she got to do with it?'

'Well, Briony got pretty fond of the kid during those months in England. And she's always rather had it in for Marion ... doesn't think she's fit to care for Lynn and all that. And now she's promised Wendover that she would look after her in the future ... adopt her.'

Vanessa sized up the situation. She could see that Charles's pride and self-esteem had been hurt by Briony's behaviour – that this was upsetting him more than the fact that his wife had admitted to being in love with someone else!

'And you don't cotton on to the idea?'

'Dash it all, Vanessa, how can I be enthusiastic? Apart from the fact that I'm not particularly fond of children, there's the question of Briony and myself. And you, Vanessa. What a beastly muddle this is!'

'I don't see that it's insoluble!' Vanessa said calmly. 'If you take the facts as they are, my dear Charles, it's easy enough to see a way out. Briony's in love with her vet and he's in love with her. Let *them* adopt the child if Marion doesn't want her, which I assume she doesn't! That leaves you ... and me, Charles. What could be nicer?'

Her voice was low and husky and her long cool fingers lay against the back of his neck, reminding him of last night – of the incredible revelation of what life with Vanessa could mean!

'But Vanessa, Briony's my wife! She's not the kind of person to – to – well, to do the sort of thing you and I did last night.'

'Oh, you mean she'd object on moral grounds?' Vanessa said smoothly. 'But I wasn't suggesting she set up home with her young man and remain married to *you!* Let her divorce you, Charles. Then she can marry her ardent lover and live happily ever after ... and so can we!'

'You don't know what you're suggesting!' Charles said nervously.

'You mean ... you couldn't care enough about me?'

He turned then and caught her roughly against him.

'You know damn well how I feel about you. But divorce, Vanessa...'

'Is that so shocking?' she asked calmly. 'You forget that I've already been divorced once myself, Charles. Am I so "low" because my erstwhile husband and I agreed to differ? You're being old-fashioned, my dear. You're no more in love with Briony than she is with you.'

'But I loved her when I married her!' Charles argued.

'Marriage doesn't guarantee everlasting love!' Vanessa replied easily. 'Unfortunately it usually guarantees the opposite unless two people share the same interests. You and I are two of a kind, Charles – or rather we perfectly complement one another.'

The man tried desperately to marshal his thoughts. Events had moved far too swiftly for his liking. A week ago he had no thought for the future but a continuation of his quiet, uneventful life with Briony, whom he believed he loved. Now, suddenly, he was trapped in a whirlwind of events which left him breathless. He doubted now that he was ever in love with Briony. Since he had known Vanessa – discovered how different life and love could be with a woman such as she – he doubted whether he had ever loved his wife. He was deeply shocked by the realization; as much as he had been shocked to learn that Briony had fallen in love with young Baker! And he had never guessed it for a moment. What a blind idiot he had been! Now, on top of this, Vanessa was suggesting divorce – a way out which he had been brought up to despise. One married 'for better or for worse'. Yet if one considered it from Vanessa's point of view – most Americans' point of view, no doubt –

what was the point of carrying on with a marriage neither partner wanted?

His own desires were clear. He wanted Vanessa – more than ever now. But they battled with his moral upbringing and the struggle was all the harder for his being unprepared for it.

'Well, Charles?'

She had released herself from his arms some minutes ago and was standing now with her back to the large window, the light filtering through the transparent chiffon of her négligé, leaving her a shadowy silhouette. Looking at her, knowing the full force of his desire to possess this lovely creature – to make her his own for always, Charles began to forget his principles. Briony might despise him – his friends might condemn him – he would probably in a moment of sanity condemn himself – but now he knew he could not fight against this force that was Vanessa. *He must have her.* In the whole of his forty years of living, he had never wanted anything more than he wanted her. Life might not be easy with this fierce, sensuous, temperamental, yet controlled woman! Some inner sense warned him that in gaining bodily peace he might lose his peace of mind. Yet there could be no peace for him without her. His whole being cried out for her and he knew that the barriers between them were as nothing beside his desire.

'Vanessa!' he cried, and as she moved swiftly towards him he rose to his feet and held wide his arms to reach for and hold the warm, living, loving woman who was to replace the ghost of his wife.

The cable arrived at eight o'clock. Forbes handed her the envelope telling her that it had been brought by special messenger.

'Seems odd, Mrs. Stone!' he said. 'They usually telephone them through and confirm them later. Maybe the line was engaged so they sent it this way!'

He was not to know that Charles had not wanted his wife to suffer the indignity of learning from a telephone operator that he had left her!

Gone to Mexico with Vanessa Stop Hope you will understand this the best way for all Stop Letter following Stop Please forgive and be happy Stop Charles.

Briony was stunned. She had known nothing at all of Charles's interest in Vanessa. She realized now that she had been too concerned with her own torn emotions to consider Charles. She had known, of course, that he was friendly with Vanessa but she had never for an instant believed there was anything more than a platonic friendship between them. Even now she could scarcely believe that the words she read were not misprinted – or else dreamed up by her own hysterical thoughts! Yet, slowly, she began to believe – began to see beneath the surface of those few words to the little events that made them sense. Marion and Gerald, Charles and Vanessa ... foursomes at Canasta, foursomes at bridge ... Charles and Vanessa dancing when she had danced with Robert ... Charles's apparent willingness to use his dressing-room ... his complete lack of demands on *her;* Charles's enthusiasm to come to America ... his reluctance to leave New York ... his not telephoning her last night ... his peculiar telephone conversation this morning ... yes, Vanessa explained all that. And she, Briony, had never even suspected...

Briony began suddenly to laugh. It was funny ... ironical to the extreme that she had for the last six months been forcing herself to think only of Charles ... and yet she had omitted to see the most important thing about him! She had filled herself up with righteous platitudes about 'her duty' to her husband, her duty to put his happiness before her own ... to give up Robert and all he meant to her because Charles *needed* her, loved her, because she felt she had never put into her marriage what she had taken from it!

Her laughter changed suddenly to tears. What a blind, conceited fool she had been!

Had Robert guessed? He had told her time and time again to have faith that it would all come right in the end. Had he known all along that Charles was making a fool of her?

No, that wasn't fair! Charles had not known until she told him this morning that she loved Robert. He, as she herself, had been fighting against his destiny ... Vanessa. Beautiful she might be ... but clever, cruel, ruthless no doubt, when it suited her. How could Charles believe happiness lay with Vanessa Gough? Did Vanessa love him? Was he able to find in her what she, his wife, had never been able to give him ... love? Somehow it seemed strange to think of Vanessa ... so sophisticated ... in love with the strangely child-like, good-natured Charles. But it could have happened. Charles would not have gone to Mexico with Vanessa just for fun! Briony knew him too well not to be aware that, in taking Vanessa away, he was at the same time suggesting she, Briony, divorce him and promising to marry Vanessa when he was free.

At least, then, she need not have it on her conscience that Charles had sent that cable in order to offer her a chance to – to gain her freedom from a bondage that had lost any possible spiritual or physical meaning. If he had wished merely to set her free, he would have come to her and told her outright that if she wanted a divorce, he would agree to it. No! Charles himself wanted his freedom – freedom to go to Vanessa. And in taking the irrevocable step he had done, he had at the same time set her free to go to Robert.

Robert! The thought of him came like a warm flash of sunlight, radiating her heart, her very soul. Robert! Now, at long last, she could openly acknowledge her love. There would be many sordid details to be gone through before she was really in effect free to go to him – yet now she knew her heart free from its last restraint.

Eagerly, her eyes shining, her heart glowing, she reached for the telephone and dialled his number. Hearing his voice in the next moment, she felt the hot tears suddenly sting her eyes and for a moment she could not speak. Then at last she found words:

'Robert, will you come round? I have some wonderful news for you!'

He did not question her, understanding that she wished to tell him in person, face to face, her good news. He was glad for her that it had come out right and yet, believing that this must mean the end of his own chance of happiness, was torn with conflicting emotions. He automatically assumed that Briony's news was that Charles had agreed to adopt little Lynn; that Charles had already set off on his return journey to New York, for otherwise Briony would not have asked him to come round. He could understand that she had to tell someone ... that she would want to tell him, knowing he would be pleased that she was made happy in the midst of her unhappiness. He thanked God at least for this small blessing. She could concentrate now on the little girl and find a measure of forgetfulness in her love for Lynn. For him there was no compensation.

Reaching the house, he steeled himself not to show his own desperate unhappiness. At all costs, he would not mar this small comfort he believed Fate had afforded her.

The radiance of Briony's face shone forth in a beauty that took his breath away. She flung herself into his arms and for a few moments could do no more than whisper his name.

Presently he allowed himself to be led into the living-room, where, once again, Briony flung her arms around him and hugged him as might a little girl have done. He looked down at her glowing face in a mixture of despair and tenderness. Despair that he could never now possess this lovely, ardent, emotional girl, who epitomized the very meaning of love and loveliness, both of mind and body; tenderness because he knew the depth of character that could reach to the top and fall to the lowest and so suffer as well as glory in the task of living. He longed to protect her from her own sensitive nature and to share in the fine semi-tones that only a nature such as hers and his own could attain.

'Oh, Robert, Robert, darling, darling Robert!' she whispered between laughter and tears. 'Can't you guess my good news? Can't you see in my eyes the glory that is in my heart? Robert, you stupid, wonderful, crazy man! You haven't lost me yet. I can see in your eyes that you think it is all over; you believe that Charles has agreed to have Lynn and that we shall soon be leaving you? No, dearest heart, no! Charles has gone off with Vanessa. He, too, wants his freedom. Oh, Robert, I can hardly believe myself that it is true!'

'You mean – you mean he's going to let you divorce him? He's going to – to – marry – Vanessa?'

'Yes, darling, yes!' Briony cried. Then, suddenly shy, she whispered:

'Robert, you're sure – sure you want me?'

He flung his arms round her then and hugged her in a replica of her own child-like enthusiasm as the truth penetrated his unbelieving mind.

'No!' he laughed. 'No, my own dear love – I don't want to marry you. I never have done. I've never loved you, my love, my sweet love. You are offering me heaven and I am going to choose hell instead. Oh, Briony...!' His voice broke and his face became suddenly serious and suffused with the depth of his feelings as he said: 'If you knew how very, *very* happy I am. Briony, let me ask you ... the question I have never dared believe I could ask... Darling, when you are free to do so, will you marry me?'

'Robert, you know that with all my heart I will!'

'And Lynn?' he said gently. 'She will belong to – to both of us. We'll make it up to her, won't we? We'll make her happy.'

'Perhaps it is really all due to her that you and I–' She could not trust her voice to continue. Yet it was true. If it hadn't been for Lynn, whose illness had prompted Marion's – or was it Vanessa's ? – invitation to America, Charles might never have seen Vanessa again; he might never have let himself care enough about her to want to set Briony free.

'We owe her our happiness, don't we?' Robert said for her. 'Do you think she's awake, Briony? Maybe it would make her happy to hear about us.'

Lynn was awake. She listened quietly while Briony tried to explain to her that one day soon, she and Robert would be married because Uncle Charles wished to marry her Aunt Vanessa. Slowly, the sad little face began to change, the large, tear-filled eyes to smile.

'Oh, Briony!' she said. 'It's like a fairy-tale, isn't it? Do you remember I used to call

Robert our Prince Charming? And you have always been my Princess.'

'And mine!' Robert whispered.

'You know, Lynn darling, that you will live with us – when we are married, I mean? You'll be our little girl then.'

'Oh, Briony, Robert!' was all the little girl could say to express her happiness at this news. For a moment, they sat in silence, each holding one of the hot little hands. Presently Lynn said:

'Where will we live, Briony?'

'I don't know, darling. You and I will go away for a holiday together.' For she knew that until the divorce took place, she must not see Robert.

'I'd like to live here ... in this house!' Lynn said. 'It's really a happy house, you know. Daddy and I were very happy here.'

Briony looked across the fair head and met Robert's eyes.

'I don't see why not!' he said at last. 'If Lynn would like it. It will be near my job – and it means she can stay at the same school.'

'Yes, yes, I would like to stay!' Lynn said. 'It seems as if Daddy is *near* even though he has gone to Heaven as you say, Briony. I suppose going away always means going away from Daddy to me. I think he'd *like* it if I stayed here. Do you think he'll know about it all, Briony?'

'Yes, darling, I do. People we love are always close to us even when they are in Heaven because they are near to us in our hearts.'

'Then maybe,' the child said sleepily, 'there's a sort of heaven in our hearts, too!'

As the blue eyes closed, Robert looked across at the woman he knew now would one day be his wife, and both knew that there *was* a heaven on earth; it lay within their reach, for it was in their hearts, too.

The publishers hope that this book has given you enjoyable reading. Large Print Books are especially designed to be as easy to see and hold as possible. If you wish a complete list of our books please ask at your local library or write directly to:

Dales Large Print Books
Magna House, Long Preston,
Skipton, North Yorkshire.
BD23 4ND

This Large Print Book, for people
who cannot read normal print,
is published under the auspices of

THE ULVERSCROFT FOUNDATION